The Dead Guy

Doug Hewitt

Aberdeen Bay
An Imprint of Champion Writers

Aberdeen Bay
Published by Aberdeen Bay, an imprint of Champion Writers.
www.aberdeenbay.com

Copyright © Doug Hewitt, 2008

All rights reserved. No part of this publication may be reproduced, stored in a database or retrieval system, or transmitted, in any form or by any means, without the prior written permission of the publisher. For information on obtaining permission for use of material from this publication, please visit the publisher's website at www.aberdeenbay.com.

PUBLISHER'S NOTE

This is a book of fiction. Names, characters, places, and incidents are either the product of author's imagination or are used fictitiously. Any resemblance to actual persons, living or dead, business establishments, government agencies, events, or locales is entirely coincidental.

International Standard Book Number
ISBN-13: 978-0-9814725-7-7
ISBN-10: 0-9814725-7-5

Printed in the United States of America.

This book is dedicated to my wife, Robin, for believing.

Doug Hewitt, October 2008

THE DEAD GUY

CHAPTER ONE

The name's Thigpen. Jack Thigpen. I investigate car insurance fraud. I'm not a double-nought spy, and I can't stomach martinis—no matter shaken or stirred—much to the chagrin of my wife. Martinis make me gag, but what I hate even more than olive-adorned vomit-inducing adult beverages are scammers, con men, swindlers, and cheats. These shysters, scumbags, *fraud-meisters*, who absolve their consciences with the belief their crimes are victimless, instead perpetuate illegal activities that result in injury and death.

The case that changed my life—and ended my best friend's—started with a call to my cell phone at eight o'clock in the morning.

"Jack Thigpen," I answered.

"You the guy who runs Thigpen Investigations?" the voice asked. His voice was low, broken, as though he needed to clear his throat.

"Yes, that's me."

"What kind of investigations do you do?"

"All kinds, but I specialize in auto insurance fraud."

"Experience?"

"I've been in the business for three years, and I've worked with all the major insurance companies. Can I ask who's calling?"

"Ted Meade. I run the claims department at Alliance Insurance."

"Alliance? I haven't heard of it."

"Yeah," Meade huffed. "Our company's relatively new, only five years old. We're not big, but we've been growing."

"How can I help you, Mr. Meade?"

"We've been getting flooded with claims from a specific repair shop. Most of the claims have red flags."

"What kind of red flags?" Claims adjustors were always looking over claims for anything odd such as claimants changing doctors just before accidents or being difficult to contact. Other red flags were inconsistent versions of witness testimony, X-rays conflicting with a doctor's initial diagnosis, and clearly legible doctor signatures (this one I've always found humorous, that they actually look for such a thing).

"Mostly it's the amount of the claims, over eight thousand dollars on average."

"That's high," I agreed.

"And there's one claim with an airbag replacement for a car struck on the side impact panel."

"That's not unheard of," I pointed out.

"Sure, but the police report says the impact panel just had a small dent."

I stood, sipping my instant coffee, laced with enough sugar to make it potable. *Gotta get that coffee maker soon.* "So, what is it exactly you want?"

"Stake the place out. See if there's evidence of fraud."

"That, I can do. First I'd like to meet and talk about this in more detail. I like to meet my clients before starting a case."

Meade coughed, but his raspy voice didn't change. "Let's talk in my office. Fourth floor of the Kalahan Building in Roseville. Intersection of Twelve Mile and Utica Road. Ask the receptionist for Ted Meade."

"When?"

"Let's see ..., how about nine-thirty?"

"No problem. You're not far."

"Okay, Mr. Thigpen, see you then."

I ended the call and sipped my coffee again, thankful to have another job. I often wondered why I didn't have more business. Insurance companies should've been eager to hire me, to have legions of fraud investigators on their payroll. But they were afraid of "bad faith" lawsuits. If they erroneously deny a claim, they could get sued. They figure it's easier to avoid the risk and pay the claims. I didn't mind the time between cases, though.

I'd been playing more tennis lately, and in the back of my mind, I figured a comeback wasn't completely out of the question.

My hand twitched and I dropped the coffee cup. I quickly cleaned up the spill, wondering if I had a pinched nerve.

It was a ten-minute drive to Roseville. I lived in St. Clair Shores, north of Grosse Pointe, which was one of the five ultra-wealthy "Pointe" communities just north of Detroit proper. Ellie lived in Grosse Pointe, in a roomy Tudor, which had been my home, too, until six months ago. Now I lived in a small bungalow, a "rental" inherited from a great uncle. He had left it for my sister, Lynne, and me, but I'd bought her out as she didn't want to move from Kansas. I hadn't known the great uncle very well, and from what I heard, he had died a horrible death from Creutzfeldt-Jakob Disease—CJD—a neurodegenerative disorder. In a way, it was a human version of Mad Cow Disease, and Uncle Theo had progressed within a few months from slurred speech, blurred vision, and loss of muscle coordination to mental incapacitation—dementia—and coma and death. My doctor informed me last week, when I'd gone in to see if I had a pinched nerve, the disease could be hereditary. I'd told him that my grandfather had died in a similar manner, and he'd handed me over to Dr. Cho, one of the best neuropathologists in the country. CJD was difficult to diagnose, but I'd agreed to have some additional tests done, even though statistically I was going to be fine. There were only a few hundred CJD cases a year in the United States, and the disease almost always struck people over the age of sixty.

I hadn't expected to need the house, but the inheritance had turned out to be fortunate because after three years of marriage, my wife decided she needed more "space" than our four-thousand square feet of flooring inside walls of brick and stucco. A trial separation, she had said. And because Ellie's parents owned the Tudor—one of five properties they owned in Grosse Pointe and just down the road from their home—I figured I'd play nice and move out. *A temporary move*, I had told myself, *just until we get back together and I can find a tenant.* Then we'll save our money, buy the Tudor, and live happily ever after.

At first the rental had been like a prison, my sentence of

being without Ellie to be served there, but more and more I grew into thinking of it as home. Sometimes I wondered if it was simply because no one objected when I put my feet on the coffee table. Or when I drank beers from the bottle instead of martinis in a glass ...

After finishing my coffee, I rinsed my cup, then shaved, showered, and dressed in jeans and a polo shirt. I grabbed my digital camera, walked outside, and climbed into my Explorer.

I drove out to the Kalahan Building and rode the elevator to the fourth floor. I found a glass door with the stenciled name ALLIANCE INSURANCE and went inside to the receptionist's desk.

"I'm here to see Mr. Meade," I said. "Name's Thigpen."

The receptionist stood. "Follow me, Mr. Thigpen." She was a young, attractive girl with straight black hair, too much eye makeup, and a short blue dress that swished back and forth as she walked. I was faithful to Ellie, but after so much time without her, I suddenly wondered if I was being faithful only to a memory.

Most of the workers sat at desks in a maze of cubicles. Aisles between cubicles didn't go straight for more than twenty feet before ending at another aisle at right angles to the first. I turned left and right through the maze to Ted Meade's office, which was an actual office with a door and four walls.

Meade paced behind his desk, talking on the phone. He was a tall man, a couple of inches over six feet, with a face wrinkled from a perpetual frown. He glanced over at us, covered the phone's mouthpiece, and asked, "Who's this, Janet?"

"Mr. Thigpen, sir."

Meade nodded and waved her off. He spoke briefly into the phone and hung up. "Sit down, sit down." His voice was low, congested. "Can I call you Jack?"

"That'd be fine," I said, settling into the brown upholstered chair in front of the desk.

"Good, good." Stack of folders littered Meade's desk. He nudged a few as though they'd been slightly out of place. "I'm glad you could take the case on such short notice." He sat behind his desk and studied me, hands under his chin, palm to palm.

"I don't schedule cases in advance. That would make my life too hectic."

He laughed. "In this town, you could probably schedule twenty hours of work a day. But where would that get you?"

"It'd get you rich, but too tired to enjoy it."

"Exactly. Now tell me, Jack, how do you usually operate on a case like this, a stakeout?"

"I find a place to park and then sit and watch through a telephoto lens."

"What do you drive?"

It was a common question in Detroit. In Chicago, someone might ask if you were a White Sox or Cubs fan; in New York, the Mets or Yankees; but in Detroit it was what do you drive?
"Ford Explorer."

"Good, good. And you just park out in the street?"

"Depends. I try to park where there are other vehicles so I don't stand out. Parking lots are good."

"That makes sense. No one'll notice you."

"Right. Now, about my fees ..."

Meade placed his hands on his armrests and leaned back.
"Here's the deal. I've been authorized to offer you a thousand a day. No expenses, though."

It was a generous offer, although freelancers tended to earn more per hour than company investigators because freelancers had to cover their own health insurance. "For how long?" I asked.

"Five days. Today's Monday, so if you can start today, through Friday." Meade opened his top desk drawer, took out a check, and filled it in. "Here's one day's pay. You get the rest at the end of the week."

I took the check, folded it, and put it in my wallet. "Okay, now where's this repair shop?"

Meade handed me a manila envelope with a tie closure. I opened it, reached inside, and pulled out a Metro Area map with a red circle drawn around a location in Warren. The name JOSEF'S REPAIR SHOP, 1803 NINE MILE ROAD was written beside the circle.

"Clear enough?" Meade asked.

"Seems to be. One thing, though, what about your investigators?"

"We haven't hired any, yet. We're still a young company. And hell, with what we'd have to pay in salaries and legal fees, it's been easier just to pay the claims."

"But they've been adding up," I said.

"Yes. This Josef guy, Josef Adolpho—keep a special eye out for him. He had a cousin in New York up on RICO charges a few years ago."

RICO was an acronym for the federal Racketeer Influenced and Corrupt Organizations Act. "The feds might be interested if it turns out fraud's involved."

"Maybe," Meade said. "So do a good job. Stake this place out. See if these guys are taking us for a ride."

I heard voices and glanced out the door. Three men were walking by, arguing. The man most vocal held a cup of coffee. He looked extremely young, a summer intern perhaps. The coffee cup had a black-and-gold B on it, a Boston Bruins logo.

"You let Boston Bruins coffee mugs in here?" I asked.

Meade laughed, the sound like a stuttering diesel. "Ah, Blalock. Transferred here last month from Boston. He'll learn not to bring it out during hockey season."

Detroit was not only called the Motor City, it was Hockey Town, too, home of the Detroit Red Wings. During the playoffs, octopi were thrown to the ice after each Red Wing goal and half the cars sported Red Wing flags from windows. Even the famous downtown statue "Spirit of Detroit" mysteriously donned a massive red-and-white jersey with the wheel-and-wing logo. People took their hockey seriously in Detroit, and the kid would be razzed so frequently for his Bruins coffee cup that he wouldn't have time to work.

"He's not the brightest guy in the office," Meade said. "But he's a go-getter."

"You have a Boston office, too?"

"Yeah, but not insurance. Alliance operates a number of businesses."

"I've never heard of them."

"They're not big enough to be noticed, not yet anyway."

I nodded, resealed the manila envelope, and stood. "I guess that's it, then. I'll call if I find anything."

Meade handed me a business card. "If there's no answer, leave a message."

"Right. Anything else before I go?"

"What if I need to get in touch with you?"

"Use the same number you called earlier. It's my cell phone. I keep it with me." I strode to the office door.

"Good luck, Jack."

I nodded. "I'll be in touch," I said, heading off through the maze of cubicles.

"Have a nice day, Janet," I said, passing the receptionist. She glanced up and smiled.

As the elevator descended, listening to the background music "The Girl From Ipanema," I wondered if I should start scheduling work in advance. Maybe, for now, it'd be good not to have spare time. Ellie didn't seem interested in getting back together. Until I adjusted, keeping busy wouldn't be all that bad.

CHAPTER TWO

According to Meade's map, Josef's Repair Shop was at the intersection of Nine Mile and Ryan Road. I cruised through the surrounding neighborhood, getting a feel for the area.

This wasn't the best section of town, but it wasn't the worst, either. Most of the buildings were one- and two-story structures. Many of the windows were broken and a greater number cracked. Liquor stores flashed neon promotions of booze.

There were gun shops, hock shops, crumbling brick facades. The blocks looked dirty, unwashed, with a thick build-up of soot that made the streets and cracked sidewalks grungy. Several abandoned cars dotted lots surrounded by tall chain-link fences. There were body shops, repair shops, and shops selling nothing but used tires. There were cinderblock buildings with, according to the signs, *Live Nightly Entertainment.*

Alleys behind buildings had trash cans spilling over. The entire area seemed to have a problem distinguishing trash from non-trash, where a bald tire might be on sale at one store, and in the garbage at another. Soda cans, liquor bottles, paper cups, fast food and candy wrappers, all sorts of trash were strewn along the cracks where sidewalk met building, as though stuffed in as make-shift insulation.

Despite the detritus and debris of the area, my spirits were buoyed by the weather. There wasn't a cloud in the sky, and the temperature was a comfortable seventy degrees. I've been on many stake-outs when the weather was terrible, and I had to suffer through miserable heat and fierce cold.

After twenty minutes of driving through the neighborhood, I passed Josef's Repair Shop and looked for a good place to conduct surveillance. There were several possibilities. The shop, a rectangular brick structure, was on the corner. Traffic was heavy at the intersection, providing good cover. The best place to hide, as Sherlock Holmes discovered, was in plain sight, where everyone passes by.

I circled the block and passed the shop again.

The front door, with JOSEF'S printed on the glass, appeared to open into an office area. The area between the front of the building and Nine Mile was a parking lot with close to fifty spaces, a fourth of them filled. A fence six feet high jutted out from the front corners of the building and continued around toward the back.

The shop's paved back lot was surrounded by the fence and pockmarked with holes as though lampposts had been yanked out. There were stacks of pallets and a couple of rusted fork trucks that looked about to collapse from corrosion.

On the east side of the fence, closest to me, there was a wide roll gate about forty feet in length. It had been pushed aside, and directly beyond, in the building, there were three repair bays with roll-up doors. Inside, two cars were raised on hydraulic lifts. Another car was pulling into the third bay.

I circled the block again and parked on a side street, where I could see the front parking lot, the front office door, and the side bays. Cars were parked up and down the street, which had a 25 mph speed limit.

I took my camera from the passenger seat, rolled down my window, and scooted away from it a bit, not wanting to be too obvious. I aimed the camera on the repair bays and zoomed in.

The bay floors were well-swept, painted red, although the paint had faded and looked like rust. Dozens of toolboxes and diagnostic equipment on carts cluttered the bays. Tools—socket wrenches, screwdrivers, open-end wrenches—and spare parts were strewn on other carts with no discernible order.

I took pictures of the cars in the bays. Then, even though the camera's time/date option was on, I jotted *10:53 June 18* and the license plate numbers of the cars in a notepad. The plate numbers were visible in the photos, but if I were called into court, documentation would show the jury I was credible.

As I watched the mechanics, I noted the repairs being done (a brake job, an oil change, and a tune-up) beside the license plate of each car. To substantiate these observations, I took more pictures.

Although the photos could help Ted Meade at Alliance Insurance, I'd have to get closer to record the VINs--Vehicle Identification Numbers, seventeen-character numbers that are unique to each vehicle. They were stamped in many locations, but the easiest to see was just inside the windshield, on the driver's side, at the front end of the dashboard.

Still, Meade had suspected an airbag replacement scam, and I saw no suggestion of that.

There was a lull in activity at Josef's, so I set the camera on the floorboard, picked up a *Newsweek*, resting it on the steering wheel, and idly wondered if Meade would consider insurance fraud victimless. I doubted it.

Sometimes the effect is not as dramatic as a fatal accident or the direct pilfering from purse or wallet, but at the very least, fraud drives auto insurance rates up at a painfully steep pace. Everyone pays. We're all victims.

And where better to investigate anything related to automobiles than Detroit? It's the Motor City, Motown, home of Ford, DaimlerChrysler, General Motors. Its streets are lined with shops that crank out springs, axles, engine blocks, pistons, and car bodies, a massive output that feeds larger assembly plants, from which cars roll off production lines in an endless stream of manufacturing muscle. Along its highways, billboards with bright neon numbers count off each year's total car production, a blue-collar version of the Times Square marquee. Outside of Detroit Metro Airport, a Ferris wheel from the '64 World's Fair had been converted into a giant roadside Uniroyal tire.

Although I live in a suburb, part of the greater metropolitan area, the cities of southeastern Michigan are as interconnected as gears in a vast machine. It is in this vastness that scammers operate, victimizing all of us, and I get satisfaction at collecting evidence to deny claims and put crooks behind bars.

After four years of studying criminal justice at Eastern Michigan University and two years on the pro tennis circuit, I married Ellie and opened a freelance investigation agency. That was three years ago. Since then, I've learned a lot about scams. Some are basic, routine in nature. In my first case as an investigator, I took photographs of the odometer in a Chevy minivan that had been in a serious accident. The following week, when the damage estimate came in from a repair shop, the mileage had shrunk by fifty thousand miles, increasing the value of the car and the corresponding payout.

I have on occasion had dreams, and they're not far from the truth, in which legions of paralegals and paramedics prowl city streets, on the lookout for accidents. They have standing orders to approach accident victims with names of mechanics, doctors, and chiropractors who are on the take, who inflate claims. On the street, these recruiters are called cappers. I've spotted several over the years, and they invariably lead me to repair shops that falsify damage amounts, such as five thousand dollars of repairs for what had been a five-hundred dollar fender bender.

Insurance companies need photographic evidence that claims are inflated. That's why insurers hire people like me. Pressured by Congress and competing with "low-rate" companies, they increasingly look for ways to weed out unnecessary cost. If the evidence is strong enough, the police are contacted and criminal prosecutions follow. Years ago, law enforcement viewed fraud as an insurance problem, but lately prosecutors have come to see the truth that fraud is a criminal act that affects everyone.

One type of case that fascinated me was how the cappers paid homeless people to get hit by cars—not at high speed, of course, just enough to give chiropractors an opportunity to schedule high-dollar treatments, which are paid by the insurance policies.

Sometimes accidents are staged for other reasons. Last year, a paralegal had ten insurance policies on his Lincoln Navigator. Ten policies, ten claims, ten times the payout. Ellie had asked me why there wasn't a master computer in which claims are crosschecked by VINs and stamped in multiple locations. I told her that there was indeed a national data bank ..., in theory. But many companies don't want to cooperate, which could help the competition. And the manpower to enter the data is something companies are reluctant to fund in the cost-cutting environment of big business.

I noticed a mechanic finishing the tune-up on an Impala at Josef's Repair shop. His blue overalls were oil and smudge free because it was still early. He drove the car to the front lot and fetched a Cutlass, which he hoisted up on the hydraulic jack.

I put down the magazine, picked up the camera, and took a picture, the Cutlass filling the frame, the license clearly visible. I wrote an entry in the notepad.

A man with a broad face and short blond hair that had been brushed up, making it appear erect, entered the bays from the office area. He was a muscular man wearing a blue shirt and looked about thirty years old. His chest was wide, expanding and contracting his shirt in an exaggerated manner as he breathed. His left hand was bandaged, held against his side. He crossed the bays and spoke to the mechanic at the Cutlass. I zoomed in with the camera and saw that the bandage covered two stumps where fingers had been, index and middle.

I took a picture.

The man headed back toward the office, but stopped to talk to the mechanic in the middle bay.

On impulse, I grabbed my cell phone and called information. I asked for the phone number of the repair shop, jotted it down in the notepad, and punched it into my cell phone. The man missing two fingers went to the back wall and picked up a phone.

"Josef's Repair Shop," he answered. "This is Adolpho." His voice was thick, accented. I was no scholar on dialects but it sounded Eastern European, the dol in Adolpho exaggerated.

"I had an accident," I told him. "How fast can you fix my car?"

"Depends on damage. And model."

"Chrysler Sebring. I think the front struts need replacing. And the airbag deployed."

"You have to take to dealership."

"Why?"

"We don't do airbags."

"That's a shame."

"Sorry, sir," Adolpho said. "Maybe next accident, you call us again."

He hung up and went to talk to the third mechanic.

If Ted Meade suspected illegal airbags were being installed at Josef's Repair Shop, why would Adolpho miss an opportunity to profit? It was a gimme for him. Had they run out of airbags? Had the thieves failed to keep up with demand?

Although I was curious about the answers to these questions, ultimately these were Meade's problems. I was hired to do surveillance, not set up a sting.

Adolpho was still talking to the third mechanic when a green Volvo pulled in and parked near the second repair bay. A short man hopped out, his hair dark, slick, and combed back. His white shirt and gray tie were tucked neatly into a blue buttoned vest. His short nose and thin face gave him a bird-like appearance. As he approached Adolpho, his head bobbed in rhythm with his strides, pronouncing the bird-like effect. He reminded me of a barnyard rooster.

Adolpho met him outside. They had talked for less than a minute when a tow truck pulled in, stopping in front of the bays. The truck had a Pontiac Grand Am in tow, but I couldn't see any damage. The truck's engine continued to run. On the driver side door, the words "repair" and "tow service" were painted in white.

Adolpho shouted something at the driver and pointed. The tow truck pulled into the front lot, shifted into reverse, and backed the Grand Am into a parking spot. The truck driver, a tall red-headed man, got out, released the tow bar, and returned to the cab.

After taking pictures of the driver, the tow truck, and the Grand Am, I swung the camera back and took pictures of Rooster Man and his green Volvo.

The man from the Volvo spoke for another minute to Adolpho, then returned to his car and drove off. The tow truck followed.

My suspicions were raised by the truck being escorted, but it wasn't until they both returned forty-five minutes later that I allowed those suspicions to take root. Rooster Man looked too much like a lawyer. A capper.

I took another picture and made a note—SECOND APPEARANCE OF TOW TRUCK AND VOLVO AT 1:18 pm.

This time the tow truck dropped off a blue Taurus.

After talking again to Adolpho, the capper birdwalked back to his Volvo and left again. The tow truck followed, but turned the other direction onto Nine Mile.

Did the Volvo and tow truck have a prearranged meeting place? Were they staging the accidents? Scouting for real ones? Did they have scanners in their vehicles to give them real-time reports of accident locations?

Moments later, the mechanics stopped to eat.

When they resumed work, their pace slowed.

I found myself yawning. Needing to stretch my legs, figuring to take advantage of the lull in activity at the shop, I got out and locked the Explorer. I walked casually down Nine Mile, crossed at a break in traffic, then returned on the side of the repair shop. I veered to my left, into the front lot, and began casually inspecting the cars—a Ford Ranger, Crown Vic, Windstar. A Chevy Blazer and two Cavaliers. Four Honda Accords. Other than the Cutlass and Taurus, which had been dropped off by the tow truck, I found only one vehicle with damage that appeared to result from collision, a Mustang, its front crumpled. Turning my back to the shop, in case anyone happened to glance out, I quickly wrote the Mustang's VIN in my notepad. I strolled farther across the lot, stopping at the Cutlass and the Taurus, recording their VINs, too.

Although prepared to do so, I never had to use my cover story. No one questioned me. There were people who frequented repair shops, looking for cars to buy. Sometimes if, say, a head gasket was blown on a car that was over twenty years old, the cost of repair might rival its blue book value. An entrepreneur might offer to purchase the vehicle at a higher value because then he'd own that VIN. And there were ways to transfer VINs, grinding out old ones and stamping new ones on. This was useful when cars were stolen. Grind out the old VIN, stamp in the new.

Sounds like a rap song, I told myself, imagining clanking sounds as a back rhythm. *Grind out the old, stamp in the new ...*

So for the price of an old clunker, a thief could have a premium stolen car with a VIN that didn't match any from stolen vehicles.

I glanced at my watch as though realizing I was late and hurried back down Nine Mile.

On the way, I tore out a piece of notepad paper, crumpled it, and tossed it into one of the few trash bins I'd seen. I crossed Nine Mile and headed back to my Explorer. I watched the trash bin. If anyone was following me, they'd be interested in what I was doing and would stop to retrieve the paper. But nobody went near the bin.

Figuring I hadn't been spotted, I thought about returning later to the front lot, when nobody was working, and write down VINs of other cars, in case there was damage I couldn't see. That could be risky, though. A late-night visitor would appear more suspicious.

For the next twenty minutes, I watched the progress of the repairs in the bays. There was a muffler replacement, a front-end alignment, and another brake job, nothing that would indicate repairs resulting from an accident. In fact, nothing looked illegal, no rush hour delivery of stolen airbags, no incriminating replacement of damaged car parts with other parts that were obviously used. The muffler was bright and shiny, the brake pads came out of a new box.

At 3:13 pm, for the third time that day, the Volvo and tow truck arrived. I noted the damaged vehicle behind the tow truck—a Jeep Cherokee—and took a picture.

After setting the camera down, I took out my cell phone and entered Meade's number.

"Meade here."

"Mr. Meade, this is Jack Thigpen. I'm—"

"Thigpen?"

"Yes, I'm—"

"Where are you?" Meade asked.

"I'm near Josef's Repair Shop, working."

"Yes, yes. How's it going?"

"I've got photographs of cars and license plates of the cars getting repairs. So far, though, none of the repairs are to cars that've been in accidents. And I haven't seen any sign of replacement airbags."

"How long have you been there?"

"Close to five hours. I have, though, seen a few cars towed in from accidents. Maybe they'll get into the repair bays tomorrow."

"Yes, yes. Good."

"But I can't guarantee that those cars are insured by Alliance."

"I understand that. We get four or five claims from that repair shop every week. Be persistent. If we get to deny even one claim, you'll have covered your pay for the week."

I nodded. It always came down to money. "These cars getting towed in, I believe, are involved with scams. There's a guy that shows up every time the tow truck arrives. Three times so far today. He looks like a lawyer."

"I see."

"Probably a paralegal. They know just enough about the law to take advantage of it, but not enough to make money practicing as an attorney."

"I'm sure you're right."

"So, I figure you might make better use of me if I follow this guy."

"Why?"

"If I can get pictures of him in action, and his name appears on multiple claims in your files, you'll have evidence to deny claims. And you'll have pictures that'll help protect you against bad faith lawsuits." I wanted to add, *and the police will be better able to prosecute. It'll get him off the street.* But prosecution didn't apply to Alliance's bottom line, so I kept that reason to myself.

"Just a minute, Thigpen. I've got another call. Stay where you are."

The background noise from the phone sounded more muffled. There was no click of a hold button getting pushed, so I figured Meade would make me wait only a minute or two. Instead, I waited ten.

"Thigpen, you there?"

"Yeah. Still waiting."

"You got a license plate on this paralegal?"

I glanced at my notepad and told him the number.

"Let me run a check on that," Meade said.

Patiently, I started the Explorer's engine. The waiting continued another three minutes.

"All right," Meade said. "This guy's name is Derek Sloan. And yeah, he's had numerous claims on Alliance, always a different car. I want you to follow him."

"Okay. You understand, though, that he might take the next car to a different shop. I can't guarantee anything."

"You said he's been there three times already."

"Right. He'll probably come back to Josef's, but you're signing my paycheck, so I want to be upfront with you."

"I appreciate that. And as you've said, the cars might not even be insured by Alliance. Understood."

"It looks like he's getting ready to go."

"Follow him. Follow Sloan."

"Is there anything else?"

"No, no. That's it."

"Okay, I'll call back tomorrow," I said, but Meade had already hung up.

Sloan pulled away from the repair shop. I dropped the cell phone and camera on the passenger seat and followed. Again, the tow truck went in the opposite direction.

Sloan drove over to I-696, sped into Detroit on I-75, and twenty minutes after leaving Josef's Repair Shop, he was heading directly toward the Renaissance Center. Near the RenCen, he exited and drove onto Washington Boulevard. The RenCen's gleaming glass windows towered above us. To our left, the Detroit River, which was wide enough to drain three of the Great Lakes—Michigan, Superior, and Huron—paralleled our path.

Five minutes after leaving the highway, the Volvo pulled into a parking lot near the People Mover tram route.

I took out my cell phone and called Hal Booker, my "adopted" brother. Hal's parents had died when he was seventeen, and none of his relatives volunteered to take him in. Because he was over at our house all the time anyway, my parents let him move in and finish out his high school year.

Hal was my best friend. Hal was the only tennis player in the area who consistently challenged my game. He was short and quick, playing the baseline well. And he was always ready to play me, anywhere, anytime, he maintained, and even though he always challenged, he'd never beaten me. Of course, he loved to get my brother Tom to play, both of them against me, and occasionally they'd win that way.

Hal helped me on cases sometimes, especially stakeouts, and the fact that he was black, and a dark-skinned one at that, was often advantageous when working in downtown Detroit. Let's face it, there are some inner-city neighborhoods in which a white guy draws attention, something investigators tend to want to avoid. In those situations, I'd send in Hal.

"Hal, Jack here. Busy?"

"Nah. Starting classes tomorrow, but I'm free today. You need a tennis partner?"

"Afraid it's business today. Need help with a stakeout."

"Sure."

"How soon can you make it to Joe Louis Arena?"

"Ten minutes."

"Hurry. I'm parked out front."

Luckily, Sloan appeared to be waiting for someone. I could see his head bob as he looked around, apparently searching for someone.

Eleven minutes after ending his call with me, Hal arrived, driving a battered Toyota pickup. Hal didn't have a lot of money, but he didn't need much, being single and living meagerly. His jeans and green shirt that had been tie-died with orange streaks seemed to contradict the cowboy hat and expensive alligator-skin boots he wore. Hal had dreams of becoming a cowboy one day, something Tom and I teased him about through high school. There's lot's of black cowboys, he'd said. Ain't you ever hear of Nate Love? That's Deadwood Dick, man. And well, of course, we had never heard of him. That didn't spoil Hal's enthusiasm, though. He was determined to buy a ranch out west one day and live the cowboy life. His determination enabled him to be a top-of-the-line computer programmer, work from home, and have a ballooning bank account. Last year, he'd even convinced Tom and I to go to a traveling rodeo show, the Bill Pickett Invitational Rodeo. It was amusing to watch Hal whoopin' and hollerin', just like a real cowboy.

Hal strode over and tapped on my window.

I rolled it down. "You are one ugly fella."

He pulled off his hat, which appeared worn and dusty, and wiped his hand over his clean-shaven head. "That's not what the ladies are sayin'."

"Do you tell them you're an honorary Thigpen?"

"Only if I hear you say you're an honorary *brother*."

I laughed. "Hop in. Wait—the guy I'm following is getting out."

Sloan climbed out and marched away, head bobbing.

"Quick—need to lose the cowboy hat."

Hal tossed it through the window, and it landed on the passenger seat. Imitating John Wayne, he said, "A man ought to have a hat on when he's outside."

"Yeah, well, we'll retrieve it at the roundup."

Bringing my camera, I got out. Hal and I followed Sloan carefully, at a distance, and I filled Hal in on the case. Sloan stopped a few times and surveyed the afternoon traffic like a befuddled mall pedestrian searching for his parked car.

"How's Tanya?" I asked.

"You're not gonna believe this," Hal said. "She left me."

"Really?" Hal didn't have many friends, feeling more comfortable in front of a computer than out socializing. He'd been serious about Tanya, though. She'd even bought a cowboy hat. "Well, forget about it. You're too good for her anyway."

"She ran off with some Mexican stud, a kid really, but he was big into drugs. I think she liked that."

"The drugs?"

"Yeah. Too heavy for me, man. Anyway, it's no big deal. I've forgotten about her already. Just thought I'd mention it."

I nodded, seeing Sloan turn and stride into a narrow alley between warehouses on Shelby Street.

"Whatcha think?" Hal asked, squinting into the alley.

"He might be trying to shake anyone following. I don't think he's noticed us, though. Probably just being cautious."

"I'd rather be playin' tennis."

"Yeah, but you're getting paid for this. No one pays you for me beating your ass in a tennis match."

"More fun, though," Hal said, grinning, his pearl-white teeth gleaming.

"Let's cut the chatter and move out."

Following far behind, we hugged a warehouse wall. The wall's red brick was caked with gray dust so that the original color shone through in spots like open sores.

Imitating John Wayne again, Hal said, "Courage is being scared to death but saddling up anyway."

"Can't argue with that," I whispered.

Sloan never glanced back. Instead, head bobbing, he began jogging and soon reached the other end of the alley, Griswold Street, where he turned right. Hal and I sprinted in pursuit, stopped at the corner, and peered around the blistered beige paint of a corner post.

A woman caught my attention.

Her white dress was sheer, cut low enough to make the fabric nearly insignificant as far as her breasts were concerned. She must have prepared by massaging an ice cube over her nipples, a quick way to make them stiff, so that they pressed out against the fabric. She appeared to be studying her right ankle, bent over near the curb, blonde curls splayed over her shoulders. Her red shoes and red lipstick looked wet.

A man driving a Mercedes gawked at the woman. He apparently didn't know how to divvy up his attention between driving a motor vehicle and leering at a beautiful woman, because he failed to see a white van swerve in front of him, failed to hit the brakes.

Crash, bam, thank you, ma'am.

It wasn't a severe accident, but it was more than a fender bender. There was damage to the Mercedes grill. A taillight was out on the van. With a generous adjuster and multiple policies, the owner of the van could make a tidy sum of money. I took a picture of the van's driver—an overweight man with an overgrown mustache that must have made breathing difficult. He reached behind him, grabbed an already deployed airbag from the back seat, and stuck it to the steering wheel.

I zoomed in with my camera and took another picture.

Miss Veneer Dress walked crisply away.

Another picture.

The van's driver was running the same basic scam that had crippled Melissa Jamison.

Melissa Jamison had been a young college girl at home for the Christmas holidays. I was on a stakeout, parked at a Burger King, waiting with a zoom camera in my Explorer on a cold, windy night, near a stretch of Gratiot Avenue with an unusual number of late-night rear-end accidents. There'd been a flood of claims to State Farm, which hired me to check it out.

Melissa should've taken her car. Her father said she'd gone out to get a notebook from the Revco across the street. That's all it was. She could just scoot across, get the notebook, and come home lickety split.

I saw her standing on the edge of Gratiot Avenue, which was four lanes plus a median. Car headlights glared by, and I noticed Melissa's breaths, wispy white puffs in the moonlight. At the next gap in traffic, she started across. The rain was light, just a sprinkle, enough to make the pavement slick.

She paused in the median, waiting for two cars to pass. After the two cars, there was a clear stretch, no traffic for a quarter-mile.

The front car hit its brakes. The scam was typical—the first car causes a fender bender with enough damage to make the accident profitable. This time, though, the second vehicle swerved, avoiding rear-ending the first. The driver didn't see her until it was too late. Melissa tried jumping out of the way, but the station wagon slammed into her. She crashed against the windshield. The impact propelled her, blood intermingling with droplets of rain, into a broken, bleeding heap dozens of yards away.

I called 9-1-1 and ran to help her. It was a chaotic scene. Cars pulled over. People shouted. Headlights from stopped cars lit the scene. Rain fell harder and people cried. I had enough sense to make sure no one moved Melissa, but the damage to her spine had already been done.

The cops arrived within three minutes, the paramedics four minutes later. They saved Melissa's life. They didn't save her spinal cord.

"Whatcha thinkin' about?" Hal asked.

I shook my head. "Nothing."

"Ya look like you seen a ghost."

"Just had a bad memory replay. That's all." The van driver who was in cahoots with Miss Veneer Dress had caused what appeared to be a legitimate accident, so there would be no questioning the police report. An insurance claim would also be legitimate—but there were probably multiple policies taken out on the van. And no doubt the amount of damage would be inflated.

Sloan appeared beside the van and spoke to the driver. Then they went to the Mercedes, whose driver was examining the front of the vehicle. Sloan handed the driver of the Mercedes a business card, took out a cell phone, and made a call.

A few minutes later, the tow truck from Joseph's Repair Shop arrived. Sloan discussed the situation with the red-headed driver.

That was the moment I got the call that changed my life. Of course, my cell was on vibrate. I pulled it from my pocket, looked at the display, and saw that the call was from Dr. Cho. My mind flashed through all the tests he had performed—the EEG, MRI, and spinal tap—and how I had insisted he call me the moment he knew anything and tell me over the phone.

My hand shaking suddenly, I answered the call. "Dr. Cho, this is Jack Thigpen."

"I'm afraid I've made a tentative diagnosis, Jack. It's Creutzfeldt-Jakob Disease."

I couldn't move. Dr. Cho had affirmed my own research. CJD was fatal and there was no treatment. Proteins called prions that were behaving badly—folding incorrectly like beach chairs sometimes do, was how Dr. Cho explained it—making microscopic holes in the brain until it resembled a sponge. It was a death sentence.

"I'm sorry, Jack," Dr. Cho said. "I'm running more tests, and there are clinical trials starting in a couple of months."

"You think I'll live that long?"

"Based on past cases, probably not."

"If I'm alive, I'll call."

I slipped the phone back into my pocket.

"What the hell, Jack," Hal said. "Tell me, man. What's going on."

"Later."

I was in shock. Not knowing what to do, how to tell Hal, I was frozen on the spot. I hadn't processed the news yet, not deep down, so it wasn't real. It couldn't be.

Then Sloan abruptly headed toward the alley in which Hal and I stood.

My legs shaking now, too, we hurried back and pressed ourselves into the shadow of a vertical I-beam that supported the warehouse walls, typical of old Detroit warehouses with supports on the outside.

Seconds after Sloan passed us, we spun around the I-beam so that now we were hidden from him again. We waited patiently. But as Sloan neared the end of the alley, we ran to see if he would meet anyone else. Sloan touched the wall as he rounded the corner, which struck me as odd. He didn't seem the type to get his hands dirty. Dirt was most likely anathema to him, a reminder of the level of his morals, and he would refuse to acknowledge such truth.

Hal pulled slightly ahead of me.

I sidestepped a puddle and ran faster.

Near the middle of the alley, just as I spotted a flicker of movement at the end of the alley, I tripped and started pitching forward.

That's when I heard a loud *crack*, followed quickly by another, and I ended up face down, staring at a pebble, with a bullet hole in my shirt and my best friend dead.

CHAPTER THREE

I would die.

It was as though when my body impacted the street after my fall, the news sank in.

For a while I raged at the world, at the unfairness of life. I had so much left to do, so many goals. Getting back with Ellie. Expanding my investigation business. Starting a family. Making a tennis comeback. Now my life was over, ending as suddenly as a bug's future under the heel of a shoe.

A depression swept through me that was so dark I would've contemplated suicide had I known I wouldn't soon die. The news darkened my thoughts, weighted my soul.

Body movement is a strange subject to think about when one is slated for death, but that was precisely the subject I found myself pondering after my rage and sadness settled.

There had been times when I was stretched out late at night, listening to soft music, the lights dimmed, my thoughts slowing into noncommittal reverie. There would be something I wanted to do, grab another beer or go join Ellie in the living room. First would come the thought, then the consideration. Even after deciding movement was desirable, it didn't come right away. Momentum had to build up within my will, like a cascading stream of neurons across synapses, until the electrical charge demanded the contraction of muscle tissue.

I wanted to get up.

But second after second passed and still I had not budged. Maybe I had no control over my body now.

I didn't believe it, though. Something inside me told me I could move. I only had to want it enough. (*I think I can,* tooted a little red engine.)

I turned my head—I could move!—and looked up at the

sunlight above the alley. The light comforted me. Although it wasn't the acclaimed tunnel of light to lead me to my afterlife, it was light nonetheless. The shadow of my death was a veil through which I now viewed the world, and sunlight helped dispel the darkness.

Placed in a new situation, the world of the soon-to-be-dead, I endeavored to take stock of the situation. Lying in the grit that had witnessed generations of assembly line workers making repetitive motions that numbed their brains (how much better I could now relate!), I tried to take inventory.

My five senses were intact. I could feel gritty dirt, smell exhaust fumes, hear a car horn's blare, see the pebble (thank you, Stanley Kubrik), and taste dry fear in my mouth.

Yet I was intensely aware, my sense of being never stronger. Some days in my life had seemed a blur, and not just the college days of drugs. No, there were days of mediocre awareness when I had to catch up on paperwork or drive long distances. These were take-it-or-leave-it days of yada yada yada, when I wasn't particularly impressed to be alive. There weren't a lot of them. Many pursuits inspired me, not just tennis. But the ho-hum days were still there in my memory. Now, though, my awareness of my presence in the world was enhanced to a point that made all of my former days ho-hum. I was in the here and now. I had never been so conscious of how miraculous that was.

That was the positive aspect of my condition.

All else was a dark, slow undercurrent of despair.

This was new to me. Normally I rolled with punches, played the cards dealt, never sulked or wished for a better life, and I didn't want to start now. Ironic, that when I felt the deepest stab of despair in my life, I had little life left.

Hal …

Why wasn't he asking me if I was all right?

Not sure why—clutching at straws—I grabbed the pebble as I stood. Hal was prone, just ahead of me, not moving in a too-wide pool of blood. I knelt beside him, staring at the sickening squishy soup of fabric, flesh, and blood that was directly above his heart. Hal was dead. There was no need to check further. A single drop of blood plopped down into the pool. He was no longer gushing blood, only dribbling, like a man at a urinal waiting for the last few drops before zipping up.

Voices drifted to me from the end of the alley. I turned. There were seven young black men, teenagers probably. Two of them were carrying short lengths of chain. Another flipped out a switchblade.

And here I was, a white guy in downtown Detroit, standing over a black man who'd just been shot. Something told me explanations would come later, after they bashed my head in, if I lived.

Wanting to come to terms with my death in my own time, I picked up my camera, turned, and ran.

I felt a breeze against my skin, just below my left armpit. There was a bullet hole there. Hal hadn't been the only one targeted. The fact that I had fallen could've made the shooter believe he'd hit me, too, that both of his targets had taken bullets.

I slipped the pebble into my pocket (in case it later decided to transmit). Near the end of the alley, where there had been a flicker of movement, I stopped a moment and bent down, staring at a puddle. In the muck at the bottom, there was a murky impression. The imprint of a tennis shoe. There were two circles near the heel and smaller circles at the toe end. At the ball of the foot there was a "W" imprint. It was slanted, aerodynamically fashioned for speed. The rightmost serif was extended, as though faster than the rest of the letter.

(In my mind, I confronted my killer while Nancy Sinatra sang, "One of these days these boots are gonna walk all over you!")

Only one shoe manufacturer carried such a design, Winner Athletics, which specialized in sports shoes. Many tennis pros wore the brand. I kept up with trends in equipment, a responsibility I took seriously because a few of the tennis players still asked for tips at the Grosse Pointe Athletic Club, where I'd been welcomed because of Ellie's membership.

The gang of youths were quickly gaining on me. They were halfway through the alley, shouting obscenities and what they intended to do to me, all of it sounding very painful.

I ran.

Although the teenagers looked to be in good shape, I was in excellent condition (other than that nasty little fatal disease brewing in my brain), and soon I had put enough distance between us to safely head back to my Explorer.

On the way, I called 9-1-1 from a pay phone and reported the murder. I didn't volunteer any information about myself, saying I was a passerby who had heard the shot, seen the body. The lady seemed to understand my wanting to remain uninvolved, although she tried to get my name. I ended the call when she persisted. There was nothing I could tell them that would help. Since the motive wasn't robbery, Hal still had his wallet (assuming the teens hadn't ripped him off), his ID, and the police would have no trouble identifying him. Besides, there was nothing they could do to bring him back to life.

I didn't feel any itch, but scratched my arm anyway. The thought of decomposition bothered me. After I died, how long would my skin stay intact? Would it peel away? Would I start attracting flies prior to death?

The thought of flies compelled me to shake my head.

I passed the lot where Sloan had parked. His car was gone. No surprise.

I crossed the street and walked toward my Explorer, realizing I couldn't stay at home. Whoever was out to kill me (and Hal) might think they failed when I didn't show up on the six o'clock news. That *someone* might try again. And I didn't want any more bullets passing my way.

I needed someplace to go.

Where?

My brother, Tom, would take me in. He was my half-brother, actually, with a different last name—Bass. My killer wouldn't find Tom by searching for relatives with the name of Thigpen.

So, I'd go see Tom.

But what would I say to him?

The truth, the whole truth, and nothing but it?

Nearing my Explorer, I wondered if I would have the nerve to look at myself in the mirror.

CHAPTER FOUR

About the mirror, I had no choice. If I was going to continue with my life, I had to confront myself with the truth. I was a dead man walking.

I opened the door, sat on the driver's seat, and looked at myself in the rearview mirror. My face looked the same, except paler. What startled me, though, was my eyes and how distant they seemed.

There can be something intimate about looking someone directly in the eyes. Sure, bullies try to stare down people and politicians have honed the art of eye contact to meaninglessness, but for genuine people, people who strive for understanding, looking someone in the eye is a form of acknowledgment. It's a compliment—an intimacy of souls.

Connecting with someone eye to eye, window to window, is the way one soul connects to another.

But the eye is a large area when considering the pinpoint accuracy of a stare. I might, for example, look at the subtle shading of the iris, the tinctures of gold and green that circle my wife's eyes (we're separated, and her eyes as of late are obscured by a cold haze) and not at a particular point. This would be missing the mark. If the window to the soul is an eye, then it's a particular point in the eye, somewhere in the pupil.

But the pupil, too, is enormous, with an infinite number of points along the circumference to gaze upon.

It's not an easy thing to pinpoint, the dead center of the eye.

(*Note to self: stop using the term "dead center."*)

But once it's found, a lengthy look can freeze someone. The look startles a person, as though they've been found out. For a moment, headlights are shining on them in the black of night and they can't move. There's nakedness in the soul, vulnerability.

And I couldn't find mine. I was hiding from myself. Maybe it was necessary. Otherwise I'd be facing the fact that I had involved Hal with my surveillance, and now Hal was dead. I hadn't shot him, but if not for me, he'd be walking around with that flashing white smile of his.

My guess—because of this, I couldn't look myself in the eyes. It was something of a habit of mine. It was a quirky ritual, a way of confronting myself, of cutting through the bullshit.

I had stared often at my eyes during college, wondering if I'd have the courage to pursue my dreams of playing tennis. I stared during my two years in the pro tennis circuit, failing to climb higher than a ninety-sixth ranking. Then I stared in disbelief as my ranking plummeted and my career faded into obscurity.

But I stared most often when my marriage started crumbling. Who was I? Did I love her? Did she love me? Was I being honest with myself? If you can't look yourself in the eyes, whose eyes can you look into?

My eyes now held little use for ferreting out any bullshit I might be handing myself. One thing was evident, though, in my eyes—utter despair.

I was spending too much time at the mirror. I needed to go before a curious cop noticed me and wanted a little chat.

I shut the Explorer's door, and it struck my leg.

"Damn!"

The word exploded out of my mouth with leftover air in my lungs. I had tried pulling my leg into the vehicle, but my motions weren't smooth. At least I hadn't slammed the door, otherwise I might've broken a bone. Evidently a dead guy (okay, not quite yet) could feel pain.

After stepping down onto the asphalt, testing my footing, I decided my leg would be all right.

I started the engine, checked traffic, and shifted into gear.

The Explorer jerked forward as I pressed the gas pedal down.

By the time I merged into traffic on I-94, heading northeast, my thoughts had settled down and my driving was no longer erratic.

Tom lived five miles north of Mt. Clemens, in an old farmhouse now surrounded by subdivisions. As I drove, I reached over to the glovebox, pulled out my sunglasses, and put them on. Tom didn't need to see my eyes. In fact, no one did.

The miles dragged.

Tom was three years my senior. Although he had given me advice over the years, I was the one who financially helped him from time to time. But he had stabilized his income in the last few years, gaining a reputation as a top-notch taxidermist. (Would he consider me now both a brother and a future specimen?)

We had grown up in Mt. Clemens, which at the time was on the edge of Detroit suburbia. Farmland to the north, city streets to the south.

Tom's father, Harvey Bass, came to Michigan to work in the car industry after a four-year stint in the Marine Corps. He rode a motorcycle on the European battlefields, sometimes driving between tanks for protection from sniper fire as he delivered orders from Field Command. Tom has a photograph of him in his dress uniform. It was taken near the Detroit River, four months after V-E Day, three weeks after meeting his future bride, our mother, Tom's and mine. Even though the picture was faded, the film black and white, I could see the gleam in our mother's green eyes.

The marriage lasted ten years, ending in a bitter divorce. They had Tom in the eighth year of the marriage, perhaps as an effort to make the marriage stick. It didn't work, and Tom's father drifted away, although he later moved back to within a few blocks of Mom.

Our mother quickly remarried my father, Robert Thigpen. She and my father had two children. After me, there was my sister, Lynne the Pin. She was always slight in stature but had a short career as an M.P. in the Army. I hadn't seen her in years. She lived in Kansas now, a manager in a Wichita K-Mart. Although passing on the bungalow inheritance, Lynne claimed to have a desire to return to Mt. Clemens, but I never got around to asking why it was taking so long.

We were notoriously poor at keeping in touch. Not that we

didn't care. We did care, just in a detached, non-communicative sort of way.

My mother lived near Lynne. My father moved to the Upper Peninsula. He seldom left there. He had some strange addiction to being snowed in; that, or maybe he and his second wife had just grown tired of the incessant industrialization of southeastern Michigan.

I thought about my family for the entire forty minute drive from Detroit, wishing we had spent more time together.

It wasn't until I walked up the creaky porch steps of Tom's farmhouse that I began doubting my sanity. No sane person in my condition would come into a home in which a taxidermist's dead animals are scattered about.

I knocked.

A few seconds later, the door opened.

"Come on in," Tom said, stepping back. Tom was my height, but his hair was dark and thick, almost wiry, shoulder-length and tied back, while mine was thin and blond. He wore wire-rim glasses, camouflage utility pants, and a green button shirt on which dabs of spilled white glue had dried into stiff, translucent spots.

I walked inside.

Deer and antelope heads adorned the living room walls. Their eyes didn't follow me around, but they didn't have to. They were so damn glassy, they caught my attention wherever I walked.

"What the hell happened to you?" Tom asked. "You hung over?"

"No."

"Is that blood on your shirt?"

"It's nothing. Spilled a drink."

I wanted to hug him, let him know I wished we were closer. Instead, I had to keep my distance. It was just my way of coping.

He led me into the den, where he worked, where the lighting was brighter, provided by long fluorescent tubes suspended from a tiled ceiling.

I settled onto an upholstered wingback chair in the corner. Tom sat on a stool at his workbench, where chickenwire and

Plaster of Paris showed the skeletal beginnings of a forest scene five feet wide. A mockup of some four-legged beast, possibly a cougar, stood beside the workbench. To my right, there were green fish mounted on wall plaques. To my left, a brown bear and a pair of wolverines stood near the corner of the room.

Tom reached across the bench and picked up a molded eye, which looked like a marble cut in half.

Tom had a sense of humor, but it was subdued, dark in nature. If he hadn't gone into taxidermy, he would've ended up reading depressing poetry in a dank underworld grotto (in rhythm with the snapping fingers of beatniks).

"What kind of eye is that?" I asked.

"Mountain lion. The surface is very rounded. Some animal eyes are flatter."

"Do they sell human eyes?"

"Of course. Lots of uses. Wax museums, for example. Hollywood probably uses them in those flicks where Jason or Freddie is ripping off some kid's face." He smiled and shrugged.

"Are all of your animals made out of frames? You just glue the hides over them, right? Don't you ..., I don't know, ever preserve the animal flesh?"

"You don't know much about taxidermy."

"You've never explained much."

"You never seemed interested. But since you asked, I only use the hides. Sometimes someone wants a skull with antlers. They're a mess when they come in. I use beetles to clean them off. They eat everything—skin and flesh and blood—and leave only bone and antler." He nodded toward a terrarium atop a stand in the far corner, near a trout that stared with empty eye sockets. "They're hungry little bastards."

I shuddered.

"You have a specific reason to ask about this stuff?"

"Just curious. I've been thinking about death lately."

"I thought I was the one with suicidal tendencies." He clutched his neck and rolled his head, his tongue drooping out of his mouth.

"Suicide was never an option with me, and it isn't now," I said, trying to sound convincing.

Tom nodded. "Yeah, right, because now you've got so much to live for."

"Not really. I can't comprehend it anymore."

He glanced at my sunglasses. "Hey, if your eyes are too sensitive, maybe these will work better." He offered me the halves of the eye he had cut and chuckled.

"No. Thanks, anyway." I adjusted my sunglasses. They were starting to feel awkward.

Tom peered at me. "You come all the way out here to ask me this stuff?"

I had never felt farther away from home. "I was in the area, so I figured I'd drop by."

"Bullshit."

"What?"

"You heard me. You haven't 'dropped by' since Ellie left and you needed someone to get shit-faced drunk with. Something's wrong, Jack. Tell me what it is."

I reached up to my sunglasses, paused, and said, "You'd better get a drink for this."

Tom peered at me. He seemed about to object, then walked to the kitchen and returned with a bottle of Jack Daniel's whiskey and two shot glasses. He filled the glasses and leaned back against his workbench. "Go ahead. I'm waiting."

"Okay, hold on a minute." I went out and returned with Hal's hat, setting it in the center of the table. I told Tom what happened in Detroit, how Hal was shot and killed and how I'd left him face down in a puddle-spattered alley.

Tom's jaw dropped. "You sure he's dead?"

"Yes."

"Hal ..., it's just hard to take in. Dammit, he was too good a guy to get murdered like this. It's too damn senseless."

"It was my case. Hal was helping. It should've been me that died."

"Christ, Jack, it could've been both of you."

"That's not all."

"There's more?"

"I got a diagnosis today. Creutzfeldt-Jakob Disease."

"I'm not familiar with it."

"It's fatal and quick. First I'll be a babbling idiot, then a stumbling, twitching mental patient, then a comatose body while these proteins chop holes in my brain."

"We've gotta get you to a hospital!"

"No. There's no treatment, other than for pain. And I'm not hurting, not yet."

"So how many years are we talking about?"

"Two months."

Tom's face paled, his eyebrows furrowed. He lifted the shot glass to his mouth and swallowed the whiskey in one gulp. "You're joking, right?"

"You think I enjoy telling you this? Do you see me laughing? Christ! I've just been given a death sentence. Take a look, Tom, a good look. If I weren't so nearly dead already, I'd blow my head off."

Tom turned away. He ran his fingers through his hair, rocked his head to the left then the right as though silently arguing with himself.

"Good, Tom. That's the way I had to accept it, just a bit at a time."

"More bullshit. I don't believe you."

I grabbed his shoulder and swung him around. "It's true, dammit."

He shook his head. "No."

"I'm practically dead, Tom. I will cease to be."

"But—"

"Deceased, bereft of life, expired."

He shook his head. "Stop!"

I took off my sunglasses and looked him in the eyes. "I'll be a dead parrot!"

Tom turned away, downed another shot of whiskey, and turned to me. There was fear in his eyes. His mouth quivered.

It seemed odd that he accepted Hal's murder but found it difficult to swallow the fact that I would die. But then, he hadn't known Hal as well as I had. "Just call it CJD, Tom, if you want to refer to it. I don't want to have to hear the entire name."

He opened his mouth and then abruptly shut it. He turned away and drank from the bottle. Muttering "CJD, CJD ...," he went to his workbench and began shifting items an inch here, an inch there. He picked up an eyeball, scowled, and flung it into the kitchen.

Faster and faster he shifted the items until his back stiffened and he stomped back to the bottle and took another swig. He faced me again. "I don't believe it," he said, voice trembling. "I don't care what ... condition you're in, what name you call it, you're going to live a full life. Understand?"

"Tom—"

From the corner of his eye, a tear rolled gently down his cheek. But his voice grew steady. "That's it. I can't—I won't—handle this any other way."

Already, within a few hours of my death sentence, I had learned much. For someone in my condition, basically a dead guy, there were two kinds of pain. The door shutting on my leg proved that physical pain was still a reality. And now I knew that emotional pain was real, too. It was still centered in the heart. Beating or not, a heart could be broken. As far as pain went, I supposed, dead guys weren't all that different from anyone else.

CHAPTER FIVE

"So, going to help me out?" I asked.

Tom peered at me. "How?"

"For starters, I need a place to stay. Whoever shot Hal might try to finish me off."

"At least you haven't lost your will to survive. Sure—I'll help."

The will to survive. Tom was right, at least at the moment. But I wasn't sure my will to survive would last. Already I could sense it losing substance, like a pile of sand on a beach eroding under the assault of a strong wind.

Tom took the shot glass and the Jack Daniel's bottle into the kitchen. He played with the shot glass, rolling it between his fingers.

I followed him part of the way and stood quietly, straddling the dividing strip between the carpeted den and the tiled kitchen. Tom sat at the kitchen table. I stared at the floor tile pattern, thinking there was a hidden connect-the-dot pattern that would present a picture, a Eureka! Thereby enlightened, I would comprehend what would happen to me. I needed to know. Confusion breeds fear. And the fluttering sense in my stomach, the squeezing tightness in my chest, the weakness in my knees, told me that panic and fear still affected my body. The dying, it appeared, could sense the approach of panic, the dread of fear. Would I be aware of my body as it started to malfunction?

Just throw yourself on a bonfire, Jack – that'll solve everything.

Would that be considered suicide?

Everything was difficult in death. Life hadn't been this complicated, had it?

Yes, yes it had. My death would mirror my life—a struggle.

And now, a struggle for what? My future sure wasn't what it used to be.

The floor tiles failed to register a picture in my mind, but I figured out at least one thing that was bothering me. I wanted to feel connected to my brother.

The dead raccoon in the den stared at me with black marble eyes. Opposite the raccoon, a fox with a skulking tail peered. The entire collection of dead creatures formed a collective roadblock to my desire to tell Tom how much I cared for him. In a way, I was just like them now, one of his stuffed animals.

I began rocking side to side, one foot in the den, one in the kitchen, alternately edging into a room of nourishment and one filled with death stares of the inanimate.

I looked at the hallway on the other side of the kitchen. The utility room door was open. Tom kept his motorcycle there, a 750 cc Triumph. It was the cleanest motorcycle I'd ever seen, not a speck of dirt. The chrome shined like mirrors. The tires didn't even have carpet lint. The red gas tank was painted with white cursive letters: *Tom Terrific*. I vaguely remembered the cartoon character from which Tom had derived the name.

On a shelf in the same room, trophies from motorcycle shows were aligned in perfect order. The fact that Tom drove the motorcycle (his "Trump") to the shows and cleaned it onsite impressed the judges.

Tom took another drink. "Where'd you say you were shot?"

"An alley in downtown Detroit, off Shelby Street. It happened while I was working on a case, following someone."

"Is the case why you were shot? Insurance fraud?"

"I don't know. If a lot of money is involved, it certainly provides a motive. But I haven't thought about it much more than that. I've got other things on my mind."

"Yeah."

"I've been thinking," Tom said. "I mean, I don't accept your ... CJD, but if it's true, you've got to find a reason to go on, something important."

"You're the one who noticed I still had a will to survive."

He shook his head. "You'll need more than that. Something like a mission."

"Like a divine mission, a mission from God?"

"That's *not* exactly how I would put it, but yeah. If there's one thing I believe in, it's cosmic balance. Karma, in a way."

"I'd say things are unbalanced right now."

"But you're alive. Hal's dead, and for some reason you're still alive. Someone had a clean shot at you and missed. Why? I believe it's because you're meant to do something. You have something important to accomplish. That's why you're still here."

He made sense, at least superficially. But my mind was getting numb, and I couldn't focus my thoughts.

He filled another shot glass and downed it. "Tell me what else I can do."

I shook my head. "This might sound strange, but I just want to be alone for a while." It didn't sound strange to me. Nothing ever would again.

"You shouldn't be alone."

"I need to think."

Tom paused. "Okay, you can stay in the spare bedroom." He pointed down the hallway. "You know where it is. There's a TV in it now."

"To think a while—that's what I need."

"And get some rest. You need it."

"Yeah."

"I'm just worried about you. Can't help it."

"I know." I walked into the hallway, stopped, and looked back. Tom stood looking at me, the whiskey bottle in his hand, his knuckles white, his face almost as drained of blood as mine. I wanted to apologize for putting him through this. "Thanks again."

"Let me know if you need anything. Just call for me. I'll be here."

I nodded and went to the spare bedroom.

I turned on the overhead light and closed the door behind me.

There was a single bed, a nightstand with a small lamp, and a desk on which sat a small TV and an aquarium with two angelfish. I grabbed the remote control that was atop the TV, sat on the edge of the bed, and for a moment listened to the faint chortle of the aquarium filter in an otherwise silent house.

A sense of fatigue fell over me. This was confusing, because I couldn't fathom why I felt tired. But I could no longer fathom my existence, either, so I figured that sleep might overtake me. The prospect frightened me. Maybe the CJD would advance at a record pace. I might not wake up. And if I did wake, perhaps I would find myself in such a deteriorated state, a sludge of detritus, that I would physically be able only to wriggle on the mattress, to wallow in my own failing flesh.

So, afraid of sleep, I turned on the TV.

For hours, I channel surfed through news shows and sitcoms and nature documentaries, the images nearly meaningless to me, but keeping my mind off my condition. I didn't want to think about it, as though doing so would hasten my ultimate demise. I had thought I'd wanted to think; instead, I'd wanted to *not* think, just to *be*.

Near midnight, I settled on hitting the PREV CHAN button, flipping back and forth between reruns of Letterman and Leno. The L men. Stupid pet tricks and Leno's version of Karnac the Magnificent.

PREV CHAN – Letterman.

PREV CHAN – Leno.

The worst thing about a death sentence was not being able to laugh, I decided.

It wasn't that I couldn't see the humor in a dog that looked like his thin, long-haired owner, or another dog that howled at his owner, who was performing an impression of a Presidential acceptance speech. Also funny: Leno's version of an Army general explaining the contradictory nature of the term "military intelligence." I could see how these things were funny, but something wasn't clicking. There was a disconnect in me.

I don't think there's anything that saddened me more than the thought that I would never laugh again. Somehow, this seemed worse than dying.

But I kept watching. Fearing I might not ever wake up, I couldn't allow myself to fall asleep.

I watched Leno, and then I watched Letterman. I vowed to keep myself awake.

I failed.

CHAPTER SIX

"Jack—"

Someone shook my shoulder.

I opened my eyes.

A face peered at me from the side of the bed. "Thank God."

"Tom?" I asked.

"I had to find out ..."

"If I was coherent?"

"I couldn't tell if you were breathing. And I was worried you weren't going to wake up."

I sat up. "How do I look?"

"No different than yesterday. A bit rough, but it's not like you're getting noticeably worse."

"That's good." I stretched my arms. "Christ, you wouldn't believe how stiff I feel."

Tom smiled, my joke relaxing him. "It's good to see you, Jack." He hugged me.

"You too, Tom."

The warmth of his body felt good and flowed into me as though he were feeding me some of his life force.

He stepped away from the bed. "I'll be in the kitchen." He walked to the door and pointed at a gym bag on the floor near the nightstand. "I brought you some clothes.

"Good. Just what I need. I'll be out in a few minutes."

Tom left, and I turned my attention to the TV and a morning news program.

A brunette with straight hair and too much make-up was describing how warm and wonderful the day was going to be—low humidity, high in the upper seventies.

The forecast filled me with optimism. The weather girl's disposition was infectious. The world was grand when the weather was this good.

Except, the effect was pure fantasy.

Reality settled in. I was going to die

I dug the remote out from the crumpled blanket and clicked the TV off. I climbed out of bed and stretched. My legs felt tight, as did my arms, but all limbs moved well enough. I'd be able to continue my existence a while longer. But for how long? A week? Two? A couple of months?

I took a quick shower and dressed in the clothes Tom had brought, a lightweight cotton athletic jogging suit—sweat pants and shirt, dark gray with blue trim. Good. My movements would be least hampered by loose-fitting clothes. The last item in the bag was a small penknife with a folding blade. I slipped it into my pocket.

I put on my sunglasses and walked to the kitchen. Tom sat at the table, a full glass of orange juice and a plate of untouched toast in front of him. His head was resting face down on his forearm. Hal's hat was hanging on the back of his kitchen chair. Hearing me come in, he stood, walked hesitantly to me, raised his arms, and hugged me. I would miss him.

He broke away, sat back down at the table, and pushed the toast away.

"Can't eat?" I asked.

"Not hungry."

I sat across from him. "There's something I need to say."

"Go ahead," Tom told me.

"Given my current condition, you've got to make sure I'm not just sleeping if you think anything's happened to me."

"I get it. Don't worry, I'm not going to be taking you to the funeral home any time soon."

I glanced to my left, at the stuffed raccoon. "It'll be soon enough."

"Jack, I—I ..." He stood, walked behind his chair, and leaned against the counter. "Did you get the knife?"

I tapped my pocket. "Yeah."

"I figure you could use it. But maybe you need a gun. Someone's trying to kill you."

"I've had enough of guns."

He nodded, and we began eating. I managed a couple of pieces of toast and half a glass of orange juice, doubling what Tom consumed.

"Did I ever tell you that Hal was my first taxidermy customer?" Tom asked.

"No."

"I guess he was a little embarrassed about it, later. See, once he heard I'd bought my first taxidermy tools, he brought me a dead rat. Said he'd pay me ten bucks to mount it."

"A rat?"

"He told me not to worry, that he'd sprayed the hell out of it with a bug spray that killed fleas and ticks."

"Still, a rat ..."

"I was proud of it at the time. I still have the ten bucks in a frame somewhere. Probably a desk drawer."

I found myself missing Hal, and I didn't have the time for that. "I need to borrow your truck," I told Tom. "You can use mine. Keys are on the nightstand."

"But—"

"Whoever shot me might want to finish the job. He'll be on the lookout for my car."

"Whoever shot you might think you're dead."

"I didn't show up on the six o'clock news. Just Hal. A single murder victim. This guy might've figured I was wearing a Kevlar vest."

Tom reached into his pocket and handed me his keys. "Where're you going?"

"I was following a guy named Sloan when this happened. I figure he's the one who ordered the hit. He wasn't the shooter; Sloan's shorter than me."

"You saw your killer?"

"A brief look. About my height, wearing a raincoat. I was in the process of tripping, so I didn't see much more than that."

"Do you know where Sloan lives?"

"I have his plate number, so I can look up his address on your computer. You're still online, right?"

"Yeah, computer's back in the utility room."

"With your motorcycle."

"Yeah."

"I also know he shows up a lot at Josef's Repair Shop. It might be that Adolpho ordered the hit. I don't know, but Sloan does."

"Be careful."

"I'm not sure what 'being careful' means anymore." I turned to the front door. "I left my notepad in my car. It's got Sloan's plate number."

Tom headed for the utility room. "I'll boot up the computer."

When I returned with the notepad—and my camera and cell phone—Tom had finished booting the computer. I opened a browser, logged on to my plate tracing service, and typed in Sloan's number. A moment later, Sloan's address was displayed. I copied it into the notepad and stood. "I wonder if a motorcycle would improve my outlook."

Tom rubbed his hand over the metalflake gas tank. "I take a drive whenever I'm down. Sometimes it helps."

I nodded. We stood in silence a moment. There was so much more I wanted to talk about, so much more I wanted to express. But there wasn't time. "I've got to go." I strode to the front door and down the steps, Tom right behind me.

Reaching his truck, a white Ford pickup, I said, "Of course, there's something else I have to do first."

"What's that?"

"I've got to go the Club and say good-bye to Ellie." I grabbed the door handle and pulled.

"How do know she's there?" Tom asked.

"She meets her clients there. Schmoozing's part of her job. She's there every day at nine sharp. Before our separation, I'd begun to wonder if she was seeing someone, having an affair."

And maybe now they want me out of the way .... No, they wouldn't shoot Hal, too. Unless they hired someone who got carried away.

There, I'd thought it. Maybe she and her lover wanted me dead. Seeing her face-to-face was the only way to gauge her surprise at the sight of me. Would she be shocked? *Jack! I thought you were dead!*

"Hold on," Tom said. "This plan of yours ..., I'm just not sure about it."

"What do you mean?"

"You're coming back, aren't you?"

"In my condition, I can't guarantee anything."

Tom hesitated. "Before you go, take a look behind the seat."

I turned, stooped, and pulled out a baseball bat, a Louisville Slugger.

"You once hit a home run with that bat," Tom said. "It might come in handy. It's got a better reach than your knife."

I tested it, a light swing. I doubted I could generate much power, but with a blow to Sloan's head, I wouldn't need to. Despite its nicks and dents, it still had a lot of life in it and would pack quite a wallop. (Now, somehow, I had a better affinity to the piece of lumber.)

I slid it back behind the seat, turned to Tom, and said, "See you tonight."

"See ya, Jack."

I pulled out of the driveway, and a few minutes later I was driving south, toward Grosse Pointe and the Grosse Pointe Athletic Club, where Ellie had been a long-standing member. Our marriage had given me club rights, although since our separation, I'd begun noticing a few uninviting stares.

During the drive, I varied my speed, watchful for anyone following me. A couple of times I exited the freeway, certain my killer was in the car behind me, but each time I was proven wrong.

Halfway to Grosse Pointe, speeding along at 65 mph, I was filled with an awareness of how I was now in the world of the living, actively participating. In a way, I was an intruder. But I didn't want to leave. Tom had said I needed a mission. Right now, I had three: say good-bye to Ellie, remain among the living, and find out who killed Hal.

I arrived in Grosse Pointe without incident.

The homes in Ellie's neighborhood were mansions, the yards expansive, the shrubbery well manicured. Her home—our home—was one of the smallest, even though its insured value was well over a million dollars. It couldn't be replaced for that amount of money (it would probably cost twice that), but insured value and replacement value are two separate quantities, as any insurance fraud investigator knows.

Seeing the house now, in my new condition, I was reminded of my hopes for a home that had only briefly been realized. During my tennis playing days, we had traveled a lot, never really feeling at home.

The week after Ellie and I moved in, I found myself staring at the mirror. Was this a home I could picture myself raising children in? Would a family thrive on this plot of land? Would I be happy here?

I became convinced—yes. This was my home. My happiness could take root on this land.

For a few years, Ellie agreed.

But then she began to see things differently. She said she'd changed. There was nothing wrong with me, she claimed. In fact, she never said a bad word about me.

She didn't want a dime of my tennis winnings.

And I would ask, what exactly did she want?

She would look away and say, *I only want out.*

That's when I learned how pain really felt, how raw it was, how devastating.

I was working hard at establishing my investigation service, a job I discovered I was good at. I made a better investigator than a tennis player, and so I felt appreciated. Besides, I hoped to soon have a family to support. I figured Ellie was going through a phase. She would want me to come back. She hadn't even known why she wanted out of the marriage. Simply to be single again? To be free? I didn't smother her, and I didn't neglect her, either. As far as I knew, we'd had a wonderful marriage.

But love doesn't listen to logic.

And no one can tell a heart what to feel.

The Grosse Pointe Athletic Club was only a few blocks away from Ellie's house. I drove the remaining distance slowly. I turned into its maple-lined driveway, which curved to the right of the clubhouse, into a parking lot hidden by tall shrubs. The club had a golf course, which was well manicured (but the landscape was too flat to be very interesting), and sixteen tennis courts, three with small sets of grandstands.

I parked Tom's truck and noticed a man looking at me from the sidewalk. He was casually dressed, his hair hinting gray. He'd been walking toward the club entrance, but once he'd seen me, he started coming my way.

I opened the truck door, stepped out, and faced him.

"Jack Thigpen?"

"Yeah."

"The tennis pro?"

"Used to be."

"You gave tennis lessons to Octavia Popadakis, correct?" the man asked.

"Yeah, but I don't give lessons anymore."

"Oh. See, I have a granddaughter. And, well, since Octavia's going to the Nationals, I figured you were good. I'll pay whatever you want."

"No. Sorry."

The man frowned, unable to understand a refusal of money. "All right, Mr. Thigpen. I apologize for disturbing you." He walked away.

The fluttering sensation returned to my stomach. Slowly, deliberately, I closed the door and walked toward the club, but then I veered toward the back. Instead of going through the main entrance, I went in through the locker room by the tennis courts. A few of the regulars were there, executive retirees, each of whom, in the spirit of leading an active life, maintained a presence at the country club. Sometimes they played golf. Sometimes they played tennis. Most often, they sat in the lounge, drank martinis, and compared notes on their bulging stock portfolios.

A couple of the older regulars nodded briefly at me, the ones I'd given lessons to. Others ignored me. Ellie was "old money" and therefore popular at the club, and they evidently valued her membership more than mine.

I continued walking through the locker room to the other side, entering the rear hallway, past the sauna and massage rooms, the sky lighted atrium. I took a deep breath as I entered the lounge, where I would in all likelihood see my wife for the last time.

CHAPTER SEVEN

Standing on plush burgundy carpeting, I sidled against the wall to a potted plant, hoping its large fronds would provide cover. I looked around the lounge for Ellie.

The room was spacious, with three chandeliers, two hand-crafted stone fireplaces, cloisters of overstuffed armchairs, coffee tables, and sofas. To my left, there were large windows near a custom bar with brass rails. There, tables were scattered, the lighting subdued. Waiters took orders. There was a low conversational buzz suggestive of wealth, quiet enough so as not to give away secrets, loud enough to be noticed.

I estimated about fifty members were here. Most were dressed in business attire, perhaps having social moments after early morning exercise. Some drank coffee, some tea, others juice (freshly squeezed, of course). Trays of bagels, toast, scones, and pastries were being carried to a private conference room past the fireplace.

Outside, there was a large patio with scattered wooden poles and trellises, through which vines weaved. I didn't know what kind of vines. (I knew more about anatomy than botany.) Many of the club patrons were having brunch outside. It was a nice day for it, a gentle breeze, not overly humid.

Framed in the sunlight, sitting at a table by the long glass window, my wife spoke to a waiter, who nodded perfunctorily.

I walked toward her, the background piano music sounding like it was broadcast from a funeral, the kind of music that plays when people are distressed and crushed, hopeless—polite music that attempts in vain to be soothing, but instead only adds to the sadness.

What would I say?

I wished I had planned better.

Ellie, we're through. Ellie, it's been fun. Ellie, as far as you're concerned, I'm dead.

No. It didn't matter how cold she'd been. I would do this as a favor, take the pressure of making a decision about our marriage away from her.

"Jack!"

Startled, I turned too quickly. My legs tangled. I lurched to the left, almost falling, but managing to regain my balance. "Octavia, what are you doing here?"

Of course, Octavia had every right to be here. She was the club's tennis representative at the Nationals, quite an accomplishment for an eleven-year-old. Octavia Papadakis had played tennis since the age of three. I'd been giving her tips since she turned eight.

"I'm here to play tennis, silly." She swung her tennis racquet. Her braided hair swished behind her. Her pleated white skirt swayed gracefully, as though choreographed by her sense of rhythm.

"You snuck up on me," I said.

She was full of energy, so that as she moved to her left, then her right, peering at me, her eyes narrowing, she seemed to be bouncing. "You all right? You got a hangover or somethin'?"

"I've had an injury, that's all."

"You'll be okay, won't you?"

"I think so. We'll see."

"Oh. Good. Anyway, I was going out to hit a few balls and I saw you, and well, I wanted to know if you have any last-minute tips."

"Yeah, that's right—the Nationals are next week. Tips? Right. Let me think a minute."

I'd given her three weeks of lessons a few years back, and she claimed it had started her on the path to success. She had more than talent; she had the drive needed to win.

"Enjoy the matches," I said. "Have fun."

"Huh? I'm always having fun, Jack. I want to win."

"I know you do. I wanted to win, too. But there comes a day when you realize there are more important things than trophies."

She harrumphed. "You must be really sick. You don't look good, you know." She squinted. "You got a fever? You look burned up."

"Yes, that's it. A fever. I'm going to talk to Ellie, then I'll go see a doctor."

"Good." She swung her racquet and headed toward the tennis courts. "Tell Miss Ellie I said hi."

"Good luck, Octavia."

She bounded toward the same door I'd come through, toward the tennis courts, but stopped to say something to Harold Ellis, the club's social director. Then she shook hands with Shelly Howe, Octavia's neighbor. Near the exit door, she stopped to talk to the man who'd funded an indoor court behind the club. His name was LaPointe, a tall man with impeccable clothes and manners. Not only was he one of Detroit's most ambitious (and rich) land developers, he seemed to remember the name of anyone he had ever met and always had a warm greeting. Octavia gestured at me with her racquet. LaPointe nodded at me with a warm smile. Appreciating his gesture (much nicer than Ellis's sneer or Shelly Howe's upturned nose), I returned the nod and looked back at Ellie.

Let's get this over with.

I strode quickly across the room.

She blinked when I sat across from her. "Oh!" she said.

"Just passing by. Sorry if I startled you."

She was wearing a light blue pleated skirt and white blouse. I couldn't help myself from admiring her legs as she scooted her chair closer to the table. Her hair was still beautiful, what was left of it, shimmering goldenrodlike in the sunlight. But the field had been harvested. The longest hairs didn't drop below the lobes of her ears.

"I-I'm okay," Ellie said. "I was just expecting Bonnie. We meet every day, and she's rarely late."

"I knew you met someone. Didn't realize it was Bonnie."

"Well who else would it be?"

I shrugged, wondering about that very question. "Clients."

"I meet clients, too."

The amazing thing about my relationship with Ellie (she

despised being called Elizabeth and would scorn anyone making such a mistake) was that we were connected on some higher plane of existence. At least it seemed that way to me. Our lives were entwined with intimacy. Watching TV, we would both rise at the same instant to head for the fridge and a snack. We had the same reactions to movies we watched, the same tastes. I'd even say that she detested chick flicks because they were too schmaltzy. What man couldn't feel affection for a woman like that? She enjoyed sports, liked quiet evenings, and loved to read. We were the J & E show, and we were the only audience that mattered.

"I wanted to have a word with you," I said.

Her narrow nose twitched, as it often did when she searched for the right words. "I'm glad you came by. I wanted to talk, too. I've been meaning to call. I've just been so busy."

"Me, too."

Instead of telling her our marriage was over, I wanted everything to be like it was before, to hold her in my arms, feel her warmth.

No matter why she had wanted to talk, I'd have to tell her that the trial separation had proven we weren't meant to be. We needed to end our marriage and file for divorce. And the sooner we did it, the easier my death would be for her.

Her mouth twisted, a sort of scrunched-up look that came close to resembling a pout, a sexy blossoming of the lips, but it was more of a follow-up to the nose twitch, another search for words. "Are you all right?" she asked.

"I feel a little stiff, that's all."

She was trying to see past the shaded lenses of my sunglasses.

I looked around the club. Most of the people here knew about our marriage problems, and they most likely took Ellie's side. Their frowns were of that special frown that only the rich have mastered.

As my gaze swung Ellie's way, she looked down. Her eyes looked heavy, weighted by sadness.

"How's the consulting firm going?" I asked.

She began arranging her silverware, tugging at the linen table cover, glancing out the window, occasionally cocking her head as though trying to see me at different angles.

"It's more work than I can handle," she said. "I might hire someone soon."

If Ellie needed help, she would hire someone at exactly the right time. She had a knack for running operations smoothly. I had sometimes wondered if the occasional bumps in our relationship were so alien to her exemplary history of project successes that she'd wanted the separation more out of bewilderment than anything else. It wasn't that she worked in an easy environment, either. She was a consultant in a male dominated field, and her projects were always high pressure.

Ellie had worked at a small start-up company that specialized in setting up warehouse shelves and ordering products from suppliers. She was so successful that she caught the attention of management at the Eddie Bauer chain. She worked there a year. Then, with industry people pleading for her services, she set up her own consulting firm. For relaxation, she played tennis. That's how I met her, on the courts in college. We've been together ever since, at least until six months ago.

"I'm glad business is good," I told her. "I've no doubt you'll figure out the workload."

"Thanks, Jack." She nudged a spoon. "Is anything *wrong*?"

"What do you mean, wrong?"

"You look like you've lost weight. Are you all right?"

"Sure."

"You don't look well."

"I lost a friend yesterday. Hal Booker. Murdered." And it was my fault.

"Oh. I'm so sorry." Ellie nodded and fiddled with her water glass. "What was it you wanted to talk about?"

I tried not to grimace, realizing that I should preempt her speech about wanting to give our marriage another try. I didn't want to hear about reconciliation. Help from a counselor could fix the marriage, she would say.

She stared out the window. Before I could say anything, she said, "I signed papers last week requesting a divorce."

"What?"

"We've been apart six months now, so—"

"It was a trial separation."

"The point is, it's time we get on with our lives."

People had once believed Earth was the center of the universe—and I had once believed Ellie cared. "You're right," I said suddenly. "It's over. I can see that now."

"I'm sorry, Jack."

"I won't fight the divorce. It's what I want, too."

She took a deep breath and ran fingers through her hair, which looked darker, probably because it was so damn short. She reached into her briefcase and pulled out a bundle of papers wrapped with a rubber band. "I found some things of yours in one of the file cabinets."

I took the papers. The bundle seemed extraordinarily heavy.

"And I made some copies of our tax returns."

"I'm sure they'll come in handy."

"Also, there are warranties on the appliances you bought for your house."

So it was my house now, not our rental.

"And a copy of the life insurance policy we took out on you."

Life insurance?

"I've got something else we need to talk about," Ellie said.

Ellie was my beneficiary.

"I should've told you sooner."

We increased the policy payout not long before the separation.

"Jack—are you listening?"

Condensation slipped down her water glass, leaving trails, which I studied, avoiding Ellie's eyes. "Are you suggesting that because I don't look healthy, this policy might pay out soon?"

"What?"

"You're still the policy beneficiary, in case I meet my maker, right?"

"I don't know. Maybe you updated the policy. What does this have to do with anything?"

"You said I didn't look well."

"You know I don't want your money."

"I don't know anything."

"Come on, Jack, you know me better than that, don't you?"

"I don't think I know you at all. I only thought I did."

Her nose twitched. She gripped her briefcase, holding it in front of her as though clutching a shield, trying to angle it to deflect an approaching arrow.

When I looked into her eyes, I realized how foolish I was. Even a soon-to-be dead guy can have an ego. I hadn't wanted mine bruised. Rejection tended to hurt, to leave wounds and scars. Ellie loved me—she just couldn't live with me.

"I'm sorry," I said. "I didn't mean that. I've been under the weather. I love you, Ellie. I always will. And the thought of us not being together ..., well, it hurts."

"I understand, Jack. I hurt, too. And I'm sorry."

"Don't be." I stood. "I've got to go. Separate ways, right?"

She nodded. "We'll talk again, okay?"

"I'd like that," I said. I walked across the carpeting, out the main entrance, and into the sunshine that, despite the current absence of clouds, was subdued.

"Bye, Ellie," I whispered.

CHAPTER EIGHT

As I drove toward Sloan's house, I thought about what Ellie had said. She still loved me. It was time, though, to go our separate ways. Fair enough. I imagined our relationship would've been good after divorce, not as blissful as those euphoric early days of the J & E Show, but good. The problem was that I wouldn't be around (not after I was in a casket for viewing).

Ellie needed space. I understood her need now. I needed space, too. I was like a creature who, knowing death was imminent, felt an urge to leave the pack, go to a distant field, and die alone. There was no good reason to subject others to watching death, a process quite possibly agonizing. No, if I had any respect for the living, I'd let them go on with their lives and not force them to dwell on the dead. Besides, I'd always viewed death as a ship to be sailed solo. The ship of death had only one captain, and everyone had to chart a unique course into the vast darkness of the afterlife.

First though, before I went off on any sort of Caribbean cruise, there were a few interactions with my fellow human beings I wanted to complete, the first being a chat with Sloan.

I could stake out his house, of course, wait for him to come home. But I wanted to know more about him before we *chatted*. A search of his house could tell much about him, give me clues about his lifestyle, his hobbies, his debts, the size of his shoes (and whether or not any bore a Winner Athletics logo). I'd know the contents of his refrigerator, the color of his shower curtain, his brand of coffee, what kind of weapons he might have lying around.

Other that the last bit of information, each detail by itself was innocuous, but having such a store of information at hand would not only give me a psychological edge, I could use the details of them during a conversation with Sloan to make him think his operation had been compromised.

I pulled off I-94 onto Metro Parkway. I slowed, watching my rearview mirror. No one followed.

Unless they were farther back.

Stop it. You've got enough to be frightened of without imaginary pursuers.

Except, I pointed out to myself, there was indeed someone out there somewhere who might try to kill me again.

After another mile, I took out my cell phone and called my brother. "Tom, it's me—Jack."

"Anything wrong?" he asked. "Where are you?"

"I'm all right, considering. I'm almost to Sloan's house."

"I could come and watch your back."

"Like I said, too dangerous. But I do need a favor."

"Anything."

I hesitated. "I'll eventually go into a coma. After that, death. Make sure I'm really dead, okay?"

"What do you mean?"

"I've heard of people waking up in morgues. Evidently, there can be deep comas that resemble death. I don't want to wake up in a morgue. Worse yet, an autopsy room."

"Jack, I couldn't tell if you were asleep or in a coma this morning."

"I know, but you shook my shoulder and woke me."

"What if that doesn't work?"

"Have the doctors inject me with morphine. A deadly dose. They do that anyway, from what I hear, for people dying in hospices. It's for pain, yes, but it's to end the pain. It just hastens the process. I just want to make sure."

"Jack ..."

"Just promise. Please."

"Okay, you can count on me."

"And I want to be cremated, not buried."

"Sure, Jack."

"Now listen, if I don't call back within two hours, come and look for me." I gave him Sloan's address. I had to repeat it because he didn't have pen and paper nearby.

"All right, Jack. Call me. I'll be waiting."

"Thanks, Tom."

A half-mile later, I turned off Metro Parkway into the Lakeland subdivision. The houses were middle class, the yards just big enough for owners to break a sweat mowing.

I turned right, onto Lake Lure Road and passed Sloan's house. Like all the others in the neighborhood, it was ranch style. Unlike most others, it was on a corner lot. Most of the lawns were cut, but there was little in the way of shrubs, few examples of dedication to landscaping. This was a working class neighborhood, an abundance of same-design houses, many with basketball backboards mounted above garage doors.

I parked around the corner from Sloan's and watched. I waited, feeling exposed, vulnerable, for twenty minutes. There was no activity in the house, no vehicles in the driveway. A few cars drove by, but the occupants appeared self-absorbed and didn't even look my way. Sloan, judging by the pace of his appearances people who'd been involved with Josef's Repair Shop, was probably a workaholic when it came to scams, and he would be out making money at it. Deciding nobody was home, I put on the work gloves I'd spotted on the passenger floorboard (making me think about fingerprints) and walked to the back of his property. A five-foot chain-link fence completely enclosed his back yard, with a gate to the driveway out front. There was a small in-ground pool behind the house. Next to the garage, there was a pair of doghouses.

The front yard was too open for me to break in that way. I'd be spotted. Here, at the back, there was an abundance of trees, tall and numerous, sentinels of subversion and concealment. A drainage ditch ran behind Sloan's house, in front of a line of pines. The ditch's banks were filled with brush and debris and so much litter—paper, empty plastic containers, aluminum cans—the ditch looked like it doubled as a dumping ground whenever the sanitation department fell behind.

I eyed the doghouses. The grass hadn't been trampled into dirt around them. There were no water or food dishes. I stepped sideways for a better view. I could see partially into the doghouses, but not all the way. Still, I saw no trace of a dog.

I didn't want to make too much noise, but I rattled the fence and in a slightly louder than normal voice said, "Hey!"

No dogs.

Good.

And still no activity from the house.

The street clear of traffic, no one in sight, I put my hands on the fence and hoisted myself up, managing to swing my leg to the top of the fence. My shoelace caught a wire. I tumbled into the back yard.

I lay there, jarred.

I had rattled the fence and fallen over; but it wasn't those sounds, it was my presence on their territory that provoked the doghouse inhabitants—a Doberman and a German shepherd. They ran toward me, barking, bristling, ears drawn back. Their teeth clacked as they snapped their mouths shut. Their paws dug into the grass. I pushed myself up to my knees and fumbled for my knife.

A few feet away from me, they stopped. They no longer barked, no longer bared their teeth. Their heads cocked side to side. The Doberman whimpered. The German Shepherd whined.

A moment later, they slunk back to their doghouses as though they'd come face to face with a great dog-killing monster and retreated in terror.

They cowered in their doghouses, whimpering, whining.

They must've recognized something in me they feared. Death? Something beyond death? Maybe they sensed the underworld, the River Styx, the dragon-tailed guardian dog Cerberus.

Hey dogs, did you glimpse the ferry man Charon? Helluva ride, I hear. And for the most part, a one-way trip.

I stood and brushed dry grass from my shirt. Eyeing the doghouses, I walked beside the pool to the back door and listened. The dogs' whimpers were beyond earshot. The only sound was the distant traffic on Metro Parkway.

I peered through the window in the back door, which led into the kitchen. The lights were off. An air conditioning window unit in the living room, which was at the front of the house, just beyond the kitchen, blew the edge of slightly rippling drapes.

I pressed my ear against the glass, waited a minute, then

decided it was safe to go inside. I turned, pressed my back against the door, and jabbed my elbow through the glass. Shards fell to the kitchen floor and scattered.

After pulling up my sleeve, examining my elbow, and seeing it wasn't cut—lucky me—I reached in, unlocked the door, and went inside.

I paused, listening for footsteps, then walked noiselessly through the kitchen—taking a quick peek in the fridge, seeing leftover pizza, cranberry juice, and two bottles of vodka—turned right, and headed down the carpeted hallway. I glanced in each of the three bedrooms, the bathroom, and the den. No one, except me, was home. But that didn't mean I wanted to take my time. I didn't want Sloan to surprise me. He might be bringing home a couple of his scamming scumbag friends. I didn't want to be outnumbered, and I didn't want to meet him on his turf. No, I wanted to meet Sloan on my terms.

I examined his closets. There were dress shoes, leather work shoes, a pair of hiking boots, sandals, and deck shoes. None had a Winner Athletics logo.

On top of his dresser, there was a small TV/VCR set. I ruffled through the dresser drawers, through the socks and shirts and underwear drawer, and in the bottom left drawer, I found a shoebox with porno tapes. Sloan had a fascination with promiscuous vixens "doing" various urban centers. *Debbie Does Dallas. Suzie Does Seattle. Mona Does Miami.* The videos' vocabulary of title verbs expanded with *Betty Bangs Boston.*

The clothes and videotapes hadn't been so neatly arranged that Sloan would notice they'd been disturbed. (I hoped.) But I carefully closed the drawers, trying as much as possible to keep everything in its original position.

The other two bedrooms were empty. Their empty walls made me realize how sparsely the house was decorated. There were no paintings, no wall hangings, no mirrors on any wall. The TV in the living room, though, was a 42-inch plasma wide screen. The stereo had wafer-thin speakers that were four feet high and a display with enough LEDs to rival a 747 control panel.

Sloan wasn't a neat person. A pizza box sat on the coffee table in the living room. A couple of stiff slices remained. His bed wasn't made, and his bathtub looked like it hadn't been scrubbed in years, the white porcelain bearing multiple rings, the bottom one the darkest.

In the bathroom, I discovered Sloan had a problem with headaches. Along with the Band-Aids, toothpaste, and shaving supplies, not only were there three bottle of aspirin, there were two bottles of prescription migraine medicine sandwiched between Ibuprofin and Goody's headache powder and a few herbal remedy capsules.

In the den, I saw that Sloan enjoyed high-end electronics. He had the latest computer, a high-end LCD display, and a deluxe combination printer/fax/copier/scanner.

I skimmed through the filing cabinet in the den, finding tax records, insurance policies (none with Alliance), and other legit-looking paperwork.

I moved over to the desk drawers. I found stamps, envelopes, and pens in the top drawer, other office supplies in the second, and in the third—bank statements from five separate banks. I browsed though them, getting a sense of the account histories.

Last year, his largest account balance was only three thousand dollars. Since then, it had grown to nearly twenty thousand. Farther back in the drawer was a portfolio of stocks that had been opened five months ago. The current value was over a hundred thousand dollars. I found two checks, one for twelve hundred, the other a thousand, both from the account of Bill Dunn at the Dunn Ford dealership.

So, Sloan really has been a workaholic, a real eager beaver this past year.

He was scamming insurance companies—at least Alliance Insurance, according to Ted Meade—and he had hefty paychecks from Dunn Ford. I'd found no pay stubs or any other reference to Josef's Repair Shop. If I considered the checks only, I'd have to conclude Sloan was working for Bill Dunn, whose name was well known in the area from the "It's a Dunn deal!" commercials. But that didn't seem rational. If a car dealership wanted to illegally increase profits, there had to be better, less risky ways.

Perhaps not.

Insurance payouts were easy for the street savvy. And, with

what I knew, the risks weren't all that high. If Dunn employed Sloan, and Sloan was the active participant in the scams, Dunn might be able to claim plausible deniability.

But why would Sloan be working for Bill Dunn? Because the pay's good. Yeah, but Sloan looked capable. Wouldn't he make more if he set out on his own?

Something's wrong.

Of course something was wrong! Everything was wrong. The entire world was moving on like traffic on an autobahn and I was a shoeless transient stuck on the side of the road with my thumb out.

Think! What is it?

I shifted my weight uneasily, looked up, and expanded my chest, drawing air through my nose, smelling smoke.

Three explosions came in quick succession—*whoomph whoomph whoomph*—muffled but almost concussive in their effect on me. They'd been just outside the house, two in front, one in back.

I hurried into the hallway and saw dancing orange-yellow light at both ends. Thick black smoke pressed down from the ceiling.

I ran to the kitchen.

Flames billowed in through the door's broken window with blast furnace intensity. The window above the sink—also looking out to the back yard—was equally engulfed by fire, just not broken. It looked instead about to melt, glowing with heat.

In the living room, curtains were ablaze. Whatever held the air conditioner in place suddenly failed and the window unit tumbled out. Flames spread along the walls, scaling them, lapping at the ceiling.

I turned, ready to head down the hallway and find an escape route. The fourth explosion came from the utility room—the gas water heater—shattering the window above the sink, blowing me onto my back in the living room. Above me, the white textured ceiling was being consumed by greedy sheets of flames that surged farther inward like hellish tidal waves.

Time to move, Jack, or that cremation option you mentioned to your brother will become reality by default.

I rolled to my left, pushed myself up, scrambled into the hallway, which was smoke-filled, pressurized, like smoldering tinder ready to burst into flames. A constant roar droned, the heated air creating a massive wind. Timbers crackled. Support beams groaned.

It'd been only a minute since the initial explosions, but already Sloan's house was nearly consumed. I figured some kind of gasoline-mixture bombs—super-sized Molotov cocktails—had been used along with the fuses I'd smelled.

Only a minute, but if I didn't get out in the next thirty seconds, I'd be going by a new name—toast.

I ran into the den. The flames outside its window were high, but not raging like in the kitchen. I pulled out the top desk drawer, ran to the window, and smashed the glass. I raked the drawer quickly around the window frame, scraping away shards. I dropped the drawer, took a step back, then propelled myself forward and dove through the opening, through fire and smoke and heat, and for a moment felt suspended like a dead pig on a spit. Then gravity had its way with me and I fell to earth with a deadened thump.

Wisps of smoke rose from my sweats.

I tumbled forward, rolled, and strode away from the heat.

Smoke churned skyward, belching as parts of the roof caved inward. Timbers groaned under weights that were becoming unevenly distributed. Shouts approached, neighbors rushing to the scene.

I climbed the fence, ran to Tom's truck, and climbed in. I hoped the neighbors, focused on the flames, hadn't noticed me scurrying away.

After tossing aside the gloves, I started the engine and sped down the road, opening the window. The cab reeked of smoke.

For the second time, *someone* had failed to kill me.

Had I been the target this time, though? Or could someone have tried to kill Sloan? Maybe the someone had thought I was Sloan.

I didn't know the answer, but I bet I knew who did.

Bill Dunn.

CHAPTER NINE

Driving west on Metro Parkway toward the Dunn Ford dealership, I pulled out my cell phone and called my brother. "Tom, I made it okay." I continued glancing at the rearview mirror, making sure I wasn't followed.

"I can hardly hear you."

I rolled up the window. "That better? I had to air out. Someone torched Sloan's house while I was inside. It only took a few minutes to turn it into cinders, almost me, too."

"How'd you get out?"

"Jumped through a window."

"Did you get hurt?"

I hesitated. "No. I'm all right." Truth was, I was beginning to believe my body was not feeling pain so intensely anymore. That made sense, I supposed. CJD attached the central nervous system. Mine was being degraded, so it wasn't transmitting pain as efficiently as a healthy body.

"What's the plan now?" Tom asked.

"I found out Sloan's working for Bill Dunn. I'm heading out to Dunn Ford."

"That the one on Van Dyke?"

"Yeah. I need you to stay by the phone again. If I don't call back in a couple of hours, you know the routine."

"Okay. Be careful."

"I will. Talk to you soon."

Thirty minutes later, I pulled into the Dunn Ford dealership. I cruised through the lot. Triangular flags of red, white, and blue plastic flapped and snapped in a growing breeze, hung from canvas ropes strung between light poles. I kept glancing at the flags, trying not to catch the eyes of sales people. Eye contact would give someone a reason to greet me and make a sales pitch.

At the moment, I had no patience for it.

I avoided them by parking in back and entering the dealership at the parts department, past a banner that claimed ALL CREDIT APPLICATIONS ACCEPTED.

They certainly accepted all applications, but they didn't approve them all. Car dealerships weren't showcases for truth in advertising. Far from it. But maybe today I'd get more truth out of Bill Dunn than he'd anticipated dealing with when he got out of bed this morning.

A man gesticulated at the parts counter, trying to describe the part he needed, using hand motions to support his limited mechanical vocabulary. "The little doohickey beside the thingamajig. It's round and bolted to the frame." Two older men behind him ran impatient fingers through hair.

I slipped past them into the repair bays.

Mechanics were busy, their pneumatic tools filling the bays with *whirr whirr* sounds beneath cars raised on hydraulic lifts. The service manager sat in an alcove office, signing paperwork. Pretending to spot my car, I marched across the bays, keeping an eye out for Sloan.

The bay doors faced west, letting in enough sunlight to offset the darkness of my glasses. The only people I saw were mechanics; and they were a noisy bunch. I walked amid the whirs of pneumatic devices and metallic clanks of tools and stopped between the last two bays, which were filled with stacks of tread-bare tires, round stacks that looked like phalanxes of Michelin Man wannabes.

Even though I didn't see Sloan, I checked everyone's shoes as I walked through. Winner Athletics wasn't exactly a household name, but I would've thought I'd see a few people wearing them. But I saw only Nike, Adidas, Converse, and brands for work boots with steel toes.

"Can I help you?" a mechanic asked.

"Just looking for my car," I said. "I think it's out front."

I turned, left the service area, and walked toward the front showroom. Hand in pocket, I slowly rolled the pebble between my fingers. It had been with me since the alley in Detroit, the start of my adventure, and the feel of it relaxed me, perhaps because it verified that I still had my sense of touch. (Or perhaps because my hand was closer to the knife.)

In the hallway leading to the showroom, I saw Dunn's name on an office door. Hesitating only an instant, I stepped in.

Dunn had a square jaw and box-like face. Wearing a white shirt and blue tie, he was sitting at his desk, typing on a keyboard. He looked fairly fit, but the bulge at his midsection suggested he'd have problems completing a three-mile run. He wore brown loafers, not running shoes, not Winner Athletics. His belly pressed against the edge of the desk, he reached over without looking and picked up a sub sandwich. He bit into it and shook his head. His square face and broad shoulders made me think of him as an overconfident pit bull.

He glanced up, slapped the sandwich down, and stood. Chewing quickly, he continued to squint at me. "You look like you're lost."

"Hello, my name's Jack Thigpen. I'm looking for one of your employees, a guy named Sloan."

His eyes widened slightly. "Sloan doesn't work here."

"Then why are you cutting him checks?"

"Maybe he did some contract work. Hell, I can't remember every name of every contractor. I'm telling you, though, he's not an employee of mine." He peered at me. "You smell like smoke."

"I just came from a fire."

Dunn carefully placed his sandwich beside the keyboard. He pointed at the chair in front of his desk. "Care to sit, Mr. Pigpen?"

"That's Thigpen. And no thanks."

"You know, it's not all that bright in here. Your sunglasses—are those prescription lenses?"

"I have sensitive eyes. Now, about Sloan—"

"Doesn't work here."

"But you recognize his name?"

Dunn rubbed his chin, which jutted out. Wrinkles in his forehead deepened. "Care to give me a reason why I should let you come in here and start asking about my business?"

I thought about telling him I was an undercover cop. But,

truth was best, I decided. I pulled out my wallet and showed him a business card. "I'm involved with an insurance fraud case."

"That still doesn't answer my question," Dunn said.

"First, I don't give a damn about your business. I'm interested in Sloan, and you claim he doesn't work here. Second, I've had a real crappy day, and it'd sure help me if you cooperate. Third, I'm tired of people bullshitting me, and you don't want to see me when I'm mad."

Dunn looked amused. "Oh, is that so?"

I took a step toward the desk. "You have no idea."

Dunn rubbed his ear as though just remembering something. He appeared uncomfortable, like he had an itch and didn't know where to scratch. "I'll answer a few questions—just a few. I'm a busy man."

"I'm sure you are."

"So go ahead. I don't have all day."

Slowly I said, "Derek Sloan. Recognize the name?"

"No. Next question."

"Mr. Dunn, you're lying. Now, I want you to arrange a meeting with Sloan for me. Tell him it's on the level, nothing to worry about. Tell him I have some business for him, something involving a new chop shop over on Woodward."

Dunn shook his head, a glint of alarm in his eyes. "I'm an honest businessman. I don't know anything about Sloan or chop shops."

"What about fraud?"

"Are you accusing me of something?"

I turned and closed the door. "Can we be honest, Mr. Dunn?"

"Honest? You say you're running a chop shop and you expect me to be honest?"

"Good point. You're quick on your feet. Can I ask who would give Sloan a check signed by you? Someone has to keep track of that, right?"

Dunn walked over to me and stared at my sunglasses. He leaned closer as though trying to peer through them.

I stood my ground, saying nothing, rolling the pebble in my

pocket.

A few seconds later, Dunn stepped away and sat on the corner of his desk. Folding his arms across his chest, he said, "Obviously, you think you know something."

"I'm going to come clean with you, Mr. Dunn. In return, you will cooperate."

Dunn tapped his shoe impatiently.

"That fire I came from ..., it was Sloan's house. Someone torched it."

Dunn's shoe stopped tapping.

"And I know he was running scams. Insurance fraud. He went down to Detroit with me following him, and then someone shot at me. I want to talk to Sloan, and you're going to set up a meeting." I didn't mention Hal, figuring it might scare Dunn into silence.

"I've never met anyone named Sloan," Dunn insisted.

"You expect me to believe that? Next you'll try selling me a car."

Dunn's breathing deepened. His voice grew angry, defiant. "I answered your questions. Now you answer one for me. Who do you work for?"

"What're you going to do—file a complaint with my supervisor?"

"Just curious. I like to know who's pumping me for information. Besides, Mr. Thigpen—"

"Call me Jack."

"That's an old sales ploy, Jack. Get the conversation to a first-name basis. Disarms the buyer. Seems like you're a bit of a salesman yourself."

"I'm not here to sell anything."

"But we're always selling ourselves to other people, Jack. That's what life's all about."

"That might be a reasonable philosophy for someone in sales, but personally, I have trouble figuring out who I am, so selling myself isn't an option."

"Then you're hiding the truth from yourself, Jack. But, no matter. As I was saying, I'd like to know who you work for. Maybe you're employed by one of my competitors."

"I told you, I investigate fraud. I work for an insurance company."

"You expect me to believe that?"

I strode to his desk and pulled out my knife.

Dunn flinched. He put his hands on the desk as though preparing to push himself to his feet.

I held the knife with my left hand and extracted the blade with my right. I ran my index finger along its edge.

"Are you threatening me, Thigpen?" He laughed, although it sounded more like a snort. "Hell, maybe instead of selling yourself, you should sell knives."

I tapped the blade against my palm.

"You don't expect me to be afraid, do you? You're so fucking pale, I figure you're going to keel over any second now."

I remained silent, tapping the blade, tap tap tap.

Dunn glanced at his phone. "Don't threaten me, Thigpen. You'll be sorry."

I jabbed the tip of the blade into the desk. "I'm through with your lies."

"I'll call the police. I'll get you arrested."

"Go ahead. Call. I'll tell them what I know." Dunn wouldn't call. He was too afraid. I could see it in his eyes, a sort of nervous quiver. But there was another reason he wouldn't call. He wanted to find out if anyone else knew what I'd been telling him.

Dunn sneered. "Maybe I'll just kick your ass instead."

I took the knife and stepped back. "Call Sloan. Arrange a meeting."

Dunn hopped off the desk, stepped forward, and shoved me back. "You're wasting my time. Get out."

I placed my left hand, palm down, on the desktop. "Wasting your time? I'm going to show you something, Mr. Dunn. It's about pain. Watch closely."

I spread my fingers and swung my right hand down, planting the blade into the fleshy part of my left hand, between thumb and index finger. Blood ran out, across his desk.

I looked at Dunn. His jaw descended several inches.

Pulling the knife out, I turned.

Dunn backpedaled.

I thrust my left hand in front of his face. "See that? I'm not afraid of a little blood. Are you?"

"Take it easy, Jack. I'm not a bad guy. I've never hurt anyone, not a soul. If anything, I'm guilty only of victimless crimes."

Dunn reached the wall behind his desk. He flattened himself against it. Beads of sweat appeared on his brow.

I stood in front of him, inches away, and held the blade against his neck.

"Don't," Dunn whispered. Sweat began dripping down his face.

"Then call Sloan."

Dunn didn't move.

"My hand's getting twitchy," I said, tapping the blade against his neck.

Dunn nodded. "Okay. Yes. I'll call him. I'll arrange a meeting. Just put that knife away."

I took a step back. "The knife stays out until you call and the meeting's arranged." I stared into his eyes. He blinked twice and squinted. "Do it," I said.

Dunn walked slowly, as though afraid of falling and slitting his throat on the knife. He reached his desk, picked up the phone, and punched in a number.

"Sloan, it's Dunn. Listen, I've got someone who needs to talk to you. It's a good deal."

I poked him in the shoulder with my free hand. "Tell him it has to be now."

Dunn nodded. "Yeah, Sloan, I'll vouch for him. But he needs to see you right away. It's now or never with this deal, and he promises to make it worth your while."

I nodded approvingly.

"Okay," Dunn said. "Yeah. I'll tell him."

Dunn held his hand over the mouthpiece and said, "Sloan says he can meet you tomorrow."

Waving the knife back and forth near his neck, I said, "No deal. It has to be now."

"I did the best I could!"

"Tell him I'm insistent.

Speaking into the phone, Dunn said, "Look, Sloan, this guy's not screwing around. If I were you, I wouldn't pass this one up."

A moment later, he covered the mouthpiece again and said, "Tomorrow."

I stuck the knife through the slit in my hand and held the point of the blade an inch away from his left eye. "Convince him," I said.

Dunn leaned back and spoke into the phone. "Now listen up, Sloan, you son of a bitch. You're going to do this or else. This guy's pissed at me and it's your fault. People who offer this kind of money don't take 'no' for an answer. So stop what you're doing and see this guy, and if anyone's got a problem with that, have him see me."

Dunn listened, nodding. After he hung up, he said, "Go down Gratiot to the center of Mt. Clemens, to the Clinton River. There's a boardwalk in the city park. Sloan'll be sitting on a bench. He'll be there in thirty minutes."

I smiled, although it was from satisfaction, not mirth.

Dunn was shaking, phone in hand, sweat dripping onto his desk, probably afraid of my mojo coming down on him.

I put the knife in my pocket, blood spattering my sweat pants, stepped to the door, and paused. "If I were you, I'd learn how to appreciate life, not money. Jump out of the rat race while you can, while you have a choice."

I walked out and headed for parts department exit.

"I've got to stop cutting myself," I muttered, looking at my hand.

Not a pretty picture.

CHAPTER TEN

After grabbing a handful of paper towels to stem the bleeding from my hand, I walked out of the dealership and headed for Tom's truck, holding my hand against my side, compressing the paper towels against both sides of the wound.

The confrontation with Dunn had left me exhausted, spent, ... a bit tattered around the edges.

The phrase not only depicted the wound to my hand, it described my mental state. Tattered. My thoughts were roiling, and the chaos was taking its toll.

I stopped beside the truck and looked in the side view mirror. I was looking pretty damn scary.

I climbed into the truck and managed to construct a makeshift bandage out of the paper towels. The blood flow slowing, I pulled out onto Van Dyke, and called Tom. "I've got a meeting set up with Sloan," I told him.

"Are you going to whack him?" he asked.

"With what, the knife?"

"It has an extremely sharp blade, Jack."

"I know. And I'm not planning to whack him. Sloan knows who shot me. I intend to find out."

"Sounds like you need my help on this one."

"I can handle it."

"If he's involved with street crime, he could be hardnosed about some things."

"Yeah."

"He might think he's a tough guy."

"I'm sure he does," I said. "Don't worry. I'm ready for this."

"Well, call me when you're done, whack or no whack. Where are you meeting?"

"Mt. Clemens city park, by the river."

"If I don't hear from you, I'll come and make sure you're okay."

"Good."

I ended the call just as I entered Mt. Clemens. I drove through the city, past the river, circled back, and parked on Crocker Avenue, in a residential area on the east side of the river. I got out and headed west on the sidewalk, which continued over the two-lane bridge into the downtown business section. Halfway across the bridge, I stopped and looked down at the murky, slow-moving river, which was only a hundred feet wide here. It widened gradually as it wound its way to Lake St. Clair, into which it emptied.

I'd never seen the river so sluggish. There'd been little rain as of late, slowing the current and causing the water to smell like dead catfish.

If water was a metaphor for life, then the muddy, listless river below best symbolized mine. (Although I smelled of smoke, not dead catfish.)

I took the pebble out of my pocket, wanting to let it fall into the river, to plop and disappear into the gloom. But it had been with me this far, I thought, studying its grainy surface, and it would see me through my meeting with Sloan.

I returned the pebble to my pocket, crossed the bridge, and reached the "boardwalk," which was actually a paved pedestrian path ten feet above the water, atop the long, sloping riverbank.

Fifty yards ahead, a lone man sat on a bench.

Sloan.

Even when he was sitting, his head bobbed.

I wanted to make it stop.

Walking along the path, I studied him.

His hair was slicked back. His narrow nose and chin reminded me that I'd originally thought of him as Rooster Man. He wore a loose-fitting business suit with a beige shirt. His shoes were black and polished. If not employed by Dunn, Sloan's appearance was slick enough for him to find a job with Satan Inc., a la *The Devil's Advocate.*

Sloan's head continued to bob as I approached, about once per second. Bob, bob, bob. In this way, the bobs appeared self-congratulatory, affirmations of his criminal existence.

I reached Sloan's bench and sat beside him. There were few other people on the walkway. Sloan had picked a good spot, in his eyes at least, because across the river, about two hundred yards away, stood the one-story brick Municipal Court building. A dozen police cars were parked there. Sloan wasn't taking any chances, despite Dunn's vouching for me.

Sloan's head stopped bobbing. He looked at me briefly, wide-eyed, as though searching his memory for my name. Then he looked ahead. "I've seen you before."

I wagged my finger at him. "You haven't seen anything yet."

"What do you want?" he asked.

"Just wondering if you gave the trigger man his orders."

"Who are you?"

"Doesn't matter." I leaned back so that the sun shone directly into his eyes.

Sloan's eyes narrowed into slits. He shaded them. "I know I've seen you somewhere."

I shrugged.

"What's this about a chop shop on Woodward?"

"I'll get to that."

"Get to that?" He shifted his weight and under his breath said, "Why do I get these goddam idiots to work with? Fuck."

"I wanted to talk about something else," I said.

He winced suddenly. From a migraine, perhaps? "You the one who burned down my house, asshole?"

"So you've heard about that."

"Fuck you."

"I didn't torch your house."

"Then tell me about the chop shop. I know what's going on over on fuckin' Woodward."

"Don't discount me so quickly. This might be a legitimate business offer."

"If it was, I'm not the one you'd be wanting to talk to."

I leaned toward him. "And who precisely would I be wanting to talk to, Sloan?"

He peered at me. "Who are you?"

I wanted to quote a line from a movie—your worst

nightmare. Hell, maybe I was.

"You know who I am," I said. "You just didn't expect to see me walking around. Right?"

"Hey, fuckwad, you wanted to meet me. You know my house was burned down. You say I should know who you are. I say you look familiar, but—"

He stopped, bobbed his head, then said, "Yeah, I saw you in Detroit the other day."

"You led me to Detroit."

"So you admit to following me. Why? Who the fuck do you work for? You ain't a cop."

"I'm self-employed."

"Bullshit."

"I want to know if you shot any firearms yesterday."

Sloan stood and started to leave.

I jumped up, pulled out the knife, and blocked his path. "I'd stay if I were you."

He surveyed the footpath and glanced across the river at the Municipal Building before sitting back down. He scratched the side of his face, his fingers twitching, occasionally glancing at the bloody wad of paper towels encircling my hand. "I've done nothing wrong. And you'd better come up with a better reason than a knife for why I should listen to you. You're pissing me off, and you won't like me when I'm pissed."

"I've got evidence."

"What kind of evidence?"

"Pictures." I sat down on the edge of the bench, set the knife in my lap, and began drumming my fingers on the blade.

"Big fucking deal," Sloan said, bobbing his head once for each word.

"To be more specific, pictures of you at Josef's Repair Shop. I've got pictures of you and that red-headed tow truck driver. I've got pictures of the cars you brought in, the license plates, and I've recorded the VINs."

Sloan laughed.

I wanted to kill him.

"You've got nothing!" he said.

My hand was grasping the knife handle, almost against my

will. Almost.

"If you're trying to get money out of me, you need to show me what you've got."

"I'll show you when I'm damn well ready."

"How much did you think I'd pay?"

Ignoring his question, I said, "I've got the basic scam down, capper. I just want to know if you're the one running the show."

And who tried to kill me, I wanted to add, and murdered my best friend.

"You're making all of this up."

"I have proof."

"I don't see any."

Even if I had the pictures with me, I wouldn't have shown him. Let him sweat.

He stood and pushed my arm away. "Just as I thought. A bluff."

I rose and faced him, pointing the knife at his gut. "What were you doing down by the RenCen yesterday?"

Sloan cleared his throat but said nothing.

"The blonde's new, right? Did you get a good peek?"

"Shut up."

"Never hurts to look at a beautiful woman, no matter if she's from Dallas, Boston, or Miami. But there was another reason you went to Detroit, right?"

Sloan glanced at his watch and looked to his right, appearing to ignore me.

"You make a great sounding board," I said. "I enjoy talking to you. Really."

"Fuck off."

I hadn't thought Sloan tall enough to be the one who left the Winner Athletics imprint, the man who shot me. But, hell, I was suspicious of everyone. And Sloan had not only been there, he had motive. "Did you lead me into an ambush? Or are you the one who pulled the trigger?"

"I don't think you're going to use that knife."

I slashed with the blade, tearing his jacket. "When you went into that alley by the RenCen, did you know you were being followed?"

Sloan was turning red.

"Know what I think? You caught on to the fact I knew about the scams. So you figure it's time to shut down the operation, move on to something else, but first you need to get rid of me. You figure I know too much, so you set me up to have me shot."

Sloan's lips parted. Instead of a rooster, he now looked like a weasel, with meaner, nastier eyes, or an animal searching for weakened prey like a hyena on the Serengeti, hunting weakened zebras. His right hand was clenched, ready to strike.

"You're breathing hard," I noted.

"I've run out of patience."

"Sounds like an anger-management problem."

"And you look tired and sick, like you're about to pass out."

I didn't feel sick, but Sloan had a point. I'd seen healthier moments.

"Why did Bob Dunn sign those checks in your desk drawer?"

"You did fuckin' torch my house!"

"Why do you hide your porno tapes in the bottom dresser drawer? Why do you have only pizza and vodka in the fridge?" I reached with my free hand and slapped the side of his head. "And why do you get so many goddam headaches?"

Sloan's teeth were gnashing. His words hissed out between them. "You're dead, asshole. You son of a bitch—dead!"

I grabbed his suit jacket and pushed him back, tripping him with my left foot. We fell with me on top. I pushed the point of the blade against his neck. "I don't care what happens to me. I don't care if the police see me kill you. I don't care."

He pushed me off, stood, and pulled a handgun from a shoulder holster beneath his jacket. "Don't fuckin' move."

"Yeah, sure," I said, standing. I shook off the paper-towel bandage and inserted the knife into the wound, re-opening it. I flicked my hand at Sloan, spraying him with blood. I passed the knife in and out of the wound. "I'm not feeling much pain anymore, and I'm betting that I can gouge out your eye before I die if you shoot me. Now, I don't care if I die, but I'm betting you want to keep your full vision."

It was the truth of my statement—I don't care if I die—that appeared to affect Sloan the most.

Sloan backstepped.

I strode forward. "Take a good look at my hand. Nasty wound, huh?"

"I–I ..."

"Tell me what I want to know. Now, or I'm going to fuck with you the rest of your life."

"Look, buddy, I didn't shoot at you. Okay? You gotta believe that. It wasn't me."

"But you know who did."

"I'm not sure. I–I think, maybe. Yes. Yeah, I think I know."

"Tell me."

"Okay. It had to be– "

Blood sprayed out from Sloan's chest, a greater amount from his back, misty red clouds like smoke from cannons, and I heard the gunshot, indicating the shot had been from long range.

Sloan clutched his chest, stared down in disbelief, his knees buckling. He fell onto the walkway, curling into a fetal position. Blood poured from his back. His eyes widened. His head, instead of bobbing, jerked forcibly as though short circuiting.

I stared, waiting for the name of my killer, thinking that because Sloan had been about to say it, the name would somehow come to me.

It didn't.

I got down on my knees and grabbed his shoulders. "Sloan!"

He convulsed and stopped breathing.

"C'mon, Sloan, get up!"

Sloan didn't move.

"Try bobbing your head."

The flow of blood onto the walkway ebbed. A fly buzzed over my shoulder, circled, and landed on Sloan's chest wound.

That's when I knew he was really, really dead.

I let go of Sloan's shoulder and stood.

Slowly, I walked along the path toward Tom's truck.

CHAPTER ELEVEN

After climbing behind the wheel of Tom's pickup, I bandaged my wound again. Waiting for it to close, I sat and stared across the passenger seat, out the window at Sloan's body. The corpse was just as I'd left it, a clump of lifeless flesh and bone, motionless on the grass near a park bench. True, nobody else had been in the park when Sloan was shot, but I was astonished that the murder was going unnoticed.

(So much for Sloan's reliance on meeting in a public place, near a municipal building and a dozen police cars!)

I looked away and stared ahead at the crawl of traffic into downtown Mt. Clemens. I put the key in the ignition and tried to think of a reason to start the engine.

There'd been three items on my list of desired things (and I remembered thinking that having desires was a good indicator I had life left in me). At the moment, desire was fool's gold, vastly overrated, bling on the catwalk of life. I no longer wanted to continue my existence among the living. Strike that from the list. I'd already said good-bye to Ellie. Strike two. So if I could find Hal's killer, I'd have my third strike and I'd be *out.*

I decided not to wallow in despair. I had a direction – identify the guy who put a slug through Hal Booker.

Okay then, where to?

I started the engine. To my right, a jogger approached Sloan's body. Her ponytail's rhythmic bounce ebbed as she slowed to a walk. She stopped and began backpedaling, looking wildly around as though anticipating an ambush.

Time to go ...

I slipped the gear into drive and pulled away from the curb. I turned left on Gratiot, heading toward Warren and a repair shop belonging to Mr. Josef Adolpho. The Dunn Ford dealership had been my other option. Besides me, only one person had known Sloan would be in the park—Bill Dunn. Initially, when I was questioning him, Dunn had denied even knowing Sloan. A liar—and someone whose business sold used cars! That didn't make him a killer, but it didn't place him high on the morality chart, either. Why would Dunn deny knowing Sloan? What was his motive for keeping it quiet? Did those checks in Sloan's house point to something illegal, something that I could use to my advantage?

Honestly, though, I'd already confronted Dunn once today, and I was getting tired of putting a knife through my hand.

Adolpho had worked with Sloan, too. I was curious if he also knew Dunn. Perhaps I'd get a better understanding of the working relationships by visiting the repair shop.

Besides, if I knew more about the work that Sloan was doing at Josef's, I might be able to figure out who gained the most by Sloan's death (and, for that matter, mine).

Also, there'd been three attempted murders of people who'd been at Josef's Repair Shop yesterday, two of them successful.

A coincidence?

Doubtful.

Traffic was heavy. People were heading back to work from their lunch breaks. Most of them drove like they were worried about being late, driving recklessly, with little regard to safety.

After turning onto Nine Mile Road, the traffic flow grew calmer. I took out my cell phone and called my brother.

"Jack, where are you?" Tom asked.

"Heading back to Josef's Repair Shop."

"Are you ..., has your condition changed?"

"No. I'm all right."

"Why don't you come back to my house? I've been thinking—we should go at this problem of finding the person who shot you in a different way. What if we posed as a couple of underworld gamblers who needed someone knocked off?"

"Try to hire a hit man?" I asked.

"Yeah," Tom said. "That way, we can get a list of suspects."

"And just how do you plan to do this? Place an ad in the paper?"

Tom didn't answer right away. I imagined he was uncomfortable with deciding how to respond to my attempt at humor. Should he laugh? How does one laugh along with a guy who's slated for death? Was he holding back? I hoped he didn't go the emotional route. Then it would be my turn at not knowing how to respond. Emotions were best suppressed at this stage in my *life*.

"We can talk about it when you get here," Tom suggested.

"I'm going to the repair shop. Tom, don't get involved in this. That guy I was going to meet—Sloan—was shot while I was talking to him."

Tom hesitated. "Is he ..."

"He's really very truly dead," I said, mimicking a Munchkin voice. "He's not moving anymore."

"Did you get shot, too?"

"No. And I didn't see anyone, so it was a long-range weapon. Maybe a sniper rifle."

"A professional hit man," Tom said.

"Seems likely," I agreed.

"All the more reason to try my plan."

I knew Tom wanted to help. If there was anyone in the world who felt more helpless than me, it was my brother. "I'm almost at Josef's. I'll call in a couple of hours. Come and check on me if I don't."

"Okay, Jack. I'll wait by the phone."

I slipped the cell phone into my pocket.

Ryan Road was only a couple of intersections ahead. I tried formulating a plan. Precisely how did I intend to go about questioning Adolpho? Using a knife as a means of persuasion was getting old fast.

A direct approach was best, I figured.

I turned right onto Ryan, drove past the rolled aside fence in front of the repair bays, and parked on the other side of the street about thirty yards from the Nine Mile Road intersection. Not wanting to give Adolpho time to reflect on my arrival, I threw open the door, quickly reached behind the seat, and pulled out the baseball bat. I swung the bat onto my shoulder and walked toward the repair bays, trying to look like a heavy hitter approaching home plate. I'm not sure how much the sunglasses and baggy sweatsuit detracted from the image, but perhaps the bat would be enough to carry the proverbial load.

Nearing the repair bays, I realized that the activity in the shop wasn't just an indication of an unusually high volume of repair work. There were two moving trucks—one out front and one near the bays. Ramps were positioned at the backs of the trucks, and workers scurried up and down, carrying boxes and tools and tires. Out front, a man wearing overalls walked out the front door with a tilting hand cart, a filing cabinet strapped to it, and steered it toward a ramp.

From inside the truck near the repair bays, a voice called, "I can't strap down this fucking tool cart!"

Josef Adolpho was standing at the back of the bays, his chest even wider than I remembered. He was breathing heavily, his chest expanding and contracting in an almost exaggerated manner as he struggled with a wrench on a hydraulic fitting. He wiped his forehead, brushing back the short outcropping of sweaty blond hair. He sneered at the truck. "Use a rope ya dumbass!" he shouted.

I walked right up to him and waited.

Adolpho pulled the wrench away from the fitting, spat on the floor, and faced me. Gripping the wrench as though it were a weapon, he pointed it at me. (I also noticed that two of the mechanics were watching me, their hands in their pockets ..., holding handguns?)

"What you want?" Adolpho asked, his accent, like his chest, thicker than I remembered. "Delovich send you?"

I didn't want to hesitate and appear unsure. Still, I had to consider my answer. These guys might not appreciate my employment with Delovich. They might consider me a threat, at least more than I presently was, an almost dead guy with a Louisville Slugger. I slowly twirled the bat handle and looked at each of the mechanics.

"Yeah," I answered. "I'm his fuckin' right-hand man."

Adolpho spat again. "What he want? I tell him I was out."

"Out?" I asked.

"Don't play game with me," Adolpho said. "My English not

so good, but I tell Delovich truth."

"Mr. Delovich just wants to make sure," I said carefully.

Adolpho grunted. He waved at the mechanics to continue their work. They resumed moving a stack of Michelin tires. From where I stood, I could see into the back of the truck near the bays. Most of the equipment I'd seen yesterday in the bays had been transferred to the truck.

"Also," I said, "there's been a problem."

"No problem here," Adolpho said. "I cooperate."

I pointed the bat at the moving van. "You sure all that stuff's yours?"

"Of course. And I give Delovich rest of lease on building. Nine months! He bring in new crew, he tell me."

"You have to understand, though, it presents ... ah, certain difficulties when someone wants out."

"I pay Delovich. He double-cross?"

"No, no," I said, shaking my head. "Your offer was generous. I'm sure Mr. Delovich wouldn't have agreed to it otherwise. But as I said, there's a problem."

"Tell me problem."

"Sloan."

Adolpho waved me off. "Sloan not here. I tell him I no longer in business."

"Yes, but—"

"Look," Adolpho said, taking a step toward me, again pointing at my face with the wrench, "I go New Jersey. Cousin set me up. I plan long ago do this."

"But you've moved up your plan," I noted.

"Has nothing to do with Delovich—or anyone else."

Yeah, right. Something's got you spooked, something that scares you enough to pull up stakes and run away from a lucrative business.

"This cousin of yours," I said, remembering what Ted Meade had told me at his Alliance Insurance office, "he the one up on RICO charges?"

"No," Adolpho said. Raising his voice, he added, "And no more talk about cousins."

"Fine," I said. "Let's talk about Sloan. He's dead."

Adolpho's mouth twisted. He wagged the wrench at me.

"You no threaten me."

"I'm just pointing out a fact. Sloan's no longer breathing. His heart's given out—probably because someone shot him in the chest. Yeah, that's gotta be it. He was murdered less than an hour ago. Surprised?"

Adolpho briefly looked away and shook his head. "This dangerous business. Maybe you die next."

That was most likely true.

Adolpho turned to the mechanics. "Hurry! One hour, we go." He returned to the hydraulic fitting, turning it so that the lifts would have no pressure and be inoperative.

I took a step toward him. "Who shot Sloan?" I asked.

"How I know?"

"Because you said this was a dangerous business, and well, I see you've lost a few fingers there, and—"

"You no talk!" Adolpho yelled. He strode to me and held the wrench inches away from my sunglasses. As he spoke, he tapped the wrench against the left lens. "You no talk or I kick ass."

I held up my hands. "Okay, don't get your panties in a knot. I was just curious, that's all."

Adolpho flung the wrench into the back of the moving truck.

"Hey, watch it!" someone yelled from inside.

"Move faster or maybe next time I hit you," Adolpho responded. He sneered at me and went over to the third repair bay, where a mechanic was checking off items on a clipboard.

I spotted the tall red-headed man who'd driven the tow truck yesterday while working with Sloan. He was standing near the cab of the moving truck, munching on a bag of Doritos. A designated driver, I reasoned, wondering if he was going to stay in New Jersey, too. Then I noticed an overweight man with an overgrown mustache. He'd been the driver in the car that had been in the accident just before Hal was shot. He was walking up the truck's ramp, carrying a box with a flap of a deployed airbag hanging over the edge.

I turned to Adolpho. "What about Bill Dunn?" I asked.

Adolpho glanced at me and grunted dismissively.

I considered pressing the issue, but figured that unless I was willing to use the bat—*C'mon, Jack, take a swing or two.*—and intimidate him, I'd get little information of any value. Adolpho didn't seem to know who had killed Sloan. It seemed reasonable to me, though, that the reason for Adolpho's hasty departure from Michigan had something to do with the same threat that had ended Sloan's life.

I walked out to Tom's pickup. Leaning against the door, I watched the mechanics load the moving trucks. They worked nonstop, faster and faster at Adolpho's urgings, like ants storing food for an early winter. I didn't want to leave, losing what might be my last opportunity to talk to Josef Adolpho. He'd be in New Jersey by tomorrow, and I doubted he'd be keeping in touch with anyone in the area.

Except maybe Delovich.

Although I'd been lucky in getting Adolpho to reveal as much as he had, I was disappointed, frustrated, and felt that even with so much luck, I was no closer to finding out who'd killed Hal. For every answer I got, I could think of two more questions—the main one being, who the hell was Delovich?

Two black Land Rovers with tinted windows turned off Nine Mile Road. They parked in front of the repair bays, beside the moving truck. Mechanics stopped what they were doing and stared. Adolpho squinted, peering. The Rovers' doors opened, and two men got out of each car, one from each passenger seat, one from each back seat, leaving the drivers inside. Their mouths were tightly shut, nearly grim, their hair blond and cut short enough to pass a military inspection. They glanced at the bays, adjusted their sunglasses, and tugged at their business suits (no ties, just white dress shirts). They looked like they were either athletic businessmen or friends of Adolpho's cousin in New Jersey.

One of them wore two gold chains around his neck. He said something and one of the other three stepped to the roll-aside fence, where he folded his arms across his chest as though standing guard.

The other two were short and stocky. One of them carried a molded plastic suitcase, the kind carried on scientific expeditions. Those two went through the bays toward the front office area while the gold-chained man approached Adolpho.

None of the four had Winner Athletics shoes.

I hurried toward the bays, wanting to be a part of the discussion, or at least listen in.

The guard standing near the fence held out a hand abruptly, striking my shoulder, jolting me to a stop. "*Wait here,*" he said. I noticed his accent sounded much like Adolpho's, the "w" sounding more like a "v." Vait here.

"I've got business inside," I told him, thumping the bat up and down on my shoulder.

"What your business?"

I took the bat off my shoulder, planted it on the asphalt in front of my shoes, and leaned on it with the palm of one hand (the one without a knife-hole in it). "Although I'm certain that I have business here, I'm not so sure that you do."

"What your name, Mr. Baseball Player?"

"Tell me yours first," I said.

"My name? Yah, sure, it's Harry Bela-fuckin'-fonte."

"Very funny. Why don't you sing me a song then?"

Adolpho and Gold-Chain were arguing. Loudly. My problem was, they were speaking in a foreign language. It sounded Eastern European. Maybe they'd only recently immigrated to the Jersey Shore.

Whatever the language, the new arrivals were thugs of some sort. But what was their problem?

Adolpho glanced at the mechanics and switched to English. "I tell you no."

The mechanics edged closer, apparently wanting to join the discussion. The red-headed man ate one last Dorito, threw down the bag, and edged closer, too.

"Why you cause trouble?" the gold-chained thug asked Adolpho.

"We cause no trouble," Adolpho said. "We leaving. You take whatever's left."

"Yeah," the redheaded man said, stopping at the back of the truck. "Then take a fuckin' hike."

Every few seconds, the gold-chained man twirled a loose-fitting watch around his wrist. It was either a nervous habit or a psychological indication he was working on a tight deadline. He held his hands out and shrugged as though Adolpho's offer was of little value. "We won't, as your man say, take fuckin' hike. There are contracts, relationships, quotas to turn over."

"Not my problem," Adolpho said.

"You hold on," the gold-chained goon said. "I make call." He took out a cell phone and spoke briefly into it. He listened a minute and then tucked the phone away. "I wait for instructions. You wait, too."

Adolpho shook his head. "No wait. Schedule to meet. We move. You take up with Delovich."

"Why you move?"

"Better location."

The thug smiled.

I was surprised at the chill up my spine in response to that mirthless smile. This was a man who enjoyed inflicting pain, and he was beginning to suspect he'd be able to administer a good deal of it soon. "You were made offer. What your answer?"

"No answer," Adolpho said. "I no longer in business. Make offer to Delovich."

The gold-chained man reached out and lightly slapped Adolpho's face. "You no understand me. I make you understand, yes?"

One of the mechanics clanged a wrench against a pipe and took a step forward. "You guys go fuck yourselves. You don't want to push this. Not today."

"No—but I get angry. I don't want to push, as you say, but you are pushing first."

The redheaded man stepped up to the thug and pushed him. "*Swinya.*"

The gold-chained goon glared and wiped his hand across his nose. "*Suka.*"

"Wait," Adolpho said, "I say we—"

The goon hit the redheaded man so swiftly that I barely saw the punch. The redheaded man certainly didn't. He collapsed to the floor.

Adolpho stepped over to the fallen man and shook him. "Get

up! Idiot! Get up and get out."

The redheaded man began crawling toward the front office area. One of the two shorter, stockier thugs emerged from the front and stood beside the gold-chained man.

The mechanics and two thugs began pointing at one another and speaking terse sentences in their own language. Faces turned red. Hands reached repeatedly into pockets as though to draw out weapons. I didn't think any of them had expected the confrontation to escalate into violence, but sometimes emotions vetoed intentions (and reason, for that matter).

Suddenly Adolpho pointed at me and in English said, "You talk to him. He Delovich's right-hand man. Delovich do whatever he say."

The guard beside me poked my shoulder. "You cause trouble?"

"No," I said. "I was just leaving. I'm not with them." I backstepped away from the repair bays. The man who had poked me grunted.

The next second played in slow motion in my mind. It was like a television replay of a score in a sporting event. Except that the event involved me. And as I watched, I was thinking, *hey, I ought to move—*

The other shorter, stockier man emerged from the front office area. A mechanic pushed him. He fell. The suitcase banged to the ground, popped open, and a canister—about the size of a household fire extinguisher—rolled onto the repair bay floor. The men from the Land Rovers realized something was wrong and dove for cover, Adolpho and his mechanics following suit. The canister banged against the back wall, against a drum of hydraulic fluid. There was a flash of light, tremendously bright, a cosmic flash—an explosion. I was blown backward. I staggered, catching my balance by using the bat as a brace.

Smoke billowed, a dense, roiling blackness.

Something screeched, an unnerving hellish sound of metal scraping on metal. There was another explosion from somewhere within the cloud of smoke. Debris rained down around me. Bumpers. Side view mirrors. Hoods. The entire scene was a junkyard dog's nightmare. Tires fell. They impacted the ground and rolled by, dozens of them, a wheel-only version of a soapbox derby.

The shower of auto parts dwindled. I peered ahead. In the thick smoke, tinged red with flames, the back half of the repair shop groaned as it began to cave in. I saw people trying to crawl out of the fiery darkness, fugitives from the River Styx who were escaping from a hell that was wicked and shadowy and flickering with flames.

The back of the building collapsed.

Debris was blown out.

Something flew at me—a piece of lumber, a section of an I-beam ..., hell, how was I supposed to know? It happened so fast. It whipped against my left arm first, then one end flipped over and struck me in the head. I fell, losing consciousness.

But I was only stunned. True, I couldn't move, but I could still hear and smell and see. *Maybe this is what I will become before I die ...*

I lay motionless for what I thought was a few minutes. I heard sirens, saw flashers, but I was floating in a curious emptiness, like in those half-awake, half-asleep moments of the morning when dreams felt all too real.

Eventually I pulled up my sleeve and glanced down. I grimaced, seeing a deep-blue bruise in my arm. Blood spilled out of an eight-inch laceration.

(*Not long now, Jack, before you swim with the fishes. It's only for those people near death that intense physical harm causes no duress.*)

Finally I stood, picked up the baseball bat, and staggered away. A police car was out front, along with a fire truck from which firefighters sprayed streams of water that hissed upon meeting the flames. An EMS truck was parked on Ryan Road, near the rolled aside fence.

"Look at his arm!" a paramedic said. He ran to me, gently grabbed my uninjured arm, and began leading me toward his vehicle, where his partner was unloading a collapsible gurney.

"I don't need help," I said, stumbling along.

"Everything'll be all right, mister," the paramedic said. "You're in a bit of shock. Try to breathe slowly."

I jerked my arm away from him. "I don't want to breathe,

dammit. And I'm not going with you."

"You're going to lose that arm."

"Back off," I warned.

"I'm here to help you."

I dropped the bat and threw a punch across his chin. It wasn't a heavyweight strike, but it took him by surprise. He turned limp and fell. "Help yourself," I said, pulling my sleeve down, covering the fracture.

I looked up. The other paramedic was frantically working on the gurney, which apparently had suffered a malfunction. (Yeah, haven't we all?)

I picked up the bat again and walked to Tom's truck, uninterrupted this time. I started the engine, shifted into gear, and sped away for the last time from Josef's Repair Shop.

CHAPTER TWELEVE

A song went through my head as I turned right on Ten Mile Road, heading toward Gratiot, wondering what I should do next.

Pick yourself up, dust yourself off, start all over again.

If only I could. The "dusting off" part would be difficult enough, let alone the starting over. My jogging suit was covered with grit and dirt and smelled like smoke. I felt like a cinder, crispy and burnt, with only a slightly higher water content.

How many had died in the explosion at Josef's Repair Shop? Who'd been the target? It couldn't have been me. No one would've risked so many other casualties. Then who had done it? Delovich? Just what was his connection to Adolpho? The Rovers' windshields had been smashed, but what had happened to the drivers?

Nothing made sense. The entire episode had been like some irate deity throwing another cosmic wrench into the order of things—my continuation on the planet being the first wrench. Maybe that's how God did things. If things aren't going well, just blow it up! Destroy it! Why not? It worked for Noah. Except there's no ark this time.

Not all had died in the explosion. I was sure I'd seen a few crawl out. One had been the redheaded man.

But how could I have been so stunned? I'd been conscious yet incapable of movement for at least twenty minutes. I figured the explosion happened a few minutes before one o'clock. Now it was almost one-thirty. Was it a result of the explosion or the first manifestation of CJD?

The investigation into Hal's murder was going nowhere fast, so fast that I'd fall apart before I learned the name of the man who shot him. Hell, maybe it was all a big mistake that I was even trying. Maybe I should accept my fate and sit quietly in a corner and wait for the cosmic hammer to whack me out of existence. (Or would it be a wrench?)

I glanced down at my arm, which hung limply at my side, at the gash, visible through the cut in the sweatshirt sleeve. I could raise the arm, wiggle my fingers, but when I exerted any pressure on it, such as pushing against the dashboard, I could see the movement of tendons.

The injury, on another man, might've made him more aware of his mortality. Mortality? (What a load of crap!) There was a universal clock ticking somewhere, and when the alarm went off, my body would falter and fail and soon after turn to dust.

A traffic light turned red and I stopped. With my good arm, I took out my cell phone, which indicated a phone message from Tom. I listened to the message—Tom wanted me to call him as soon as possible. But with my arm the way it was, I had to wait until I got out of traffic. I returned the phone to my pocket. The light turned green and I pressed the gas pedal.

I drove another ten minutes. Then, at the Gratiot intersection, I awkwardly turned the steering wheel, pulling into the parking lot of Philmont's Pharmacy. I found a spot near the entrance, parked the pickup, took out my cell phone, and called my brother.

"Tom, I'm not at the repair shop anymore."

"I know you didn't want me to call, but I tried anyway. You didn't answer. It's all over the news."

"Hal's murder?"

"No, the fire at Josef's Repair Shop. I didn't want to call because I have no idea what you're up to, how you're doing this investigation of yours. I figure maybe you're under a table somewhere, eavesdropping, and it wouldn't be good for your cell phone to start chirping."

"I know it's tough to wait," I said, "but you're right, a phone call at the wrong time could be hazardous, at least as hazardous as anything can be in my condition. But my cell phone's on vibrate."

"You're coming back here, aren't you?" Tom asked.

"I don't know."

"C'mon, Jack, you need to rest."

I changed the subject. "What's the news say about the fire?"

Tom sighed. "There's no official statement yet, but one of the firefighters was quoted as saying it looked suspicious, and people in the area say they heard an explosion."

"There was."

"What happened?"

I explained how I'd gone into shop with the bat, about the arrival of the Land Rovers, the ensuing discussion. I described everything I could remember except my injury and the encounter with the EMS guy. I was growing weary of unloading my problems on Tom.

"So what're you going to do next?" he asked.

"I don't know."

"You should come here. It's too dangerous out there, Jack."

I realized I needed to have Tom repair my arm. He stitched together animal skins for his taxidermy work, so why couldn't he sew up a gash? It's not like he'd need to medicate me for the pain. No anesthesia required.

"All right, I'm coming," I said. "It'll be an hour or so. I have to make a pit stop first."

"Good, Jack. That's good that you're coming. I'll be here."

"Hey—anything on the news about Sloan's death in Mt. Clemens?"

"Nothing about any death in Mt. Clemens."

"That's odd," I said, wondering if the story was being purposefully buried. "Keep watching—it has to show up. See you in a bit."

I turned the cell phone off, slipped it into my pocket, and began patting my sweatsuit, trying to air it out, knock the smoke and grit loose from the fabric.

C'mon, Jack, Tom's not giving up. Why should you?

(I hated when I was right, at least the part of me that wouldn't give up. Sometimes that part, when right, was just too damn certain of it.)

I looked in the mirror and tried straightening my sunglasses. They were bent. The lenses were scratched. I needed a new pair.

So what's next after you stock up on eyewear?

I took out the cell phone, got the number for the Dunn Ford

dealership from information, and punched it in.

"I'd like to speak to Bill Dunn," I said, wanting to ask if he knew Delovich, or Adolpho. He'd known Sloan, and Sloan was dead now.

"Mr. Dunn left about twenty minutes ago," a woman said cheerily. "May I take a message?"

"Where'd he go?" I asked.

"I don't know, sir. Is it important?"

I hesitated. "No. Besides, I'd rather see him in person for this. What about Mr. Delovich?"

"No, sir. He's not here either. Were you expecting him? He only comes by once a month or so, and I just saw him last week."

"I see."

"Would you like to leave a message, sir?" the woman asked, her voice tilting slightly away from cheeriness toward impatience.

I considering asking about Sloan, but I decided I'd wait until I could do it in person. "No. That's all right. Have a wonderful day."

I put the phone away and checked my wallet to see how much money I had. One hundred and twenty-nine dollars. I had credit cards, of course, but those transactions could be traced, and I had no idea who might be trying to hunt me down.

Gathering my nerve to face the public, I closed my eyes a moment.

My thoughts drifted.

Deadwood, dead center, dead in the water.

Perhaps people needed to be almost dead in order to fully understand how thoroughly the word had infiltrated our language.

Dead spot, dead ringer, dead to the world.

It was a word that lost its potency through overuse. People bandied it about carelessly, being much more cautious with other words, such as murder and mutilation. People said the word "dead" so often that when they used it to describe the termination of life, other people are confused. When a police officer tells someone that a relative is dead, the person will inevitably say, "What?" The word "dead" doesn't register. That's because it's abused, denigrated, stripped of its power, cast into the casual realm of everyday use.

There was no doubt—the word "dead" had lost its potency.

And I was dead on target about that.

After using the end of my sweatshirt sleeve, tying it around my arm to at least partially close the wound, I went inside, the cashier and the two patrons in line staring at me like I was a Martian with a bad fashion sense, picked up a shopping basket, and headed for the first aid aisle. I had to set the basket down when I picked out an item, having only one good arm. I picked out a couple of Ace bandages and dropped them in the basket.

That would help with the arm, but what about tomorrow? What other part of me would be cut or broken, given my tendency toward reckless behavior, even to the point of stabbing myself? I picked up the basket and continued to the next aisle, expanding my shopping list. Elbow and ankle wraps. Knee braces. Athletic tape. A back support.

Next, I picked out a pair of sunglasses that closely matched the pair I was wearing (except for the damage) along with a strap to help keep them on.

In another aisle, I picked out a pair of shoe inserts, thinking they would help reduce the impact force that walking imposed on my spine. My entire central nervous system was deteriorating and in danger of breakdown. I needed to reduce the stress on my body as much as possible.

Instead of thinking about living a healthy lifestyle in order to prolong my existence, I needed to think of it more as preventive maintenance.

I picked up a box of Epson salts (figuring if I took a bath, the salts might help rejuvenate my body, rehydrate it somewhat), a bottle of mouthwash, and a box of wet wipes.

Instinctively, I knew I needed something else. I stared at the Ace bandages in my basket. They might work at holding my wounds together, but something stronger seemed appropriate.

Duct tape.

I went back the hardware aisle and grabbed a couple of rolls. Hell, if Tom couldn't repair my arm, maybe I could just wrap it with duct tape. It wouldn't last long, but then again, I probably wouldn't either.

On my way to the checkout counter, I picked up two more

items: eye drops and deodorant. I paused at the end of the aisle and waited until the cashier finished with someone buying a disposable camera. I hurried to the counter and set the basket down, holding my bloody arm behind my back. "I'm in a hurry," I told her. "And I don't have a loyalty card."

She swiped a loyalty card that was beside the cash drawer.

I glanced down and picked up a tube of breath mints. "These might come in handy."

"Yeah, bad breath's a turn-off."

She finished ringing everything up and said, "Seventy-two, fifty."

I gave her four twenties. After getting my change, I left, wishing her a good day.

Outside, I set the bags down, opened the pickup's door, and set my supplies on the passenger seat. I took out the new sunglasses and attached the strap. I put them on, then opened the mouthwash and gargled. I took out the box of wet wipes and cleaned myself off as best as I good. I ended up smelling like a mixture of Listerene and isopropyl alcohol.

Better than smelling like road kill, I reasoned.

I put away the supplies, pulled back out onto Ten Mile Road, and continued driving to I-94, where I got on the highway, heading toward Mt. Clemens.

Gradually, as the flow of traffic seemed to sweep me along without any effort on my part, the cars mesmerized me. I imagined that I was a viral strain in a channel of corpuscles, part of a vast motorized intravenous system. The ebb and flow of the cars, the tapping of brakes, the accelerations were being caused by the massive beating of an unseen heart at the end the artery.

I was an intruder here, not wanted, a virus unable to escape or be killed by the normal defense of the universe—the autoimmune system. No white cells came to attack me, to defend the corpuscles. I was a transgressor, a pestilence, and the autoimmune system had voided itself into oblivion, leaving me—a dead guy, almost—here among the respected, living parts of capillary roadways.

I was the ultimate outsider, fitting in with neither the living nor the dead.

And just what could I do about it?

Not a damn thing.

CHAPTER THIRTEEN

When I stepped up to Tom's front door, I set the pharmacy bag down and reached for the door knob. Instead of opening the door, though, I knocked. I was, after all, still an outsider.

The door opened mid-knock. "Next time, just come in," Tom said. His jeans looked clean, his T-shirt unblemished by dabs of paint, but he had a haggard, unshaven appearance with dark, heavy bags under his eyes. His rattail seemed to be under pressure to unravel, hairs springing out in every direction.

"I, uh, just wanted to make sure you were here before I came in," I told him.

Tom stepped aside, holding the door open. "You're arm," he said. "It's bleeding."

"It's cut bad." I picked up the bag, walked inside, and headed toward the den. "I need you to operate."

Tom closed the door and followed. "There's a hospital nearby."

"I don't need the publicity at the moment." I set the Philmont's Pharmacy bag on the worktable. The stuffed wolverines looked less menacing, less intimidating than yesterday. They seemed almost ... well, like they pitied me. At least they had some assurance of remaining intact for the foreseeable future.

Tom entered the den but stood about as far away from me as one could while remaining in the same room. It was like he wanted to slip into the kitchen and forget about the den, about anything dead that might be in there. "What's in the bag?" he asked.

"First aid kit," I answered, setting the bag on the end of the workbench. I pulled out the duct tape. "For emergency repairs."

"Jack—"

"You've got to do this for me, Tom." I sat at the workbench and pulled off my sweatshirt, not an easy task given that I had to do it mostly with just one arm.

"Christ, Jack."

"I need the use of both of my arms. This one's going to keep bleeding unless you stitch it shut."

Tom walked into the kitchen, made a drink (orange juice and vodka) and returned. He took a sip. "Let me get this straight. You want me to sew this long gash in your arm?"

"You might have to make additional cuts so the two sides will stitch neatly together."

Tom took a bigger drink. I figured alcohol would improve his operating skills, such as they were. He'd probably need to be as numb as possible. He set the glass on the workbench and started emptying the pharmacy bag, laying the braces and bandages beside his drink.

"You can do this, Tom."

He nodded, turned, and opened a cabinet below the workbench. He rummaged through a drawer and took out a razor knife, a spool of the strong thread, and a sewing needle.

I set my arm on the workbench. A few dry specks of blood fell. Several thick drops oozed out onto my skin.

"Got any rubbing alcohol?" I asked, setting the knife down.

Tom wordlessly left the room and returned a few seconds later with a half-filled plastic bottle.

"Towel?" I asked.

He brought one from the kitchen and sterilized the needle and blade. The fluorescent bulbs overhead glared. The room felt warmer now than it had a few minutes ago. The dead animals in the room—badger, fish, wolverines, cougar (still in the construction phase)—seemed to give me more attention than my brother did. They, in fact, stared. Welcome, they appeared to intimate.

I stared at my arm, medical terms floating into my consciousness (terms I thought I'd never use after learning them in high school science class). Layers of skin—epidermis, dermis, and subcutaneous tissue—puckered up around the laceration.

Tom took the razor knife and cut away some of the loose threads of skin that appeared unsalvageable. "That doesn't hurt?" he asked.

"No. I wish it did."

"Not much blood now."

Tom pinched the end of the gash together and stuck the needle through the two sides of skin.

I found myself grimacing, a shiver of pain racing up my arm. I took deep breaths and grunted from throbbing discomfort. I'd thought I couldn't feel pain, but I'd been wrong. My sense of pain was diminished, but it wasn't gone.

My arm ...

It stared at me, trumpeting the unwavering nature of my mortality. I was falling apart. Death came for all (although some, like me, with an expiration date).

"Sorry about that," my brother said.

"No, you had to do it. Keep going."

I realized Tom was looking back into the kitchen, toward the sink.

"Get another drink if you need it," I said.

Tom looked at me and shook his head. "No. I forgot to sterilize my hands."

Any infection would probably outlive me, I thought.

Tom rinsed his hands with the alcohol and returned. He reached forward and pulled the flaps of skin together.

My arm looked like one of those bio-engineered jobs in the cheap movies, a cheesy version of Arnold Schwarzenegger's Terminator arm. (A cyborg, he had explained—part flesh and part machine.)

"Let's make sure everything's sterilized," he said, picking up the bottle of isopropyl alcohol. He poured the alcohol over a towel and tapped it over the edges of the wound.

"Shit, shit, shit," I said, wincing, my face contorting.

"I thought you might feel that," Tom said.

My thoughts swirled. My mouth twisted as I tried to form words. "Apparently severe pain hurts just as much as my pre-CJD days."

Tom nodded. "I'd say that's good, but I figure you don't

want to hear that at the moment." He set the bottle down and picked up the needle and thread.

My mind reeled, and I felt unconsciousness tugging at me. "Can you please hurry?"

"Sure." He began pushing the needle through my skin, again and again, lacing his way down the length of the wound. I didn't feel any tugs of skin this time. Pain had numbed my arm.

"I was thinking about what you said happened to Sloan and what happened at the repair shop," Tom said. "And well, you did say you were conducting an insurance fraud investigation."

"That's right."

"Ever hear of the Purple Gang?"

"No."

"They were a Detroit mob back in the days of Al Capone."

"Not a very menacing name for a gang," I noted.

"They were tough," Tom said. "They ran the rackets and the booze-running from Canada. Those were Prohibition days."

"How'd they get the name?"

"According to Uncle Bob—"

"I never met him, did I?"

"No, he ..., uh, still likes to keep a low profile."

"What—is he in the Mob?"

"I don't know. Never had the nerve to ask. Anyway, Uncle Bob said some shopkeepers called these young thugs the color of bad meat, a purple gang."

I shuddered. Bad meat.

(with stitches)

The image of Frankenstein's monster appeared in my head, a creature that had been animated from dead tissue. In the Hollywood version, the monster had sported quite a few stitches.

(like me)

Tom continued talking about the Purple Gang as he worked on closing the cut in my arm, making the stitches very close to each other.

"Bootleggers brought booze over the Detroit River, easy as pie during winter when it was frozen, but boats worked well enough when it wasn't. They sold the liquor to Capone in Chicago. Of course, Capone wanted to control Detroit himself, but like I said, the Purple Gang didn't fuck around. They were killers, fairly bloodthirsty from what I gather. Freelance racketeers were afraid of them, and so were the other gangs."

"What's this have to do with me?" I asked. "They sound like bootleggers, not *fraudmeisters*."

"Let me finish," Tom said, sounding like he needed to keep talking so that he wouldn't be overwhelmed by the sight of sewing together flaps of his half-brother's arm. "I'm just trying to highlight a few points. Like this was big business. There was even a booze pipeline constructed between Canada—Windsor—and Detroit."

"I bet there was a lot of money involved," I said.

"Absolutely, and when there's a lot of money involved, the stakes are raised. The Purple Gang pulled no punches. Hijacking, extortion, murder—they did it all."

"Okay, so what's that have to do with me?"

"A lot of money's at stake with fraud, yes?"

I nodded. "Are you trying to say that money's the reason Hal was killed? Sloan, too? And that's why Josef's Repair Shop was firebombed?"

"Absolutely. And the other thing about the Purple Gang is how they eventually lost their grip on the city."

"When was that?" I asked.

"The nineteen-thirties."

"What happened?"

"Well, it's kinda like globalization today. The smaller companies get gobbled up by the bigger corporations. Lucky Luciano's East Coast Syndicate moved in. It was a national crime syndicate, and the Purple Gang just couldn't compete."

"I think I see where you're going with this," I said.

"Yeah, you've stumbled onto something big, some kind of organized crime ring. With so much money at stake, maybe even billions of dollars if it's a national crime ring, they don't take any chances, especially with some—from their viewpoint—two-bit insurance fraud investigator poking around."

"I agree that there's got to be more going on than a simple scam," I said. "But if it's organized crime, wouldn't the attempt to murder me have been done by a professional hit man?"

"Sure."

"But the guy who shot me didn't use a silencer. Neither did the guy who shot Sloan."

"I don't know," Tom said. "I've heard silencers can throw off the aim. Sloan was a long-range shot, didn't you say?"

"Yeah."

"So a silencer wouldn't be a good idea. And as for when you were shot at in Detroit, maybe a hit man wouldn't want to carry around a silencer, which would be pretty suspicious if a cop ever saw it. But a handgun, well, they have permits to carry those, so it's not that big a deal."

"You think some kind of reincarnation of the Purple Gang is involved?"

"No. What I'm saying is, I think there's more than one gang. That's why your Mr. Josef Adolpho was leaving. He saw the writing on the wall. And your telling him about Sloan's death just confirmed his suspicions. It's the Big Squeeze."

"Who's doing the squeezing?"

"Someone with a bigger organization than his. See, it's a lose-lose decision for Adolpho."

"Which decision is that?" I asked.

"It's like the East Coast Syndicate moving in on the Purple Gang. Now, do you join up with them as they're moving in and risk getting killed for double-crossing the Purple Gang? Or, do you stay loyal and get killed or your arm broken by the syndicate? Lose-lose. Adolpho decided to move to New Jersey. He opted out."

"It sounds like you're suggesting a turf war."

"That's it—a turf war."

"But how does knowing this help me?"

Tom grunted. "I'm still working on that."

"Let me know if you come up with something."

My arm resembled, more and more, the arm of Frankenstein's monster. Maybe villagers would come after me, too, like they had come for that particular abomination, with torches and intentions to destroy me.

Tom began talking about what he'd learned from the news

reports on the fire at the repair shop. There were a couple of eyewitness accounts on the local news. The national news was carrying the story, too, but not as extensively as the local channels. There'd been five people killed, according to one report, although there were no official announcements yet. One survivor had died on the way to the hospital. The cause of the blaze wasn't known yet, but a couple of Land Rovers had been spotted leaving the scene. An EMS guy reported being attacked at the scene by some big thug.

Big thug? Well, it made sense. No one wanted to report being knocked over by a lightweight tennis player.

Finished with his account of the news, Tom switched the subject dramatically and began talking about ingrown toenails.

I didn't want to stop him, but I grew tired of listening. A sense of fatigue was draping itself over me.

As Tom continued talking, he got into a rhythm and began working more quickly. Within twenty minutes of starting on the toenail reverie, he made the last stitch. After tying off the end of the thread, he cut the remainder with scissors and ran lines of Krazy Glue over the jagged cuts.

"Eighty-three stitches," Tom said. "That ought to hold you together."

"For a while, anyway," I said, flexing my fingers. I raised my arm, swiveled it forward and back. "Good job, Tom. Thanks."

"No problem, Jack. What're you gonna do now?"

"This might sound strange, but I think I want to take a bath."

"Doesn't sound strange to me."

I shrugged. It sounded more than strange to me; it sounded insane. "Can you wash these clothes while I'm in the tub?"

"Sure, Jack."

I stood, a wave of dizziness sweeping through me. "I just need to relax a while." I'd always felt better after a bath. Maybe it'd still work.

"I'll get the water started," Tom said, heading for the hallway. He hesitated. "What water temperature?"

"Make it warm, Tom. It's starting to feel cold in here."

Tom looked like he was about to say something, but he

simply nodded and went down the hallway, toward the bathroom.

If my nervous system would allow me to cry, I wanted to then and there. Instead, I collected my pharmacy supplies into the bag and walked down the hallway toward the sound of running water. I remembered a movie quote from one of the Frankenstein movies, *Knowledge of mortality is a uniquely human gift.* Yes, I thought, a gift out of Pandora's box, along with all of the other nasty little gifts.

CHAPTER FOURTEEN

On my way to the bathroom, I glanced at Tom's motorcycle, the Triumph, and the lettering on the fuel tank—*Tom Terrific*.

The bathroom was large for a farmhouse, with a wide sink, a set of cabinets, and a claw-foot bathtub. Tom had taken a couple of towels and set them on the counter beside the sink. Water gurgled into the tub, which was nearly half full.

"That's enough water, Tom. I want to keep my arm out."

He turned off the water. "What else can I get for you?"

"Some privacy?" I suggested.

"Yeah, just leaving." He stepped outside, and I closed the door.

"Hey, Tom, I said, cracking the door open. "There are a few things you can bring me."

"Sure."

"Hold on." I emptied my pockets onto the counter, beside the towels—penknife, cell phone, wallet, keys, and the pebble. I carefully removed shoes, socks, and sweatpants, not wanting to put too much strain on my arm.

I opened the door farther and tossed out the sweatpants and socks. "Can you wash those quick?"

"I'll short-cycle them."

"Good, and can you bring me that thread and needle?"

"Why?"

"Just a little touch up on another wound." True enough. I'd work on my hand by myself. "Oh, and scissors to cut the thread."

"What's going on, Jack?"

"You don't think I'm going to slit my wrists, do you?"

"No, I was just curious. That's all."

I showed him my hand. "Minor, relative to the arm. I can

handle this one. By the way, there's Epson salts in the pharmacy bag. Can you bring me the box?"

"Yeah. I'll be right back."

I walked over behind the sink, took off my sunglasses, and stared in the mirror. The bags under my eyes were drooping dangerously low, and I worried my eyes—dull and looking lifeless—would simply fall out. My lips were dry. I drank a glass of water, using the rinse glass on the sink, but it didn't seem to help.

"Here you go, Jack."

I'd left the door open a few inches. Tom's hand was poking through the doorway, holding the duffel bag he'd left the sweatsuit in yesterday. I took the bag and set it beside the toilet. "Thanks, Tom. I'll be out in half an hour."

"All right. Call if you need anything."

I took the Epson salts out of the bag, poured a couple of handfuls in the tub, and swished the water around for a few seconds. I figured maybe the high concentration of salts would help the water to rejuvenate my skin (at least a little, which was about all I could hope for).

Next, I took out the thread, needle, and scissors and set them on the commode lid. After watching Tom, I knew how to stitch together a wound, although I had to do it twice, on the top of my hand and on my palm (the exit wound).

I returned the thread, needle, and scissors to the duffel bag. I put the pebble on the faucet. It looked lonely, so I figured I'd keep it close to me. Careful to keep my left arm out of the water (not wanting to fill the wound with water like a hull-damaged ship), I settled myself into the tub. The water was warm, like amniotic fluid. I wanted to relax, to forget about everything, which of course was impossible. Still, the water had a soothing effect.

My energy level was fading quickly. It amazed me to have any amount of energy at all. Wherever my energy came from, I knew that the end result was my being like a fuse, burning lower and lower. The day and hour was approaching when I'd reach the end of that fuse and burn completely out.

I stared at the pebble, grabbed it, and dipped it briefly in the water. No meaning came to me from the pebble, although I'd been hoping that perhaps some sort of "pebble philosophy" would bubble up. People tended to agree that life had meaning, but to what end? That was the crux of the dilemma of life. Religions answered with the concept of God, but the word "God" (like "death") was overused and had lost its power. The art of soul-searching – prayer, meditation, whatever – was being lost not because of secularism, but because of capitalism, from years of overuse of the word "God." Hell, it was printed on the money, for Christ's sake! How could someone not become inured to its meaning?

The pebble, sitting there without questioning its purpose, hinted at a larger meaning, but I failed to grasp it. Answers seemed submerged, lost in the undercurrents, although I could feel their presence.

And so the pebble, ultimately, failed to transmit (sorry, Mr. Kubrick).

No *Grok!* for me.

The door opened partially, and Tom laid a clean sweatsuit and new socks on the floor.

"That was fast," I said.

"I had another pair. I hope that's okay."

"Yeah, you did good. I'll be out in a few minutes." I grabbed the bar of soap and quickly washed myself. The water turned murky, like I'd been covered with a thick coat of dust. I leaned forward and pushed the lever to open the drain. Water began chortling down.

After climbing out and drying myself, I dressed in the sweatsuit. I put on socks and shoes and repocketed the items that I'd removed (included the non-transmitting pebble). As the last of the water in the tub gurgled down the drain, I grabbed the duffel bag and returned to the den. Tom was in the kitchen, sitting at the table, reading a Bible. He looked frazzled and frantic, harried, like a man who was taking a final exam the next day and hadn't yet studied. That, or he needed another drink.

"You're not going to find answers there," I said.

He glanced up. "Just looking for clues."

"What happened to your Zen idea? You know – the one

about the balanced universe. You said I was canceling out something bad that had happened."

"I haven't given up on that yet. It's just, ... well, it doesn't seem like a good idea to limit myself to one concept of the afterlife."

"Yeah, I know what you mean."

I set the duffel bag on the workbench in the den and began loading it with everything I'd purchased at Philmont's Pharmacy. I didn't want to use any of the supports or braces until I had evidence of joints failing. I popped a breath mint into my mouth and swiped my underarms with the deodorant, worried that CJD carried with it the stench of death. *Try to keep the stench down, okay? That's good. Don't want to smell like a carcass.*

"I'm going to use this duffel bag as a repair kit, okay?"

"Sure, Jack. Need anything else in it?"

"No, this should be enough."

My legs began shaking, and I suddenly felt like I was going to die. "I'm going to sit in the living room a minute," I said.

Tom flipped a page of the Bible. "Okay."

I walked into the living room and sat in a lounge chair, beside a window, thinking I'd have time to rest.

I was mistaken.

CHAPTER FIFTEEN

I'd been sitting for just over five minutes when my cell phone vibrated. I took it from my pocket and stared at it, seeing Ellie's number, thinking that perhaps (like God) I shouldn't answer.

But what the hell, I missed her.

"Hello?" I answered.

"Jack, it's me, Ellie."

"What do you want?"

"I'm worried – I think someone's following me."

"Have you called the police?"

"What are they going to do, Jack? This guy hasn't done anything illegal."

"Then why are you worried?"

"I don't know. There's something about the way he looks at me. Could you please just check him out? Please."

I was never very good at saying no to Ellie, and today was no different. Besides, I'd never heard Ellie sound so concerned. She was a good judge of character, and I didn't doubt that the man allegedly following her was up to no good. Still, that didn't mean he had evil designs on Ellie.

"Where are you?" I asked.

"St. Clair Shores. At a friend's condo. I just came over to pick up a few things."

She gave me the address. It wasn't far from my rental. Suspicion stabbed at me – maybe Ellie was staking out the rental and was unable to find me (after trying to have me killed), so she called. Maybe that look of surprise when I saw her at the Club hadn't been a reaction to how ragged I looked – maybe she was surprised at seeing me still alive. And maybe her call was a setup. She was going to have me killed.

But I quickly shook off doubts of her intentions. I was being too suspicious. Besides, I had plenty of more likely suspects. Bill Dunn, for example.

"Whose condo is it?" I asked.

"Bonnie's."

"Why do I get the feeling you're not telling me everything?"

"Listen Jack, this guy has Bonnie spooked, and she's a dear friend. I need to put her mind at ease. I've got an appointment, and I don't want to leave until she's settled down."

"All right, fine. It'll take about twenty minutes."

"He's parked beside the condo. A black BMW. There's a parking lot there for the library on Harper Avenue."

"Okay, I'll be in Tom's pickup truck. Look for me."

"Thanks, Jack. I owe you."

I put the cell phone back in my pocket and went into the den to get my repair kit, now stuffed into Tom's duffel bag. "Got to go," I said.

Tom was standing near the kitchen table, talking on the phone. He put a hand over the mouthpiece. "But I'm working on a plan," he said.

I glanced at the clock above the sink. It was 2:38. "Should be gone only about an hour. Doing a favor for a friend."

"Where'll you be?"

I told him the address.

Tom opened his mouth as though to ask me to stay, but then thought better of it. "Always on the go. You're a friggin' human dynamo."

Outside, on my way to the truck, I spit out the breath mint. My saliva quotient was too low to dissolve it.

I threw the duffel bag on the passenger seat, started the truck, and drove toward St. Clair Shores.

As I got closer, I began to get more worried about Ellie. I'd been foolish to suspect her (even though a small part of me still wondered about her motives, perhaps a natural result of divorce). In the past two days, I'd seen seven people killed, and if Ellie thought she'd spotted someone who was threatening, I ought to take her word for it.

When I got to the parking lot, I saw immediately why Ellie was concerned. The parking lot was mostly empty, with about ten cars parked near the library entrance on Harper Avenue. The BMW was parked at the back of the lot, facing the side of the condo with the address Ellie had given me. Ellie's Mustang was parked in the condo's driveway, along with an Accord that I assumed belonged to Bonnie.

There was a row of low, scraggly hedges separating the lot of the condo's yard, which was bordered by a short chain-link fence, providing a clear view from the library parking lot.

I wanted to confront the man in the BWM (with the Louisville Slugger in hand), but my last confrontation, at the repair shop, hadn't worked out quite the way I'd envisioned, so I settled for parking on the street and placing the bat in my lap.

I saw Ellie pass by the condo's front window and glance out. Her attention was on the BMW, and she didn't notice me.

She moved away from the window, but I could still see her. Her friend placed a sympathetic hand on Ellie's shoulder.

Bonnie was an attractive woman, a couple years younger than Ellie, with bright green eyes and shoulder-length red hair. When she pulled Ellie back a step and kissed her on the lips, I blinked. Then I shook my head as though trying to reestablish reality. But no, the world had already changed once when I heard my diagnosis, and it changed again, just now, when I'd seen Bonnie's probing tongue and realized that Ellie had spent the night here, with Bonnie, and they were kissing each other good-bye.

Now I knew why it had sounded like she'd been hiding something from me on the phone.

Look at it in a positive light, Jack. At least she didn't leave you for another man.

The kiss lengthened, and Ellie lightly stroked Bonnie's hair.

I told myself not to get emotional. A display of emotions would drain me, and I'd already done enough draining for one day.

Even so, emotion surged within me, erupting from some hidden well. My stomach lurched. I gripped the steering wheel, shook it, then I covered my face with my hands and sobbed. They were dry, as I could form no tears.

C'mon, Jack, now's not the time.

I leaned back and looked at the condo in time to see the kiss end.

Ellie and Bonnie moved away from the window for a few minutes, and I drove forward twenty feet so I'd be more visible. The next time Ellie looked out, she saw me and waved.

I nodded at her.

A minute later, the front door opened and Ellie stepped out. Along with her purse, she was carrying an overnight bag.

She was smiling nervously, but the smile faded as she started toward her Mustang. Her grip on the bag tightened as the BMW's door opened and the driver got out.

It seemed to be a time of recognition, because I knew I'd seen the man before. He was young, maybe early twenties, with black hair that was longer in back, almost in a mullet style. He wore a jersey with a black-and-gold B, the Boston Bruins logo. He was the guy who'd transferred to Alliance Insurance from the Boston office, at least that's what Ted Meade had claimed. Blalock.

The man approached Ellie quickly, as though on an important mission.

I hesitated only an instant before climbing out of the pickup, but in that time my head was flooded with thoughts. Blalock was only trying to locate me after I'd gone missing from the case. But no, Ted Meade had my phone number. He could've just called. Then I figured Ellie and Blalock were working together, planning my demise. Of course! She'd given me a call with a plea for help, and silly me had to come to the rescue (said the fly approaching the spider web). Then I remembered that Ted Meade at Alliance Insurance had not only hired me for the case on which I got shot at, he'd been the person who told me to follow Sloan into Detroit, where I'd been targeted.

Meade ordered the hit. It must've been him. And Blalock's working for him, and Ellie's on the take, too. It's all of them. They all conspired to have me dead.

I approached the Mustang, holding the bat in my right hand. I wondered if the stitches would hold if I needed to take a two-handed swing.

Ellie opened her car door and got in.

Blalock saw me coming, but that didn't stop him. He got

to the Mustang a few seconds before me. To Ellie, in a thick Boston accent, he said, "I need you to get out of the car." He pronounced it *cah.*

"Stay in the car, Ellie," I said. I poked Blalock with the bat. I thought about asking him what a cah was as opposed to a car. Instead, I said, "Stay the fuck away from her."

"Thigpen, I'm glad you're here. You've caused enough problems and it's going to stop now, shithead." He pronounced "here" as *he-ah* and "shithead" as *sheet head.*

"What's got to stop?"

"Don't play dumb with me," he said, thumping his chest near the Bruins logo as though nothing escaped his keen mental acuity. His jersey wasn't tucked in, and the shape of it on his hip was suggestive of a handgun underneath.

"Next, you'll ask me to play dead." I glanced at his shoes, brown leather casuals, not a Winner Athletics design. "Ain't gonna happen."

"Shut up."

I was getting confused. Nothing made sense to me. This cocky punk was trying to appear intimidating, but he seemed little more than a hooligan. "What is it precisely that you want?" I asked. "Why are you here? C'mon, Blalock, talk to me. Maybe we can work something out." *If I can understand that accent, sheet head.*

"What do I want? What are ya, a fuckin' moron? I want to kill you, Thigpen. And maybe I will. I might pull out my gun and blow your fuckin' head apaht. Whatcha think about that?"

I didn't really care much. I held up my hands and mockingly said, "Please don't shoot me!"

"Put yah hands down," Blalock said. "I don't wanna attract attention."

"Attract attention?" I asked, lowering my arms. "You stalk Ellie in broad daylight, park in an empty lot to watch her, and threaten to kill me—and you don't want to attract attention?"

"Shut your trap. For now, we're just having a little chat. Nothing wrong with that, is theah?"

"Maybe I'm not in a chatty mood," I told him.

"But see, there's consequences later, depending on how well

I think this chat goes. I'm going to lay it on the line, Thigpen. You're gonna stop your investigation. You ah gonna take a trip, a long trip, someplace fah away. Japan, maybe. Yeah. You'll go to Japan until all this blows ovah."

"All what blows over?"

"No questions. You're going to agree now, or I think Elizabeth Thigpen is gonna regret it."

Blalock might've done enough homework to know Ellie was my wife, but he didn't know her nickname. (Maybe he's just being formal for effect, I told myself.) One thing I felt fairly sure about—I could swing the Louisville Slugger faster than Blalock could draw his gun.

"You got a license for that gun?" I asked. "I mean, if you don't, you're taking a huge risk by carrying a concealed weapon. You'll notice I'm not concealing this bat."

Ignoring me, Blalock turned to the Mustang. "Listen heah, Miss Elizabeth Thigpen, I need you to tell me how much ya know. How much has your husband told ya?"

"Told me about what?" Ellie asked, hands on the steering wheel, her arms rigid.

Blalock looked skyward a moment and swiped his hand across his nose. "His investigation, dammit. Josef's Repair Shop."

"I don't know anything," Ellie told him. "We're separated. I just filed for divorce. We don't speak to each other much anymore."

"Then what's he doin' heah?"

"I called him."

He waved off the answer. "When was the last time you been to Europe?"

"I've never been to Europe. I don't even have a passport."

Blalock squinted at her as though trying to determine how high her bullshit factor was. "How bad ya wanna keep your fingahs?"

I nudged Blalock with the bat again. He turned quickly and glared at me. "She's telling you the truth," I said. "She has nothing to do with this."

"What game you playing, Thigpen?" he asked, rubbing his

chin. His dark eyes twitched.

"It ain't baseball," I told him. "Now, I want to ask you a question. I suggest you answer. Does Bill Dunn work for Ted Meade?"

Blalock peered at me. "You don't get it, do ya? This ain't no fuckin' game. You're in way ovah your head."

"Because it's bigger than I think?"

Blalock's eyes twitched again. He flexed his fingers, and his hand drifted toward the bottom of his shirt. "I oughtta shoot you now."

"Why don't you?"

"Shut your trap."

"Because you'd get caught. And I might get this bat around before you pull the trigger. Lot of ways to screw this up, Blalock."

"You'd bettah start asking yourself how much you like your fingers, shithead." He opened his mouth, then his gaze turned abruptly to his left, toward the road. His eyes widened and he whispered, "Delovich!"

I turned. A black limousine was stopping at the curb. The rear window—tinted—lowered halfway and a stern voice said, "You haven't been answering your cell phone."

Blalock nodded. "I been busy."

The voice, deep and resonant, said, "You have one minute to get in your car and leave. I will call you, and you will answer. You will then do precisely as I say. Now go."

I approached the limousine. The window closed before I could see inside. "Wait!" I demanded, raising the bat.

The limousine sped away from the curb. I swung, missing a tail light by inches—*striiiiike*!—and the bat slipped out of my hand and flew onto the grass in front of Bonnie's condo. I was able to get the license plate number, though.

An Indiana plate ...

By the time I turned, Blalock was in his car in the library parking lot. By the time I retrieved the bat, Blalock was driving down Harper Avenue.

I walked up to Ellie's Mustang. Her arms were trembling, her knuckles white from her grip on the steering wheel.

"Listen," I said, "maybe you ought to leave town for a while."

"For how long, Jack? What have you gotten yourself into?"

"A week should be long enough. And evidently, whatever I've gotten into is bigger than I think."

"I'm calling the police. He threatened me. What was his name? Blalock?"

"Ellie, I'm going to take care of Mr. Blalock." If Delovich doesn't beat me to it. "I don't want the police involved in this right now."

"Why not?"

"They'll want to question me. Extensively. And I just don't have the time. You'll just have to trust me, Ellie. Please."

"I don't know, Jack. This is serious."

"I promise in a week's time, everything will be settled."

She shivered. "All right, Jack. One week. But next time I'm calling the police." She looked at Bonnie's condo. "Bonnie should go with me." She peered at me.

I nodded at her. "That's a good idea, but you should leave now. Someone might come back looking for you."

She hesitated, then reached into her purse and pulled out a cell phone. "I'll call once I'm on the road and tell her."

"Okay."

Her nose twitched. "Jack, I ..."

"Ellie, I don't regret one minute of our marriage. The J and E show had a good run, and I'm thankful. I want you to know that."

She nodded. "We had some good times. And I want you to know that I've been worried about you, Jack. You look worse than yesterday."

"I'll be closing down my investigative business soon. Ellie, I don't know if I'll see you again."

"Why not? You make it sound like you're going away permanently."

"I have no specific plans," I told her. "Let's just say I might suddenly get called away."

"Called away? Where?"

Part of me wanted to tell her the truth, but she looked happy, deep down, and I didn't want to do anything to change that.

"I'm not sure," I told her. "Now, let's go before *Sheethead* comes back."

She nodded, her mouth twisting as though she wanted to add something else but wasn't quite sure how to say it. She turned the ignition keys, starting the Mustang's engine. "I hope you feel better soon, Jack."

I nodded. "Good-bye, Ellie."

"Bye, Jack."

She backed out of the driveway. Heading toward Harper, she raised the cell phone to her ear. She turned right, south, toward Grosse Pointe.

Without looking back at Bonnie's condo, I returned to the pickup and left, turning north on Harper, which despite the traffic, looked like a concrete riverbed in a barren landscape.

CHAPTER SIXTEEN

Driving to Tom's house didn't tax my ability to think. Trying to figure out who was running things with regard to Sloan and Blalock was an entirely different matter.

The man named Delovich certainly had power over Blalock. But what about Ted Meade? How did Meade and Alliance Insurance fit into the equation? Then there was Josef Adolpho, who might very well be one of the five killed at the repair shop explosion. And I couldn't forget about Bill don't-call-me-Pigpen Dunn.

I was betting the head honcho was either Dunn or Delovich.

One thing bothered me, though—Blalock had told me he felt like he should shoot me. If he'd played a role in setting up my murder, he'd have known I'd already been shot. Maybe he believed that the "hit" hadn't happened yet. Whatever the case, something didn't quite mesh. He'd wanted information, pressing Ellie for knowledge of what I was doing. And what about that question about going to Europe? Did Blalock think there was some kind of Parisian connection? Was this *knowledge* the reason I got shot at? What knowledge was it? Nothing made sense.

There was more than a hint of desperation in Blalock's actions. That much I was certain about.

I was on Gratiot, entering Mt. Clemens, when my cell phone vibrated.

"Hi Jack. It's me, Octavia."

Her tournament match is coming up fast, I realized. Octavia called occasionally to ask for advice, although she usually tracked me down when I was at the Club. "Shouldn't you be out practicing your tennis stroke?" I asked.

"Just came in from two hours of backhand practice," she said proudly. "Hey, Jack, are you all right?"

"Well enough," I said.

"Well, anyway," Octavia said, speaking quickly, "I was calling to ask for your special advice. I need a tournament tip."

"Shoot," I said.

"You know the Nationals are next week. Well, I've got the qualifying match against Cheryl Baine tomorrow. If I win, I'm trying to come up with a good practice schedule. I mean, these will be Nationals matches! How do I prepare? Do I take a day off? What did you do when you were on the pro circuit?"

I had no doubt she'd beat Cheryl Baine, who was stockier than Octavia and more powerful, but much less graceful. Cheryl was a good kid, but I disliked her father, who was on the Club's board of directors. He was a hard-nosed bastard who trained Cheryl incessantly.

"I'll make this simple," I said. "You change nothing. That's why it's called a pre-tournament ritual."

"Yeah, but this is Nationals!"

"Doesn't matter. Every tennis court has the same dimensions. Change nothing."

"So, the day before, just a light workout?"

"Yes." I hesitated. "Octavia, while I have you on the phone, I have to tell you something."

"Okay, go ahead."

"I won't be able to give you any more advice. No more tips from me."

She laughed mockingly. "Ha ha, very funny."

"I'm serious."

"Why, Jack? Oh, I know. You were always afraid I'd beat you one day, and you're just going to stop talking to me because of it."

"It's not that."

"Then why, huh? C'mon and tell me."

"I've, uh, had a severe injury. It's difficult for me to walk, let alone play tennis."

"But that shouldn't stop you from giving me a pointer from time to time."

"True enough," I said.

"I can still call, can't I?"

"I'd rather you not."

"Where are you going?"

"I'm not sure. Maybe Japan. But I'll be with you in spirit. Always. And at the Nationals, I want you to keep that backhand strong."

"Okay, Jack, I will. And thanks. I'll call ya later."

"I know."

We ended the call just as I pulled into Tom's driveway. By the time I parked the pickup truck, Tom was on the porch, waving at me. To the extent that I could, I hurried, bat in hand, toward the porch to ask him what he was so excited about.

CHAPTER SEVENTEEN

The fact that I could still hurry onto a porch struck me as astonishing.

How long had it been since I was given a death sentence? Nearly twenty-four hours? Maybe a little more, maybe a bit less.

I reached Tom's side, and we walked inside.

"You look excited about something," I said.

"There's nothing wrong with welcoming a brother home, is there?"

"I suppose not. I need to check a license plate on your computer."

"Go ahead. While you're doing that, I'll tell you what I've been doing. I've got a plan, Jack, a sure-fire way to catch your killer."

"Nothing's sure-fire anymore, but tell me anyway," I said, sitting down at the computer desk. I put the bat's end on the floor and balanced the handle against the edge of the desk.

"Remember what I was doing when you left?"

I found the program and logged on. "You were looking at a Bible."

"Looking for answers."

"I said that the answers aren't there."

"Exactly," Tom said. "So I started thinking, where would I find answers? That's when I called my uncle."

"Uncle Bob?" I asked, typing in the license plate number in the search window.

"Yeah. He's in town because of the union strike."

"And what answers were you looking for from Uncle Bob?"

"Better if you call him the Colonel."

"Colonel Bass?"

"Just 'the Colonel.'"

"For now let's stick to Uncle Bob. I'm having a problem with authority figures at the moment."

Tom nodded. "Anyway, I called him and kinda gave him a hypothetical question about hiring a hit man in the area."

"Tom, nobody's going to ask about those things over the phone. He'd know you're not serious."

"Actually, he didn't let me finish. He was furious that I raised the subject on the telephone. At least he sounded furious. Uncle Bob has a loud voice, and he's usually pretty boisterous."

The license plate information came up on the computer screen. The limousine was registered to a packaging company in Indianapolis. Someone else I knew had recently gone to that very same city. Bill Dunn.

"Learn anything?" Tom asked.

"Not really." I pointed at the computer screen. "I suppose I could go to Indianapolis and investigate, but I don't think it'd do any good." At best, I'd find out that Delovich was a bigwig at the company.

"Well, then, I'd say it's time to try my plan." He took a bandana out of his back jeans pocket and tied it around his forehead. "Let's go see Uncle Bob."

I hesitated. Maybe Tom was on the right track. I certainly wanted to know who'd given the order to have me killed, and if I could find the hit man, he'd be able to tell me directly, at least if he survived the encounter. Next time I swung a bat, I wasn't going to miss.

"I don't want you involved, Tom. I'll go."

"Uncle Bob won't talk to you, certainly not about something like this. Me, I'm family."

"I'm your half-brother. Doesn't that make me family, too?"

"For Uncle Bob, I don't think it works that way."

Go ahead – it'll give Tom a feeling that he's helping.

"All right," I said, standing. I grabbed the bat. "Let's go."

We walked outside. "Hey – you going to let me drive?" Tom asked.

I handed him the keys. "Try not to bounce me around too much."

He snorted, trying to hold back a laugh.

"It's okay, Tom. It's a joke."

"Yeah, I'm just ..., uh, not sure how to respond sometimes."

We climbed into Tom's pickup. He turned the truck around and pulled out on the road. In fifteen minutes, we were on 16 Mile Road, heading west.

"Hey, Tom, what's with the bandana? Some kind of disguise?"

"Not exactly. I think Uncle Bob will remember me better with it on. Make him feel more comfortable. Like you and your sunglasses." He glanced sideways at me.

"Makes sense," I admitted.

We drove about thirty minutes in silence. I was conserving my strength. I figured Tom just didn't know what to say.

He began drumming his fingers on the steering wheel.

"About five more miles," he said, his fingers skipping several beats before resuming a steady cadence.

I wanted to take the opportunity to talk more, but nothing came to mind. "So, how's everything going, otherwise?"

"What do you mean?"

"I mean with your life. You know—money, love, things like that."

Tom's fingers stopped drumming. He shrugged and leaned back, slipping his hands to the bottom of the steering wheel. "Okay, I suppose. Money-wise, the house and truck are paid for, and since I don't commute, there's not much of a gas bill. I make enough so my taxidermy jobs get me by."

"You stopped working after I came over. Won't you get behind in your schedule?"

"Nope. I called everyone and said there'd be a one-week delay in everyone's delivery date." He glanced awkwardly at me. "I'll call for a longer delay."

"Don't," I said. "This'll be all over with by then, one way or another."

We stopped at a traffic light. Tom's hand drifted to the top of the steering wheel. He began drumming his fingers briefly, then scratched his head and returned his hand to the bottom.

The light turned green. Tom matched the acceleration of the car ahead.

"Love life?" I asked.

"Nothing much to talk about. Hell, Jack, you know I've always been a loner. It's not that I'd mind having a lady around the house, but I'm okay as is."

"You should get out more," I told him.

The ensuing silence had an awkward feel to it. I wished Tom would go back to drumming his fingers.

"Tom, I'd like you to do a favor for me. When"—and if—"I'm gone, keep an eye on Ellie for me. Make sure she knows she can call you if she needs anything. And no matter who she goes out with after I'm gone, it's ..., well, I'm okay with it."

Tom nodded and began drumming his fingers. "Sure, Jack. No problem." A few seconds later, he said, "Just ahead, next intersection. We're here."

I looked to my right as we reached the Mound Road Stamping Plant, a sprawling factory that stretched farther down Mound Road than I could see. It was surrounded by a ten-foot fence topped with concertina wire. Within the fence, asphalt. No cars. Very unusual for a weekday, but then, the UAW was on strike. There were acres and acres of empty parking spaces. The gates were closed, and there were security guards posted just inside. Labor movements and strikers have, from time to time, been known to sabotage facilities if they felt management was dealing unfairly, especially if there was an influx of scabs.

Tom turned left onto Mound Road, then got in the right turn lane. "There's the union hall."

I nodded blankly, staring at the rusty oil drums at the factory's gate. They'd been filled with varied lengths of two-by-fours, and they were ablaze. The fires were hypnotic. Something about them was calling to me, something that I couldn't quite identify, but I knew that when Tom stopped, I'd have to go over and take a look.

Fine, I told myself, go and look at the fires—just don't go all Joan-of-Arc on me.

CHAPTER EIGTHTEEN

Tom found a spot in the nearly full parking lot, which had capacity of well over a hundred cars. He climbed out of the pickup and took a step toward the entrance of the union hall, a one-story brick building about the size of a small bowling alley. Circling the building, there was a small perimeter of grass, into which was stabbed dozens of ON STRIKE placards.

Detroit's been *blue collar* since the time of Henry Ford. The workman mentality was pervasive, affecting how the city's inhabitants perceived the world. They revered people like Robin Hood, a hero for the middle class and the underpaid, and Thomas Edison, who might not have been a brilliant man but was someone willing to put in tireless man-hours testing a thousand light bulb filaments before finding one that worked to his satisfaction. (Someone from MIT might argue that a smart man would've narrowed the filament choices first by employing scientific theory, but that wouldn't have been a blue collar way of looking at it.)

"Coming?" Tom asked.

I stood beside the truck and pointed across Mound Road. "I'd like to walk over there first."

"Why?"

"I-I don't know for sure." But as soon as I said this, I did know. It wasn't the Siren call of the crackling, burning wood, it was a memory.

"Just as well," Tom said. "Uncle Bob—the Colonel—will be more at ease if it's just me."

"I'll come back in a few minutes," I told him. "You'll be in the hall?"

"Yeah. When you come in, stay near the front door so I can find you."

I nodded. "Good luck."

I turned and approached Mound Road, considering the task of crossing it. I could walk down to the intersection at 16 Mile Road, or I could try dodging traffic. I winced, remembering the video game *Frogger* and how the frog got squished by traffic when it couldn't hop fast enough out of the way.

After waiting for a break, I managed to cross, dodging traffic as best I could (not particularly nimbly, but still a remarkable feat for someone staving off CJD), and headed along the sidewalk toward the nearest plant entrance, fifty yards ahead.

The memory that had been revived by the fires in the rusty oil drums was that of my father bringing me to a strike when I was five years old.

I could remember my fascination when I'd gazed at the picket line. Old men (although to a five-year-old, all adults looked old) with unshaven faces—men who looked like giants—talked glibly with one another; cheering, laughing, clapping each other on the shoulder. There was an unstated cohesion, a sense of camaraderie in those union ranks. I sensed their brotherhood, their uniting under a common cause.

But why, if the memory had provided a proverbial spark, was I drawn to the fires?

Because it's not the fires, it's the sense of community. I'm drawn because I remember the sense of belonging.

All strikers were family on a picket line, regardless of job or race or gender. I wanted to see if I could feel it.

Maybe it's like the tunnel of light, that sense of being drawn into the afterlife, into Oneness.

This was different than my kinship with Tom, with whom I had a special bond. And despite what had happened between Ellie and me, I still felt a fondness for her. I wished her well. But as for the rest of humanity (except, perhaps, for Octavia), I was suspicious of them. They appeared as greedy undertakers, feral participants in the dog-eat-dog world, willing at a moment's notice to bury the competition (and put me in my grave).

A guy with a death sentence had to attend to his business—in my case, finding Hal's killer—but he also had to take advantage of opportunities to help him understand his place in the universe. He didn't necessarily need to discover the grand meaning of life, but it would be nice to at least catch a glimpse of its significance.

I neared the gate. Cars streamed steadily beside me.

I reached the gate and stopped. There were six picketers here. One of them waved a cardboard sign at the traffic on Mound Road. The sign was painted with large neon-green letters:

ON STRIKE
AMERICAN PARTS FOR AMERICAN CARS

The other five picketers were sitting in fold-out chairs. Three held cups holding what looked like beer.

"Hey, guys," I said, "I'm with you all the way." I shook my fist in the direction of the factory.

"You come to relieve one of us?" a picketer asked. He took a drink from his cup. He was a heavyset black man with a shaved head. "The shop steward said he'd have replacements here by now."

"No, I was just passing by. I thought I'd stop and have a talk, see how things are going."

"You a reporter?" the man asked.

"No."

"Then what the fuck you want to talk about?"

He hadn't asked in a threatening tone. The "fuck" had been included like it was a linguistic tic, in the same way a Canadian might add "eh?" to the end of every other sentence.

"We could talk about cars," I suggested.

"Yeah, well, I'll tell you somethin' about this year's models. Don't buy one until well after the strike's settled."

"Yeah," another chimed in, "they got managers running some of the lines. No tellin' what kind of crap they're putting out."

"Oh, I don't know about that," I said. "I'm sure the quality is just as high as your average Hyundai economy model."

They laughed, and one of them offered me a paper cup filled with amber fluid. I took the cup and politely took a sip. I couldn't be sure, but it seemed my taste buds were dulled. Even the memory of what a good cold brew tasted like was fading.

Another car honked. The picketers waved and cheered.

I wanted to pull up a chair and join them. Nothing would ease my mind more than to forget about Hal's murder.

"I'm not an auto worker," I said, "but my father was. I remember him bringing me to a picket line when I was a little kid."

"What was his name?" one of them asked.

"Thigpen. Worked here up till about fifteen years ago."

A couple of the picketers shrugged. Others shook their heads.

I stared at the flames, the orange-red flickering, a roiling mass of combustion, chaotic and violent, smoke churning skyward. That's the nature of the universe—violence—and it all started with the Big Bang. How can there be peace of mind in a universe born by an explosion of time and space?

"Anyway," I continued, "I wanted to see if anything's changed. I remembered how tight the strikers were with each other."

"Yeah, we're tight," the bald black man said, grinning. "Ain't got a choice. If we ain't tight, the strike won't hold and management gets their way."

"And a lot of us will lose jobs," the striker who'd given me the cup added.

The one holding the sign said, "We're gonna stick together and see this thing through."

Wouldn't it be nice, I thought, if all of humanity arose as one and announced, We're all going to stick together from now on.

Yeah, right.

Someone had shot at me yesterday and had killed Hal. The brotherhood of Mankind was an illusion, a concept created by poets with no basis in reality.

Four cars drove by, all of them honking. The picketers got out of their chairs and waved and cheered. After the cars passed, the picketer holding the sign said, "When the company starts losing money, they'll start seeing things our way."

Strikes were battles of wills. They were costly to employees, which was an incentive to settle early. Although paid from a strike fund built from union dues, the checks were only a fraction of their normal pay. But strikes were costly to employers, too, and a car company's sole purpose was to make money (at least that's how stockholders usually saw things). They usually gave ground grudgingly, but they did give ground, seeking to offer as little as possible in the way of concessions in order to reach an agreement.

"You guys will win," I said. I turned and glanced across the street at the union hall, where Tom was trying to help me. It was time to return to the mission (not quest) at hand. "I have to head back. Just wanted to come over a minute and give my support."

"Thanks, man," the black guy said. "We appreciate it."

His tone was honest, and the way the others nodded made me think that I'd actually made in difference in their vigil.

Maybe that's what being alive was all about—making a difference.

I nodded at them and headed back along the sidewalk in the direction of the union hall.

After a few minutes of walking, I began to cross Mound Road again, my own particular version of a game I called *vehicular evasion*, imagining I looked like an inebriated man trying to walk a straight line for a dour-faced police officer.

It's just your imagination, Jack. You're walking fine.

I reached Tom's pickup. My trip down memory lane—and across Mound Road—over, I walked to the nearest placard in the grass surrounding the building and emptied the cup.

On my way inside, I found a trash bin and threw the cup into it.

"Jack, there you are!" Tom said. He was standing with two other people. One of them was expressing his opinion of management, setting a cadence to his criticism with the word *fuckin'*.

The union hall was smoky, full of noise, with people playing cards and eating snacks from a table full of bowls of chili and potato chips. A few flies twittered greedily on the tablecloth. At the far end of the hall, a man with stubby fingers was rubbing his chin as he stared at me. The Colonel, a.k.a. Uncle Bob. He was registering my face in his memory, I knew, for potential future reference.

"How'd it go?" I asked Tom as he sidled away from the guy who hated management (fuckin' thick-head morons).

He grabbed my elbow. "I'll tell ya outside. You're not going to believe this."

That was improbable. My skepticism was at an all-time low.

CHAPTER NINETEEN

"Tell me," I said as we stepped outside.

"You gotta understand," Tom said, "Uncle Bob didn't really come out and say anyone was a hit man. He has an odd way of making me understand things without saying anything specific."

"Are you saying he was vague?"

"Not exactly. He gave me a name. Archie Norton. And he's into guns in a big way."

"Wait—isn't Archie Norton the owner of that Chevy dealership?"

Tom nodded. "Bingo."

Archie Norton went by the nickname of Kodiak. He hunted big game, and in the Chevy dealership's showroom, there was a Kodiak bear he'd shot in Alaska. "Doesn't seem like a hit man would be any kind of overt gun enthusiast. I mean, that's like a big clue to the police."

"Best place to hide is out in the open," Tom said.

"True," I said. "You can tell me more while I drive you back to your house."

"You want to drive?"

"It'll help keep my mind off things."

Tom nodded quickly and handed me the keys. I pulled out of the parking lot, turned left on Mound, then right on 16 Mile Road, heading east toward Mt. Clemens. Rush hour traffic was winding down, but I still had to pay sharp attention to the road.

I glanced at Tom, who was staring ahead. His eyes flickered toward me, and he said, "Are you okay with talking about this now?"

"Yeah. Go ahead."

"Okay. Jack, I gotta tell ya, I was pretty slick. Uncle Bob knows I'm not a criminal or anything, so he did say he was curious about why I wanted to talk about these things. I said I was going to write a book."

"I'm not sure it's a good idea to lie to Uncle Bob," I said.

"Wasn't a lie. I am going to write a book someday, just not about this." Tom was silent for a few seconds before he continued. "So, Uncle Bob starts talking about hypothetical situations. He talked about the ways things might be in, say, New Jersey."

I remembered that's where Josef Adolpho had wanted to go. Did his life end in the repair shop today? And what's it like for a life to actually end?

"In a place like Jersey, Uncle Bob said, there'd naturally be a tendency to have turf wars because of all the money at stake with the casinos."

"There's a floating casino opening up on the Detroit River tomorrow, isn't there?" I asked.

"Yeah, on a riverboat. It'll be permanently docked, though."

"What I saw at the repair shop fits the turf war theory," I said. "But I was thinking this is all about cars."

"Ah, but if there's a crime boss in the area, he'd try to have control over all the illegal goings-on, the car thefts, chop shops, insurance fraud, numbers rackets, and especially the casinos."

I nodded. Even if the casino was audited regularly, there were ways to hijack some of the profits. And auditors could be bribed, officials paid off. With money and power at stake, a whole helluva lot of people were willing to look the other way. One aspect of a casino was particularly attractive to the underworld—the opportunity to launder money.

"Okay, so here's where it gets interesting," Tom said. "Now, if there was a turf war, and someone wanted to have, say, another crime boss whacked, there'd have to be someone trusted to do the hit. And these people don't go around handing out business cards."

"But wouldn't they just use someone in their crime organization?" I asked. "I mean, these guys would probably have hit men on their payroll."

"I guess so," Tom said. "But what if the turf war is a new thing? I mean, if there's just one gang in control and everybody's on board, there's no need for hit men."

"Whenever there's power and money, there's always someone else trying to get it from you."

Tom shrugged. "Maybe Norton's just been added to the payroll. Or, maybe this new group that's trying to move in, they've got a shortage of hit men because they're new in the area—and they're all busy applying pressure to get everybody to switch allegiance."

I remembered Adolpho's missing fingers. Pressure.

"That makes sense," I admitted.

"Uncle Bob told me that it's no secret that there's been a spike in auto thefts lately. Lots of money involved."

"What kind of cars?"

"Mostly high end models. Why?"

"If there's a spate of Taurus thefts, I'd suspect chop shop activity. If it's a fleet of Infiniti models, I might think they're being shipped overseas. You don't have anyone in Poland wanting to buy a stolen Ford Escort."

"Poland?"

"Just an example."

"It's just interesting that you used that as an example because Uncle Bob mentioned that he wouldn't be surprised if, in a place like New Jersey, there'd be some European crime kingpin trying to move in."

Ah, the wondrous benefits of globalization.

"Which would definitely start a turf war," I noted. I remembered Blalock (with a Boston accent) had asked Ellie if she'd traveled to Europe. What did Blalock suspect—that Ellie (or I) was working for a European crime boss?

"Right, a big turf war," Tom said. "So, I asked Uncle Bob if that were to happen around here, who would someone like me go to see in order to have some of this pressure eliminated."

"And?"

"That's when he said he'd probably check out Archie Norton. The guy's got more rifles that some police departments. He's got a dead eye—" Tom looked sharply out the window. "Sorry, ... he's an excellent shot. And, well, a guy like that's always looking for new sport, bigger challenges. And if the price is right, people can be talked into doing things they might not otherwise even think of."

I was beginning to suspect that Uncle Bob might've been taking his nephew for a ride on the bullshit express, but I knew I'd have to check out the story.

"When we get to your house," I said, "let's see if we can find his home address. I'd like to pay Mr. Norton a visit."

"You don't want me to go?" Tom asked.

"Nope. I have to do this myself."

"I understand, I s'pose. Anyway, I have to admit I've been getting pretty hungry. I haven't been able to eat a thing since yesterday."

"Neither have I."

Neither one of us said another word until I pulled into Tom's driveway.

"I forgot to tell you something," Tom said. "Remember when you were telling me what happened at Josef's Repair Shop?"

"Yeah, after I was able to pick myself up." And knock an EMS guy's lights out.

"While you were in the tub, I went online and looked up those words you heard. Took me a while because I didn't know the spelling."

"What'd you find out?" I asked, stopping the pickup truck. I turned off the engine.

"They're swear words, more or less. '*Svinya*' means pig, and '*Suka*' means bitch. They're Russian."

I was reaching to open the door, but I froze, my hand resting on the handle.

European crime boss. Turf war. Russian.

Mafiya.

CHAPTER TWENTY

After I explained to Tom my suspicion that the Mafiya was moving into the area, we went inside and I found the address for Archibald Norton in the telephone book, which at first surprised me, but then I realized that as the owner of Norton Chevrolet, he was somewhat of a public person.

"I'm going to stake out his house," I told Tom, who was in the kitchen.

"When should I expect you back?"

"If you don't hear from me by midnight, go to Norton's house and look for me. I'll probably call. I might stake the place out all night."

"Okay." He looked lost, probably because he wanted to say so much more (that, or he was deciding what to eat). "I'll stay near a phone."

I went outside and drove to St. Clair Shores without incident. Within a minute of turning onto Norton's street, I arrived at his address. The house was large, on a lakefront property. The lake side of his yard was curved outward, extending the impressive length of his property's shorefront.

I parked a few houses down, where I could see into the back yard, and waited. The sun was dipping toward sunset. It was six-thirty, and the heat of the day was beginning to subside.

Quickly I grew frustrated. I knew what Norton looked like from his television commercials, but he was nowhere to be seen. The driveway was crowded with four SUVs. Music was playing in the backyard, country (or western, depending on which state the musician was from), with slide-guitar sounds and the plaintive twang of a wronged cowboy's voice.

I started the truck and parked in front of Norton's house.

I walked up the driveway, across the cut-stone walkway,

and climbed the three steps to the front porch, where I rang the doorbell.

An attractive woman, no older than twenty-five, came out wearing a red bikini. Her blonde hair was styled with tight curls. Her red fingernail polish matched the color of her lipstick (and bikini). "Well, hello there," she said with a slight southern drawl. "Can I help you?"

"Yes, ma'am. I'm doing a promotion for WRIF radio. I'm looking for people who can show me their Winner Athletics shoes. If you have 'em, you'll be entered in a contest to win a thousand dollars."

"Really?" she asked, playing with a strand of curled hair.

"To be honest, I can't guarantee you'd win."

She was looking me up and down, her mouth twisting in a way that reminded me of Ellie. "You're a bit of an odd character," she said. "Something about you is ... different."

"I have my ways," I told her.

"Hmmm. Well, I don't wear Winner Athletics, but I really don't know about my husband."

"Is he home?"

She looked me up and down again, the strand of hair curling around her finger. "No. Sorry to disappoint you."

"That's all right. I'm just hoping to get the word out about Winner Athletics." I considered asking her to go and check her husband's shoes but decided against it. She might mention it to Norton later, alerting him to my visit. "Maybe I'll come back when your husband's home."

"Wait—you're looking for anyone with Winner Athletics shoes?"

"That's correct, ma'am."

"Oh please, sugar, call me Sharon. Sharon Norton."

I hesitated, not wanting to give her my real name, not if Archie Norton was a hit man. "I'm Samuel Diamond. Call me Sam."

"All right, Sam. You have a kind face, and a darn good tan, too. Not sure what it is about you, though, that I find so ... intriguing."

I shrugged.

"I bet you're cool under pressure. Right? And a big hit with the girls? You know, diamonds are a girl's best friend."

Without missing a beat, I said, "Especially when they're big."

She hesitated, then smiled, eyes fluttering. "Well, Sam, why don't you come on out back. I'm having a party, and maybe someone's wearing some of those shoes you're looking for." She held the door open and stepped aside.

Hoping to find some Winner Athletics shoes lying around—I was beginning to wonder if the killer was the only one who owned a pair, none of my suspects so far having them—I walked inside.

Sharon Norton walked toward the back of the house, and I followed.

"It's just a little pool party," Sharon said. "My husband, Archie, bagged some kind of record caribou, so he came back from Alaska early. I figured we'd throw a party for him."

I'd almost said gesundheit, such was the multi-syllabic manner in which she said her husband's name—Aaarcheeee.

"I thought he wasn't here," I said.

"He was here earlier, but he had to leave. Got a phone call, and all of a sudden he's gotta take off. It's urgent, he said."

"Is he the Archie Norton with the Chevrolet dealership?" I asked.

"Sure is, sugar. You've heard of it?"

"Yeah, but I have to admit I own a Ford."

She reached a set of sliding glass patio doors and stopped. "I hope you like country music," she said, her hand resting on the door handle. "Archie hates country. I can only play it when he's not around."

"I understand."

"Well, it's getting to be a problem," she said. She winked at me. "Fact is, we've been having quite a few problems lately. Makes a girl lonely, know what I mean?"

"I know all about being lonely."

She slowly shook her head. "I wouldn't have thought a man like you'd have any relationship problems."

"Well, Sharon, they've only come up lately."

"I've had problems from day one. I married him for his

money; he married me for the great sex. Does it shock you that I'm telling you this?"

"Not really. You seem like an open, honest young lady, and at the moment I can't think of a marriage arrangement that's any better, long-term."

Sharon was looking me up and down again. Maybe the odd thing about me that she kept wondering about was the fact that I was wearing a sweatsuit on a hot day. I glanced to my right and saw an open door that led into a study with yellowish curtain-filtered light and mahogany wood paneling. Mounted on the wall was the head of a gazelle. "Your husband must be an excellent hunter," I said.

Sharon cocked her head to see what I'd glanced at. "Oh, I'm sure he is. Talks like he is, anyway. He goes on hunting trips four or five times a year."

I took a step toward the study. "Mind if I have a look?"

"We can look in, but Archie doesn't allow anyone in his study when he's not here."

We walked to the study's door and peered inside. I counted four heads mounted on the wall: elk, moose, antelope, and the gazelle I'd already seen. Above the fireplace, a badger was positioned in an attack pose. Near the fireplace, there was a desk. Anyone who happened to find themselves in front of the desk, speaking to Norton, would be subjected to the sight of the attacking badger, a psychological disadvantage that I'm sure Norton planned. Although owning a dealership, Norton was basically a car salesman, and they were all keenly aware of psychological ploys.

"Amazing," I said.

"Oh, I really don't think he's such a great hunter. The guides probably lead him to the animals. All Archie has to do is aim and pull the trigger."

"Still, he must have a powerful gun to take down an elk."

She twirled her hair again and leaned against the doorframe. "Archie likes to think he has the biggest gun in town."

"And does he?" I asked.

Her finger twirled the lock of hair to the front of her face, tracing along the bottom of her lip. "Now, Sam, how on earth could I possibly know if he's got the biggest? That is, unless you're proposing I make a comparison ..."

I held up my hands. "For such a beautiful woman as yourself, I'd be afraid I wouldn't measure up."

"Somethin' tells me you wouldn't have a problem."

"Maybe later. I hate gun comparisons when there're so many people out back."

"You got a point there, sugar."

"Tell me something, though," I said, wanting to learn more about Norton. "What kind of thrill does hunting give Archie?"

"Beats me. All I know is that Archie likes guns more than he does sex. He spends hours polishing them."

"I wouldn't know how often a gun needs cleaning. I've never owned one."

"Oh, you've got a gun, sure enough, Sam. And if you ever need it polished, I'd be happy to lend a hand."

I could feel a stirring of blood. "I'll be sure to keep that in mind."

"Well, I don't see any wedding ring, and just to let you know, you wouldn't have to worry about any entanglements from me."

"I just don't think we'd have much of a future." I peered at her. Even if she flirted with most men, this was more than casual flirting. This was a bona fide offer. Was she tired of Archie *polishing his gun*?

Seeing no shoes, I turned back to Sharon. "Shall we meet your guests?"

"Sure. C'mon."

Sharon led me out to the patio, heading to the far side of the pool, where the guests had congregated, watching a boat race on the lake.

Suddenly my right leg stiffened. I pitched headlong into the shallow end of the pool.

Sharon jumped in and helped me toward the steps.

I gasped and took a deep breath in case anyone was looking.

"Are you all right, Sam?" she asked.

"Yeah, fine." There were plenty of reasons why my leg had suddenly cramped. Lots of exertion lately combined with low intake of fluids. That was one. Or the progression of a disease on the central nervous system. That was another.

We sloshed through the remaining distance to the steps out of the pool. Once out, I knelt, out of breath.

Sharon went to a chair that had a stack of towels on it and returned with one. "Here."

I took the towel and began drying myself. Not wanting to meet the guests, who were coming our way, I said, "I'd like to meet your guests, but really, I'm running very late. I've got to go."

Her head cocked, she said, "If that's what you want, Sam. Sure. Promise you'll call me?"

I stepped toward the patio door. "I have to go."

She led me into the house. "Wait." She went down a hallway and quickly returned. She handed me a card. "It's got my private number on it."

"Can't make any promises," I said, walking toward the front door.

"Oh, I'd be so pleased if you do, Sam."

At the front door, I stepped ahead of Sharon and instead of opening that door, I opened the door of the closet next to it.

"Wrong door," Sharon said. She giggled.

No. Not the wrong door. Because as I stared down at the shoes, I saw a pair that each had the angled W, signifying the Winner Athletics design.

As Tom might've said, Bingo.

CHAPTER TWENTY ONE

"My mistake." I handed the towel to Sharon.

"Sam, I can throw your clothes in the dryer," she said suggestively.

"Sorry, gotta run."

She reached for my arm, touched it gently, and said, "Do come again, Sam Diamond."

I said good-bye and walked out to the street.

As I drove away, I took the cell phone from my pocket, water dripping from it. I set it on the passenger seat, thinking its days were over (as mine would be soon), and set my wallet and the penknife beside it, thinking they might dry out there.

Unable to use the cell phone, I drove fast to Tom's house. I didn't want him showing up at Norton's. Archie Norton was a killer.

At Tom's, I parked the truck, gathered the items from the passenger seat, and went inside. Tom was sitting at the workbench in the den, bending wire mesh into shapes that looked somewhat like otters.

"Geez, Jack, what happened?"

It was nice being called Jack again, instead of Sam.

"Went for a swim," I said, putting the cell phone, wallet, and keys on the workbench. "Actually, I fell into Norton's pool. Getting to be a bit klutzy."

Tom hesitated. "What'd you find out?"

"Norton wasn't home, but his wife was. I went in and found a pair of Winner Athletics shoes. They looked about the right size, too."

Tom stood, strode toward the kitchen, and banged his fist against the wall. "I knew it!" His gaze darted left and right. He stormed back to the workbench, picked up a rawhide hammer, and smashed the spine of the half-constructed plaster panther. "I'm going to kill that son of a bitch."

"Tom—"

"C'mon, let's go."

"No, Tom."

He threw the hammer against the wall across the room and brushed his hand over his head. "Why the hell not, Jack?"

"Look, I'm sure Norton and me will be having a heart-to-heart discussion about it real soon—but if you and I are going to talk about killing someone, we'd better be awful damn sure about it." *And there're a few things I want to do first.*

"You're not sure it's Norton?"

"I'm almost positive it is him. Almost. I think I'll be able to get a confession out of him if he's the one. Right now, though, I'm tired. It's been a long day. We'll take care of Norton soon enough."

But I was starting to wonder just how soon it would be. I was feeling exhausted.

"So what's your next move?"

"Get some dry clothes."

Tom nodded. "Hold on." He went to his bedroom and returned with a folded set of sweats. "Washed and dried these while you were gone. Stitched up the sleeve, too."

I took the sweats, went to the bathroom, and put my penknife and pebble on the sink. While I changed clothes (after noting that the glue had held the gash in my arm closed), I pondered what my next move was. Archie Norton might very well be the hit man who had killed Hal, but who had ordered the hit? I still needed to see Bill Dunn and find out what his connection was with Sloan—and see how well he knew Delovich, the man from Indianapolis.

At the moment, though, I didn't want to do any of those things. I was tired. I needed a break from reality.

And, too, I had the sense that there needed to be a calm before the storm. When I confronted Norton, the shit was going to hit the proverbial fan.

I finished changing, put the penknife and pebble in my pocket, and dropped the wet sweats in the drier in the utility room.

When I returned to the den, (after noticing Tom had set up a portable fan to blow on my wallet and phone), I told him where I'd left them.

He nodded. "I'll get 'em later."

"Good, because right now I want to go outside and watch the sunset."

"Sure, Jack."

We went to the back porch and sat on a couple of creaking wooden rocking chairs. I took off my sunglasses and set them in my lap. Tom didn't say anything, perhaps sensing that I appreciated having him at my side and that I didn't want to talk about death anymore; and no matter what subject we tried to discuss, there'd always come a point at which my condition would be an issue.

Besides, the sunset was wondrously colorful. It didn't require a genius to know that while I was still around, walking the earth, I should take a bit of time to stop and smell the proverbial roses.

The sky was turning purplish (with, appropriately, a bit of pinkish rose tint). Clouds above the horizon were highlighted with yellows and oranges that were swept with crimson swaths. There was no clear-cut delineation in the colors. They blended smoothly, as though painted by a great artist. Clouds farther away from the horizon were deepening into darker purples and indigo blues, a rich tapestry with an inexplicably dense weave.

The sky gradually darkened.

"Did we have a good childhood, Tom?" I asked suddenly.

"What?"

"I mean, if you could change anything about our upbringing, would you?"

"Hell no."

"You sound so sure."

"No one's past is perfect—we've all screwed up at some point or another. And everyone's been screwed over, too. But if you're not happy with your past, you can't be happy with who you are."

"Sounds very Zen-like."

"Maybe so."

We sat for another thirty minutes, the only sounds the chirpings of crickets and the tires whining on Gratiot.

"What did you think you were going to do?" I asked suddenly. "Go at Norton with a hammer?"

"I don't know, Jack. I wasn't really thinking."

"If Norton's the hit man, he'll be a tough character. He'll know how to handle a gun."

"You're forgetting—we've got the element of surprise."

"I think hit men are always watching their backs. Besides, if Norton's the one who shot at me, he knows what I look like. No element of surprise."

"He doesn't know me, though," Tom pointed out.

"I don't want you involved."

"We've already had this discussion, Jack. And I'm already involved."

I sighed. There had to be a way to make Tom feel he was more involved without endangering him. "Think the wallet's dry?" I asked, putting my sunglasses back on.

"Yeah," Tom said. "Dry enough."

"Let's go back in," I told him. It was the chair (not me) that creaked as I stood.

We went inside to the den.

"I'm going to call Lynne," I told Tom.

"How much are you going to tell her?"

I shook my head. "Not much. I just want to make sure there's nothing unresolved between us."

"In that case, I better not talk to her. I'll let something slip."

I sensed that Tom, knowing Lynne would soon be getting an invitation to a funeral in the not-too-distant future, was afraid of not sounding like his usual self. Lynne was perceptive and might guess something was bothering him.

"Got her number around?"

Tom reached into a drawer and pulled out an address book. He grabbed the phone and punched in the number for me.

After four rings, a recorded message played: "Sorry, but we're out at the moment. You know what to do at the beep."

"Lynne, it's Jack. I could say that I just wanted to check in and see how you're doing, but it wouldn't be true. Something's been bothering me lately, and I need to get it off my chest. Remember how we fought when we were kids? Always arguing. Tooth and nail sometimes. Hell, I don't even remember a single thing we argued about. Mostly kid stuff, I suppose. You know—saying things like, 'You touched me!' and 'No I didn't!' That's normal for kids, right? Anyway, I want you to know that I'm sorry if I ever hurt your feelings. That's why I called, to apologize. And ..., well, I think you should move back to Michigan. Tom needs ... ah, more family in the area. Yeah. And then you can help set him up with someone nice. Remember how you used to find dates for him? I think he needs someone. Anyway, maybe you can afford to move back if Tom helps you to find a good, cheap house nearby. Please keep it in mind. We all love you and miss you. And, oh, if I can't manage to call you back, I just wanted you to know that you've been a great sister—the best ever."

I put the phone down.

"I don't know, Jack, but it sounded like you were saying good-bye for good."

"If she calls, tell her I'm not here."

"Okay, Jack. Whatever you say. She needs to know about Hal, though. She really looked up to him. He listened to her more than we did. In some ways, he was more of a brother to her than we were."

"Call her in a few days. It'll all be over then, I think. She can tell Mom and Dad. They should know, too. They were the ones who took him in."

"Listen, I think you should lie down for a while. Your voice is sounding tired."

"I need to do something first. I'd like your help, Tom."

"Anything."

"Got any classical music?"

"Just what you've given me at Christmas."

"Okay, good. Put on Mozart's *Requiem*. It sort of fits, I think, for what I need to do."

"And what's that?"

"Write my will. And you'll be my witness—or do I need

two?"

"I think it's two."

"Shit."

"No one's going to contest it, right? I mean, Ellie's not going to have a problem, is she?"

"No."

"Then I can find someone else to sign. Don't worry about it, Jack. Not a problem."

"I need pen and paper, too," I said.

Tom brought me a spiral notebook and a blue pen. I opened the notebook and as I stared at the paper, music started playing. It filled the air with a heavy timbre—mournful bassoons, wistful cellos, repeated fugues. The solemn tones reminded me that Mozart was near death when he started composing this particular work.

Requiem was as near to the music of the dead as I could imagine, as though Mozart, during the final days of his life, had glimpsed the darkness beyond the veil.

I wrote a simple declaration of my desires to be enacted upon my death, adding a stipulation that they were only to be honored upon my cremation. Knowing Tom was doing well enough financially (and Ellie was doing even better), I left all of my worldly possessions to Lynne and specified that I wanted Ellie to respect my decision (since we weren't legally divorced yet). *Wait, Jack – the Explorer's going to be here already.* Nodding, I willed the SUV to Tom. Then I wrote again that Lynne was to get the house. Maybe Lynne would realize it was an opportunity to come back to Michigan. My ashes were to be scattered from atop the Blue Water Bridge into the St. Clair River. I signed and dated the will and then added a note: *Tom and Lynne have meant the world to me. I'll miss them.*

"Tom, I need you to sign and date this as a witness."

He leaned over my shoulder. "Where?"

I pointed below my name and wrote witnessed by.

Tom signed and dated it without, I think, reading it.

I tore the sheet out of the notebook and handed it to him. "Put it somewhere safe."

Tom took the paper into his bedroom.

I went into the spare room and lay down on the bed.

Tom looked in. "Are you all right, Jack?"

"I just need to rest."

"Another break from reality?"

"Yeah."

"Want me to get you up at any particular time?"

"No. If I never get up, that'd be all right with me."

I closed my eyes and nestled my head deeper into the pillow. I thought Tom had left but a couple of minutes later, he said, "Okay, Jack. All right. I'll, uh, be here."

"Good night, Tom."

"Rest well."

The entire weight of the world seemed to press down on me. I subconsciously resisted, but the force became crushing. Something gave way, and I felt myself falling.

Still able to faintly hear *Requiem*, I fell asleep.

CHAPTER TWENTY TWO

I awoke to the sound of birds.

They're more animated than the pebble, I thought, but that doesn't make them any more meaningful.

Sunlight streamed in through the window, a few motes of dust drifting lazily near the drapes, without purpose or pattern.

I climbed out of bed and headed for the den, noticing that Tom's motorcycle was missing.

Music was playing—*Il Buone, Il Brutto, Il Cattivo*, the theme song for the Clint Eastwood movie *The Good, the Bad, and the Ugly*.

Mood music for a showdown. Very funny, Tom.

As I reached the workbench, I realized the CD was on continuous play. It must've been, because Tom had left a note saying he'd left at eight o'clock (it was now ten) for the Norton Chevrolet dealership. He promised not to do anything until I got there.

There were a few tools missing from the workbench. The rawhide hammer had been picked up from the floor and was nowhere to be seen.

Trying to hurry, I went out to the pickup and brought in the duffel bag. I slipped off the sweatsuit and put on the knee braces, the elbow braces, and back support. I didn't think my body was on the verge of collapse, but I wasn't sure. I couldn't get a feel for its condition. A knee might be about to buckle, and I wouldn't know.

I probed the Frankenstein-like wound on my arm. The glue was holding. And it didn't hurt.

After putting my sweatsuit back on, I went to the bathroom, found an unopened toothbrush, and used it to brush my teeth—not that I was worried about cavities, but I wanted to keep the smell of my breath manageable. I gargled with mouthwash, just in case the toothpaste wasn't enough.

I looked at the mirror and didn't think I looked that bad. Not dead yet.

Back in the den, I put the pebble (a.k.a., my pet rock?), keys, wallet, and penknife in my pocket. I tried using my cell phone. It wouldn't even light up. Death by drowning.

I went outside, taking my repair kit, climbed into the pickup, and drove toward Mt. Clemens.

"Go ahead, Norton," I said, "make my day."

I was nowhere close to being a Clint Eastwood look-alike, and my words sounded a little too hollow to be intimidating. Still, this would be a showdown. I'd have to make do with whatever Eastwood bravado I could muster.

And what'll you use, Jack? A rawhide hammer?

The penknife couldn't be considered a weapon of intimidation, certainly not to a Mafiya hit man. (*Wait, Jack, you don't know if he's Russian.*) But because it was small and lightweight, I could wield it quickly, which I considered important because I wasn't quite as fast as I used to be. Besides, if needed, the weightier Louisville Slugger was behind the seat.

At the Chevy dealership, I drove through the sales lot, looking for Tom or his motorcycle.

There were at least ten customers looking at cars. Some had come as couples, some alone. All were being attended to by sales staff. The customers looked ready to buy, perhaps even eager, like junkies needing a fix (but low on cash).

Near the repair bays on the side of the dealership, I saw the *Tom Terrific* motorcycle and parked beside it.

I was walking around toward the front showroom when a man with a white shirt and a flashy blue plaid tie approached.

"Sorry," I told him. "I'm not looking to buy a car."

The man grinned. "Didn't say you were."

"I'm in a hurry."

"Okay," he said, stepping aside. "I suppose salesmen just like to talk, that's all." He started following me.

"Is the strike affecting sales?" I asked.

"Yes, but sales are actually up. People figure they'll go ahead and get a new car while they're still available."

"I bet Archibald Norton is thrilled."

"Oh, we can never tell what Kodiak—that's what we call him—is feeling. Great poker face. Can't read a thing."

"Quite a nickname," I said.

The salesman spotted a car pulling into the lot. An old Beretta. It stopped beside a row of minivans, and a young couple got out.

"Have a good day," the salesman said, veering off toward the couple.

"Fuck off," I whispered.

A few seconds later, I arrived at the main entrance into the front showroom. I glanced at my hands, which I discovered were clenched.

I'm close to being dead, but at least I can be pissed off and can still clench my hands. And I'm on my way to meet the guy who shot me. Nobody better stand in my way or they're gonna get a monolith crammed up their Kubrick.

I pushed the door open and stepped inside onto a white tile floor. Ahead, there were six shiny cars equally spaced in two rows. Farther to the back, there was a blue-carpeted office area of cubicles with gray four-feet-high dividers. The corner cubicle was elevated by a raised floor section, reminding me of a conning tower. Sales manager's office, most likely.

Immediately I noticed the dead Kodiak bear to my right, near the glass showroom wall. Actually, as Sharon Norton had said, it was mounted in a display, its fur reddish brown, standing on its hind legs, over seven feet tall. Its forelegs were raised as though about to take a swipe. Its claws looked like raptor talons.

The bear was standing in a habitat display that was at least ten feet wide. The detail of the habitat was stunning. Behind the bear, there were successive layers of rising ledges. The rock looked realistic, slate-gray with pockmarks of brown. Foliage covered the rocks near the sides. In the synthetic rock three feet from the base, there was a cascading waterfall. Positioning pieces of synthetic grass near the pool at the bottom of the waterfall, Tom glanced over his shoulder and waved.

I marched over to him. A salesman was approaching me.

"I'm with him," I said, pointing at Tom. The salesman nodded and smiled.

"What the hell are you doing?" I asked Tom, kneeling at his side. I could now hear the whirr of a water pump, the waterfall self-contained, recycling water from the pool back to the top.

"Working on the habitat."

"I can see that."

"Norton's not here. They're expecting him around noon."

"Who gave you permission to make changes to the habitat?"

"Actually, I told them that Mr. Norton had hired me to do a few improvements, expand the habitat a bit—add an otter and expand the background, maybe a tree, a few shrubs, some rocks."

"You didn't tell them your name, did you?"

"I'm not stupid, Jack. I said I was Mark Stoneman."

"And what are you going to do when Norton gets here?"

Tom shrugged. "I'll say someone who claimed to be him had called me."

"He won't believe that."

"What's he going to do, shoot me?"

"Not here, he won't," I told him. I shifted my sunglasses and looked around the showroom. Nobody seemed to be paying us much attention. "Look, Tom, these guys—the Mafiya—don't screw around."

"I know that," Tom said.

I imagined Norton holding a rifle, putting Tom's head in the crosshairs. "They don't care about lives or karma or anything other than money," I said. "Their money. They'll kill anyone who's a threat."

"I can handle it," Tom said.

"I still don't understand what you plan to do here."

Tom tapped the rawhide hammer, setting the artificial grass into its base. "Back you up."

I couldn't argue with Tom's desire to have Norton pay for his crime. "If I die, turn Norton in to the police. Tell them to run ballistics on the bullet that killed Hal Booker and compare them to Norton's guns."

"What exactly would I say?" Tom asked. "Do I tell them

about you?"

"Just tell them the truth. And Tom ..., be careful."

"I will, Jack. The way I figure it, Norton's gonna threaten me when I confront him. Then it'll be self-defense. Killing Norton will be justified."

"I just wish you'd asked me about this."

"You'd have said no. Besides, this is giving me an opportunity to do something important."

"What do you mean, important?"

Tom took out a tape measure from a small toolbox, which I noted would fit in his motorcycle saddlebag. "I've just been doing quite a bit of thinking lately." He measured out a length of three feet, across the bear's hind legs, then clicked a button and the tape snapped back into its aluminum housing. "I'm not getting any younger, and it's about time that I—well, like you said—get out more."

"That's not what I meant, and you know it."

"Well, Jack, you're just going to have to get used to it." He looked over my shoulder, and I turned to see what had caught his attention.

An approaching salesman pointed at me and said, "Hey, someone's on the phone. Wants to speak to you."

"Me?" I asked.

"Jack Thigpen, right?"

I nodded.

Who knew I was here?

I followed the salesman to a cubicle and picked up the phone. I held my hand over the mouthpiece until the salesmen left, then raised it and said, "Hello?"

CHAPTER TWENTY THREE

"What the fuck are you doing to my bear?" The voice had no accent. Rather, it was forceful, each word punctuated.

"Archibald Norton?" I asked.

"That's right, fuckwad. The owner."

"I'm not doing a fuckin' thing," I said. "It's some taxidermist. Name's Mark Stoneman, I think. Said someone told him you wanted a few improvements."

"And what the fuck you doing in my car dealership?"

"I came to speak to you."

"What about?"

Guns. The Mafiya. Who gave you the order to shoot me?

"I'd say we can start with who you're working for."

"I don't know what you're talking about."

"The fact that you know who I am already confirms what I suspected about you, Aaarcheeee."

"Hey—"

"See, I know you like to go out for target practice; only sometimes—let's just say people get in the way."

"You don't know what you're talking about."

"So, let me guess, you were coming into the dealership, spotted me, and went somewhere to call. You didn't want to meet face to face, not here anyway, because I'm alive and you weren't expecting that."

"I want you out of my dealership."

"Why? Hell, maybe I'll even buy a car."

There was a pause. "Okay, Thigpen, you do that. I hardly ever come by anyway. Spend all the fuckin' time you want there. No sweat off my brow. And I suggest you tell Mark Stoneman—I saw you talking to him—to get his hands off my display or I'll have him arrested. I'm a respected figure in this community, and the police ain't gonna let someone fuck with my bear."

"Hey, Norton, I'd think you want to talk to me, considering the evidence I have."

"What evidence?"

"The bullet," I said, lying. *It's back there somewhere in the alley. Would it be worth finding so there could be a ballistics match?*

"What bullet?"

"The one meant to kill me. Got stuck in my Kevlar vest. I don't have the one used in the murder you committed, though. I admit that much."

"And just who was it that got murdered?"

"Friend of mine. Hal Booker."

"Thigpen, I'm starting to think you don't know a goddam thing."

"Oh, I know a few things. I know about Delovich. And Sloan. And I can make some strong connections between them and you."

"You'll have to be more specific."

"Tell you what, Norton, I'll make this easy on you. I want to talk, and you need to hear what I have to say. But I don't think you want to be seen with me. Perfectly understandable, given the circumstances. So you just pick a place, any place, and I'll meet you there."

"Sounds like you're trying to set me up."

"For what? Besides, you can name the place and see if anyone is following me."

Norton paused. "Okay, Thigpen, here's the deal. You want to talk? We'll talk. There's a sand pit off Twenty-Seven Mile Road near Plank Road. It's by an outdoor rifle range."

I knew about the rifle range. There were few houses in the area, the sounds of rifle shots being an effective deterrent to local housing. And as a teenager, I'd gone to a party more than once at the sandpit. Late-night bonfires and booze. At least we'd been off where we couldn't cause much damage. "Yeah, I know where it is."

"You want to talk, you meet me there."

"All right," I said.

"Be there in twenty minutes, or I'm not showing."

Norton hung up.

I went to the habitat, where Tom waited expectantly. "Got to go," I told him.

"Where?"

"I'll meet you back at your house."

"But—"

"Listen, Tom, I'm heading out to meet Norton. He knows you're not supposed to be here, so you'd better leave. Tell you what, see if you can fix my cell phone. It's waterlogged. If you can't, get me a new one."

"I can do that after helping you with Norton."

"No. I'm doing this by myself."

"What about your strength? How is it? And your reflexes?"

"Look, Tom, what's Norton going to do, kill me?"

"He's a hit man, Jack. Like you said, these guys don't fuck around."

"I'm not afraid of death. Besides, I've got to take care of Norton myself. I'm looking forward to the meeting, more than I'm willing to admit. Okay?"

Tom stared at me, his breath short and angry. He flexed his hands, then took a deeper breath. "I suppose I understand. It goes against my gut, though."

"You just get yourself out of here before the cops show up."

Tom threw the tape measure into the toolbox. "All right, Jack. But you don't have a phone. How'll I know where you are?"

I hesitated. "Remember the sandpit by the rifle range on Twenty-Seven Mile Road?"

"Yeah."

"If I'm not at your house in a couple of hours, that's where I'll be." Possibly approaching the state of rigor mortis by then ...

I turned and walked out of the dealership, flexing my shoulders and hands, preparing for my meeting with Aaarcheeee.

CHAPTER TWENTY FOUR

The place where Norton wanted to talk was isolated.

I drove along the dirt road leading into the area from Twenty-Seven Mile Road until I entered the sand pit area.

There was a main pit about thirty feet deep (currently half filled with murky, stagnant water) and a hundred feet across. Several smaller (dry) ones were off to my left. The surrounding ground had some patchy vegetation, but I suspected there'd been toxic chemicals dumped here at one time or another. The entire area was the size of a football field. Around this area, there were a few small, scattered trees that appeared too scraggly to be alive. Farther away still, taller maples and pines indicated healthier soil. The rifle range, a quarter-mile off to my right, had excavated the area's sand and dirt to make fifty-foot high berms in back of the rows of targets.

I got out and walked in front of the pickup, holding the Louisville Slugger at my side. The day was bright (although in my condition, there was a mysterious pall over everything, like a partial solar eclipse), with a few wispy clouds caressing a deep-blue sky. After a few minutes of watching flies landing on patches of sand, only to take off immediately in search of someplace more promising, and listening to the occasional crack of a shot at the rifle range, a Jeep pulled up and I got my first look at Norton.

I stared at him as he got out and approached me. He walked slowly, carefully, like a cautious predator. Not even bothering to hide his intentions, he wore a shoulder harness over a blue short-sleeve shirt, a handgun nestled under his left arm.

Still, the man didn't appear intimidating. His face was incredibly narrow. A long, thin nose gave the impression that a punch would shatter its frail bones. His hair was short, hardly longer than stubble.

Norton stopped a few feet away. Although his face looked frail, his eyes were piercing—dark brown with flecks of black. His stare was cold.

A killer's line of vision would be equally dispassionate.

"I have to admit," I said, "you don't look surprised to see me. But I hear you hide your emotions well."

Norton folded his arms across his chest and continued to stare.

"Nice shoes," I said, looking down. "Winner Athletics, right? Dress for success, that's what I always say."

As Norton spoke, I could see that he was much more physically fit than I was, even though he was about my height and weight. He seemed to project his words with entire muscle sets from diaphragm to shoulder. "Why the fuck you bringin' up shoes?"

"Because Winner Athletics has a distinctive logo in their soles. And yesterday, there was a shooting in Detroit, and I happened to see that logo in a mud puddle after the shooter ran off. Care to look at the sole of your shoe and see?"

"Listen, Thigpen, I'm going to make this easy for you, okay?"

"Start with a confession—tell me you pulled the trigger," I told him. "Then you can tell me who wanted to have me whacked."

"I don't know a fuckin' thing about any shooting. Got that? But if I did, I'm tellin' you the contract's been called off."

"What do you mean, called off?"

"If someone wanted you hit, that someone would put out some money to have it done, right?"

"Unless," I said, "you were an employee of some crime organization."

Norton thumped his chest. "I only work for me."

"So if you were the shooter, it would've been a hit; and there was a contract out on me."

"And what I'm tellin' you is that the contract's been withdrawn."

"Why? Because you fucked up the first time and didn't succeed?"

"Nobody gives a reason for putting out a contract, or for canceling it, either."

I couldn't get a feeling for his emotions. His was truly a poker face, revealing nothing. A cold, blank stare.

Hell, I don't think he had even blinked once since arriving.

I swung the bat around to hold it on my other side. He didn't flinch, didn't move an eyelash.

A man like Norton would need a steady hand ...

"Hear enough?" Norton asked. "That satisfy you?"

I picked up the bat and poked him in the shoulder, jarring him backward. "No. That doesn't satisfy me at all."

"You tryin' to get money out of me, you little shit?"

"I told you what I want," I said. I poked him again.

I figured Norton's underarms would be drenched with sweat by now. The day was warm, and there was no shade here. The hot sand reflected heat. And yet Norton stood there coolly, taking jabs with a baseball bat without flinching.

"*Swinya.*"

"What?

"*Suka.*"

"Speak English, asshole."

"They mean pig and bitch."

"Hey, you dumb fuck, if you're going to try to insult me, you need to make sure I understand the words."

"I'm not trying to insult you. I know you don't give a fuck what I think."

"How you gonna play this, Thigpen? What the fuck's your game?"

"This ain't a fuckin' game. There's no trophy at stake, and money doesn't mean a thing to me. I've told you what I want, for starters, and you seem to be having a problem in the compliance department. Confess."

"You better watch who you're messin' with, Thigpen. You never know when you're gonna end up dead."

"True enough for most people," I said.

"I've been patient with you, Thigpen. Better consider your options while you still can."

I poked him with the bat. "Maybe I'll just turn you in."

The left side of Norton's mouth curled up. "You ain't got shit, Thigpen. You're a fuckin' two-bit investigator wannabe—I knew that when I was watchin' you at Josef's Repair Shop and you threw that paper in the trash and then watched to see if anyone would pick it up."

"I hadn't realized it was such a popular ploy. Why didn't you shoot me there?"

"If anyone wanted to shoot you, they'd want someplace without so many people around."

"I still think I've got quite a story to tell the police about you. And there's still the matter of Hal Booker. I assume he was killed to eliminate the only witness."

He blinked, an indication I had nailed down the reason Hal was killed.

"No one's gonna believe you," Norton said.

"Maybe they'd believe a guy named Sam Diamond."

"Who told you ..., son of a bitch—that was you!"

"I didn't happen to see a black raincoat, but I bet you own one."

"Don't you ever come back to my house!"

"Maybe Sharon invited me back. Seems you aren't satisfying her. You aren't being a good husband. You're too busy polishing your gun."

Norton might've possessed a poker face, but it was starting to redden slightly in the cheeks. "You step one foot in my house—I'll kill your sorry ass."

"Oh, you mean try again? Aren't you afraid you'll get caught this time?"

The side of his mouth curled up again. "You're forgetting something, Thigpen. You were checked out. Nobody would worry about having you knocked off because there *ain't no one to miss you*. Live by yourself. Self-employed. Shit, nobody'd ever even report you missing."

I almost winced. Norton had a point. I was like a proverbial tree falling in a forest with no one around, making no sound.

"Yeah, you hadn't thought about that," Norton continued. His lips pulled away from his teeth and he made a sound that was nearly a growl. "Too bad. Then again, I could claim self-defense. You got fingerprints all over that bat."

... ain't no one to miss you ...

I raised the bat. "Game's over," I said, starting to swing.

Norton pulled out the handgun. I adjusted my swing, striking the gun and hand simultaneously at the instant Norton fired. Although I batted the firearms dozens of yards away, and Norton's hand dangled from the end of his arm, numerous bones broken, the shot knocked me back a step (only a step, thanks to the knee braces) and now my side was burning. I looked down at the spreading dampness on my sweatshirt.

Norton stared at me.

I smiled. "It's only a flesh wound," I said calmly.

"What the fuck ...?" Norton whispered.

I stuck my index finger through the hole in my sweatshirt, onto the wound. I pulled out my finger and showed the red wetness dripping from it. The pain had already dissipated.

"Look what you did!" I said.

I took the bat firmly in my hands, raised it, and charged Norton.

He tried scrambling away, but he slipped in the sand.

I leveled the bat and jammed it at Norton's solar plexus. Wheezing, he dropped to his knees.

I went over and picked up the handgun. Then, standing in front of Norton, I aimed it at his forehead. Far from his usual calm, he was now shaking.

My hand trembled. I set the bat on the ground and held the gun with both hands. The gun seemed to shake of its own volition.

But not enough that I'd miss his brain.

Shoot! Kill him!

His eyes were closed.

It'll be just like putting him to sleep. Hal's dead. An eye for an eye.

I wanted to shoot. I wanted to kill him. I started pulling the trigger. In Tom's voice, the word karma whispered in my mind. I'm not sure whether it was the tremble in my hand or a last-instant decision to spare the killer's life, but either way the handgun angled to the right before I squeezed tightly enough to fire a shot, and I blew off most of Norton's ear.

His eyes opened. His hand felt up toward his ear. He looked at his hand, now awash with blood. It streamed down the side of his face.

How can anyone shoot people for money? How can murder be dispassionate? The taking of life ..., the spilling of blood ...

"I guess it's your lucky day," I said. Louder, I added, "That is, if you can hear me now!"

"But I shot you," Norton said weakly.

I pointed at the wound in my side. "It appears I don't roll over easily."

Norton's mouth dropped.

I pulled up the length of my sleeve and showed him the sewed-up gash on my arm. "See those stitches? I'm a goddam walking Frankenstein monster, that's what I am. A walking dead guy."

Norton shook his head in denial.

I tapped his forehead with the business end of the handgun. "Now, answer my questions or else we'll see how well you deal with wounds like these."

"W-W-What do you want to know?" he asked, staring at my side, either transfixed by the blood or afraid to meet my eyes.

"You pull the trigger in Detroit?" I asked.

"Yeah."

"Who put out the contract?"

"I c-c-can't say for sure."

"Want me to go for the other one?" I asked, tapping the gun against his other ear.

"It's the truth! L-L-Look, I can tell you who I think it was. It's gotta be him. He's used me before, when he wasn't so high up."

"Tell me."

"His name's Delovich."

Bingo.

"How often do you do these hits?"

"Not often."

"How many hits?"

"Altogether, maybe nine total."

"You're not sure?"

"Nine. Not, um, counting you."

"Counting Hal?"

He nodded.

"Well, I think you should count me." I tapped the handle of the handgun against the top of his head. "Because you did try to kill me. It really wouldn't be fair not to be counted. Don't you think so?"

"If you s-s-say so."

"Good. Now tell me, know a man named Blalock?"

He paused. "No. Not that I remember."

"Josef Adolpho?"

"Yeah, I know Adolpho. Know him from our Jersey days. He w-w-works for Delovich. That's why I figured you were getting hit. He didn't w-w-want you getting any closer."

"Who told you to stake me out there? Delovich?"

"No, not Delovich. I don't know his name. He w-w-was just a courier, though. He didn't order the hit. He gave me a down payment."

"How much?"

"Five thousand."

"Doesn't seem like much to risk prison."

"That was ten percent of the final payment. Easy money. T-T-Tax free."

"You don't have any feelings in there, I think." I kicked him in his chest, aiming for his heart.

He rolled to his side. Dirt and sand mixed with the blood on his face. He lay on his side, coughing, wincing.

"Were you told why I was supposed to get knocked off?"

Norton shook his head.

This isn't over yet, Jack.

"So, I'm investigating insurance fraud, then I get shot at and Hal gets killed, and then someone else tells me to stop because this was bigger than I think. Know what that means, bigger than I think?"

"No."

"Listen up," I said. "I'm going to say some names. You tell me what you know. Okay?"

Norton nodded.

"Ted Meade."

"Don't know him," Norton said.

"Bill Dunn."

"He owns a Ford dealership. Actually, Delovich owns it, I think. That's all I know about D-D-Dunn, though."

"Derek Sloan."

"Don't know him."

"You kill anyone in Mt. Clemens yesterday?"

"N-N-No."

"Hear anything about a turf war?"

"Yeah, lots of people feeling p-p-pressured. Lots of 'em end up getting whacked."

"Hear anything about the Mafiya moving in?"

"Yeah, that's the word on the street. Hell, man, I thought you might be Mafiya instead of an investigator."

"You realize now I'm not Mafiya?"

"You ain't Mafiya."

"No, I'm an army of the soon-to-be dead, an army of one."

"Let me go and get my ear f-f-fixed."

"This guy who gave you the down payment. Did he say anything?"

"Yeah, a few words. Asked if I was all set."

"Did he have an accent?"

"Yeah, the guy was definitely from New England."

Blalock.

So Norton didn't know who Blalock was, but Blalock was in on the hit. That explained how Norton knew where to find me. Blalock would've been able to find out from Ted Meade where I was doing my stake out.

"P-P-Please," Norton said. "I'm gonna bleed to death."

"Who's Delovich?"

"He's, uh, head of a crime ring. Organized crime."

"The Mob?"

"Hell, man, I don't think that's what it's called anymore. It's just organized c-c-crime."

Norton was starting to look like a pig, sweating, on all fours, wheezing and coughing and looking ready to be put out of his misery. *Swinya.*

"All right, Norton, here's the deal. You get just one chance at this, understand?"

Norton nodded.

"You got money stashed away somewhere?"

"Yeah, ... Bahamas."

"How much?"

"Almost two million. I, uh, I got a second life there. Sharon thinks I go hunting."

I figured Norton had a second identity, too. Probably passports in different names. The usual hit man paraphernalia. "I want you to take all of that money and donate it to charity."

"All of it?"

"Keep fifty thousand. You earned it. The rest goes. And you're going to explain to Sharon you're leaving her. She gets everything—the house, any money you've got in town. You'll give her power of attorney. Right away. This afternoon."

"What about my guns?"

"Leave 'em."

"Yeah, okay. After today, I'm through with guns anyway."

"You'll never kill anyone again."

"No."

"You won't even harm a fuckin' fly. Got it?"

"Yeah."

Hell, Jack, you got his head teed up. Get the bat. Take a swing. Knock one out of the park.

"You're going to earn money honestly."

"That's right."

"I want you to get a job selling cars."

"Okay, yeah."

"Preferably used cars."

Norton nodded.

"Get out of here before I change my mind."

"W-W-What are you?"

I took off my sunglasses. "I'm Jack Thigpen, the dead guy."

He looked around on the ground a moment, most likely for parts of his ear, but gave up and scrambled away.

I waited until he left, then put on my sunglasses, picked up the bat, and headed toward Tom's truck. At the door, I stopped and stared at the handgun.

Part of me said I might need it. Another part wanted nothing more to do with the weapon that put a bullet through me. Still another part suggested I put it in a trophy case. It was this latter part I told, shut up.

I looked up, spotting a shadow pass over the ground. There, high above the surrounding trees, a hawk soared. He cruised on an air current, searching the ground for movement, perhaps for a tasty mouse.

I leaned back and pitched the handgun toward the sandpit, figuring I'd let destiny do with it what it wanted, and heard a splash a few moments later.

I climbed into the driver's seat and drove toward Tom's house.

CHAPTER TWENTY FIVE

As I drove toward Tom's, I wanted to tell myself that I was marveling at the human body's ability to heal itself, to regenerate blood and skin and close wounds. Instead, I only hoped that the bullet hadn't passed through any vital organs. It had passed very close to my side, almost missing me. But as with many wounds, sometimes the less serious ones can release a lot of blood.

In any case, I felt a great need to repair the hole punched into my body and hoped the Ace bandage I'd wrapped around my midsection would at least slow the loss of blood.

I ruffled through the duffel bag and grabbed the duct tape. Stopped at a red light, I ripped off a piece and put it over part of the bandage covering my wound. Duct tape could repair anything, I'd been told.

I was glad I'd let Norton go. I'd considered making him turn himself in to the police. Norton would've done anything I asked. But he was only the trigger man, a tool, and I didn't want to tip off any of the bad guys.

The person I wanted to find was the one who'd given Norton a reason to kill me, the person who'd put out the contract. That person was Delovich, and I figured I could reach him through Bill Dunn, given enough time.

First, my body needed repair.

By the time I reached Tom's, I realized that I'd experienced an adrenaline rush during my encounter with Norton. I'd been juiced up. And now I was having a letdown, a sinking withdrawal feeling—like a heroin addict after a day of rehab.

I parked, walked to the porch, climbed the steps, and stopped at the front door.

The door swung open and Tom appeared. "Was Norton the

guy?" he asked quickly. His eyes lowered to the blood on my sweatshirt. "What the hell happened?"

"Same ol' story," I told him.

"Shot?"

I nodded.

"By Norton?"

"Yeah. This time he came closer to the mark. He was the one who shot at me in Detroit, the one who killed Hal. I confronted him about it and he shot me."

"You kill him?"

"I came close, but no."

"See, if I'd come along, I could've caught him. He might be able to outrun you, but I'd get him. Damn straight, I would."

I hesitated.

I wanted to barge past Tom, find my Explorer keys, and leave. I'd go somewhere secluded. Alaska, maybe.

"If you had come along," I told him, pointing at the damp stain on my sweatshirt, "this could've happened to you. This is precisely why I wanted you to stay here."

Tom looked like he wanted to object, but he didn't. Maybe he figured I had enough baggage weighing me down without adding concern for his safety.

"I need you to stitch me up again," I said, walking in.

Tom closed the door and followed me to the workbench.

"Sit down, Jack. I'll fix you up."

I sat and watched Tom get out his taxidermy tools.

On the table, there were printouts from the Internet with articles about embalming and studies of the brain dead.

"I'm not feeling very good," I said, taking off my shirt. I yanked the duct tape off and unwrapped the bandage.

Tom tried to hide it but I saw him wince as he glanced at my wound.

"You've lost a lot of blood," Tom said.

"It's not that. It's … the disease. It's progressing. I know it."

Tom shook his head. "Jack, I couldn't do what you're doing." He leaned close to me and stuck the needle through the skin at the top of the hole.

"What do you mean?"

Tom completed a few stitches before replying. "I'd find a way out."

"An escape clause?"

"Yeah, and if there wasn't one, I'd make up my own."

A wet drop fell onto my sweatpants, and I realized Tom was crying.

"See," Tom continued, "in my mind, suicide's a bad thing—a sin, evil. But if I'm gonna be dead anyway, I'm gonna find a way to send myself on my way."

"No, you'd find some artistic release to express your feelings."

"Nope, I'd be dead already. My focus would be on punching the train ticket and leaving the station."

"Very metaphoric, but you can't say for sure what you'd do. It's like soldiers never knowing how they'll react to their first battle."

"Maybe." He grabbed the scissors and cut the thread. "Front's done. Lean forward and I'll get the one in back."

I leaned forward and heard Tom sniffing.

I thought about complimenting him on his work (yeah, Tom, you're getting better with practice), but he was probably getting tired of stitching up his brother.

"Pretty bad, huh?" I asked.

"You're lucky, I think. The bleeding's stopped. Another inch to the left, and it probably would have struck your intenstines."

I could feel the tugs on my skin. At least I hadn't lost my sense of touch.

"I shouldn't be here," I said. "You're right. I should have my ticket punched and leave the station."

"Don't think, Jack. Not right now."

Maybe Tom was right. Don't think. He'd done a lot for me, and I owed it to him to keep trying. Besides, I was working my way steadily up the food chain, having found Norton, who'd given me Delovich's name.

After Tom finished stitching the wound, he went and got another sweatshirt. "You're going to need a change of wardrobe soon."

"Yeah."

Tom left and returned with the other sweatshirt. While I put it on, he paced back and forth on the other side of the workbench. His eyes looked red, but I couldn't see any tears. "Okay, I can understand why you didn't kill Norton, but that guy should be in jail for the rest of his life. I'm going to have to figure out some way to get the police on his trail."

"Why?" I asked. "What good would it do?"

"For one, he might kill again."

I shook my head. "I made quite an impression on him. He's going to be quite the philanthropist from now on. Trust me. And you're not going to find him. He's leaving the country."

"I still think maybe he ought to have a little accident somewhere along the line."

"Maybe he will. Watch the news for anything involving used car salesmen. Otherwise, let's leave it to karma."

Tom stopped pacing, picked up a new cell phone that was lying on the workbench, and handed it to me. "Here. You have to at least keep in touch with me."

"Okay." I opened the cell phone and punched in the number for Dunn's Ford.

A woman answered.

"I need to see Mr. Bill Dunn. It's urgent."

"He's on his way in now. Can I ask who's calling?"

"Sid Noir," I said. "I'll be there in one hour. At two-thirty. Consider this an appointment. Oh yeah, tell him there's a lot of money in it for him—in my proposition, that is. I've got a shipment of courtesy cars to unload."

"But sir, I can't guarantee—"

"Mr. Dunn will be very upset with you if this opportunity slips away."

"I can get in touch with him and call you right back."

"No, I'm afraid there are reasons why that won't be acceptable. Two-thirty. Have a nice day." I ended the call.

"I have to go," I told Tom.

He began pacing again. "Jack, I'm worried about you."

"I know."

He poured a glass of orange juice. "Drink this."

I complied, feeling a bit better.

"You've got stitches and braces holding you together. You're taking bigger and bigger risks."

"I have nothing to lose."

"Let me ask one more time—bring me along."

"No. And if you ask anymore, I'm not coming back at all."

"Okay, Jack—I had to try."

I stood and headed toward the front door, deciding to forego the Explorer for now. "I'll be at Bill Dunn Ford's, working my way up the food chain. I'll call in a couple of hours; if not, you know the routine."

"I'll be here."

I paused at the door and looked back. Tom nodded and waved briefly. I opened the door and went outside, thinking I was leaving for good.

CHAPTER TWENTY SIX

I drove to the Dunn Ford dealership—stopping for twenty dollars of gas on the way, thinking it'd be enough to get me wherever the hell I was going—and parked near the repair bays.

Someone's thinking you know something, Jack. Bigger than you think. *You better figure that out. You can't leave for the Great Beyond unless everyone you know is safe. If Blalock can threaten Ellie, anyone can be threatened, anyone you know or ever knew.*

Early for Sid Noir's appointment, I waited and watched the customers walking the sales lot. I studied their eyes, my fascination of the living growing. Idly, I rolled the pebble between my fingers.

They're buying dreams, I thought. Their eyes gleamed with excitement, a sharp intensity that at the same time possessed a distant, dreamy stare.

At least they're still chasing something, Jack. The American Dream.

I'd dreamed of being a champion tennis player. I'd dreamed of Ellie, too.

More and more, I doubted I could remember those dreams with any passion.

Don't think, I told myself.

I stepped out of the truck and went inside.

I went to Dunn's office, but no one was inside. Still five minutes early.

I found a salesman in the showroom and asked him to page Mr. Dunn. "Tell him Sid Noir's waiting in his office. I have an appointment."

The salesman nodded, and I went back to the office and waited in a chair across the room from his desk.

At two-thirty, Dunn walked in, still wearing a white shirt and blue tie, carrying a Subway bag, saying, "Sorry to keep—" His square jaw dropped and color drained from his face. "You!"

I stood and smiled. "I figured Sid Noir was a good alias. Don't you agree?"

Dunn turned to leave.

"Wait," I said. "I've got news from Delovich."

Dunn froze. He turned slowly, faced me, then glanced back over his shoulder. "What news?" he asked. "I'm guessing it's not about courtesy cars."

"First, come in and have a seat. You really don't want me to be upset with you, right? You know I've got, shall we say, a certain resistance to pain. That fact might come back to haunt you if you make the wrong choices."

Dunn looked unsure.

I raised my sweatshirt and showed him the new wound. "I got shot. See? But that bullet was like the knife I put through my hand. Nothing much slows me down."

Dunn blinked at least a dozen times rapid-fire, his face still drained of color. He rubbed his chest as though responding to the onset of a heart attack. His legs began to quiver and he staggered to his desk. He put a hand on it as though to hold himself up, then worked his way around until he was at his chair, on which he sat.

"What do you want?" he asked.

I got up and closed the door. "Let's keep this private, shall we?"

"Just stay on the other side of the desk," Dunn said. He took several breaths in quick succession.

"For now, okay."

Dunn swiped his hand across his face, an effort to collect his wits. "You killed Sloan," he said, his voice more steady. "You gonna kill me next?"

"How do you know Sloan's dead? It hasn't been on the news."

"Shit—everyone's heard. And you forced me to set him up."

"Newsflash—I didn't kill Sloan, and you were the only other person who knew where Sloan was going."

"Oh, you killed him, all right. I gotta tell you, payback's a motherfucker, and someone's gonna pay you back soon. Count on it."

"People have tried," I said, thinking Dunn truly believed I'd shot Sloan. But if Dunn didn't kill him, who did? Norton hadn't known, either.

Maybe Delovich.

"Who put out the contract on me?" I asked.

Dunn worked his jaw sideways as though loosening it up. He was either nervous or he was trying to find the right words to say.

"Come on, Dunn, tell me. You don't want me to get my badass mojo out."

"I don't know anything about a contract," Dunn said. "I'm just a businessman."

"But you know a man named Delovich."

Dunn hesitated. "I know a lot of people."

"But you were going to leave until I told you I had news from him."

"So what?"

"You're starting to piss me off."

"If you have news from Delovich, I suggest you tell me."

I stepped toward the desk and sighed, taking the penknife out of my pocket.

The office door opened behind me, and as I turned, a man stepped into the doorway. He was well dressed and immaculately groomed, his thin (almost gaunt) face clean-shaven and tanned. His hair was black, graying slightly at the temples, and combed back. His black suit was well tailored and expensive. His shoes were hand-made Italian leather, with an incredible shine to them. He stepped into the office, lightly tapping a dark red-stained cane that looked like solid antique mahogany.

"I hope I'm not interrupting," the man said, his voice deep and resonating, sounding much deeper than a face as thin as his should produce. His accent was similar to Adolpho's, but not nearly as noticeable and much more cultured.

"No, Mr. Delovich," Dunn said, jumping to his feet. "I was hoping this guy was just leaving."

Delovich!

CHAPTER TWENTY SEVEN

A man rushed into the office and stood at Delovich's side. Blalock. He was still wearing the Boston Bruins jersey he'd worn when threatening Ellie. "I got heah as soon as I could," Blalock said.

"Glad you could make it," Delovich told him. "It's time we all had a chat."

"Delovich, huh?" I said, pointing the penknife at him.

He didn't appear alarmed, or even surprised for that matter. His cold blue eyes surveyed me. "Out for a jog?"

"Someone told me the casual look's coming back in fashion," I said. "You look like you don't recognize me."

"Oh, I know you were the one trying to stop Blalock yesterday." Delovich turned slightly and lightly slapped the back of Blalock's head. "He gets overanxious sometimes. He needs to learn how to bridle his ambitions. Should I know any more about you than that?"

"Don't give me that shit," I told him. "Why'd you cancel the contract? Did you figure my life wasn't worth the going rate?"

"Ah, Jack Thigpen," Delovich said. "I'd heard your name in connection with a hit. I was wondering what all the fuss was about. I have to admit that I'm a bit puzzled about it all." He nodded at my penknife. "Is that your standard weapon of intimidation?"

"For you, it's not intimidation I'm after. Care to see how much damage I can cause?"

He moved quickly (and with a certain amount of elegance, I had to admit). The cane swung up and flashed in front of my throat. There was a click and from the end of the cane, a short blade snapped out. He continued the swing, the blade retracting, until it was at his side. He leaned on it. "I don't think you want to do that. I've taken people's eyes out with less effort than you just witnessed."

"Let me kill him," Blalock said.

Delovich turned and cuffed the back of his head again. "I'll do the talking here." Facing me again, he said, "Blalock moved here from Boston. He's a relation, so I felt obligated to give him employment. He's young and still learning, but at times I wonder if he'll ever come around."

I put the penknife back in my pocket. "Blalock threatened someone I know. If he does it again, I'll kill him."

Delovich looked me up and down. He sniffed once, like an animal catching my scent. Then he walked behind the desk slowly, casually, tapping his cane, tap tap tap, as though out for a stroll. He looked at Dunn briefly, though intensely, sniff, before returning to the spot beside Blalock.

"Blalock won't be bothering you anymore, Mr. Thigpen," Delovich said. "It was a misunderstanding. His heart is in the right place, but his eagerness diminishes his capacity to think."

This was all wrong. Delovich was too clean-cut. He looked sincerely apologetic. *Unless he's just toying with me – a cat clawing an injured mouse before finishing the kill.*

I looked at Blalock, whose forehead was beginning to sheen from the buildup of sweat.

Dunn was standing behind his desk, looking down mostly, deferentially, but glancing up every few seconds.

Delovich turned to Blalock and said, "Close the door."

Blalock moved to close it, and two husky young men wearing dress slacks and open collar polo shirts stepped into the doorway. One of them put his hand on the door, stopping Blalock. "It's all right," Delovich told them. "Wait outside." Once Blalock closed the door, Delovich's demeanor took a nosedive. He pointed his cane at me. "Listen, asshole, don't you dare threaten me again."

"Threaten you?" I said. "You're trying to have me killed. Norton told me. Aaarcheeee Norton."

Delovich rubbed his chin and said nothing.

"So you don't deny it?" I said.

"I'm trying to figure out what the fuck's going on, Mr.

Thigpen."

"Archie Norton's a hit man."

Delovich gave a short wave of his hand as though it was common knowledge.

"He tried to kill me," I continued. "I confronted him and he said you were the one who put out the contract on me."

"Hit men don't know who put out their contracts."

"He admitted he wasn't sure, but it has to be you. You've got a stake in Josef's Repair Shop, right?"

Delovich stepped slowly to the desk and stared at Dunn a moment (with Dunn averting his eyes). "This guy on the level?" he asked Dunn.

Dunn shrugged. "I know he ain't a cop or anything like that. He came here and made me set up a meeting with Sloan. He, uh, can be pretty convincing when he wants to be."

Delovich raised his cane and rapped Dunn's head with the end of the cane. "You're starting to sound like a talker to me. I don't like talkers."

"I'm sorry, Mr. Delovich, sir. It won't happen again. I swear it."

"You're not convincing me," Delovich said.

Dunn bent forward, putting his forehead on top of Delovich's hand. "Please, Mr. Delovich. I swear I'm not talking. It's Thigpen. Ask him how convincing he can be. See if I'm not right."

"I don't give a fuck how convincing he is. I don't even give a fuck if he's on my side. I have simple rules. One of them is don't talk."

"I know, I know," Dunn said.

Delovich turned and began walking away. In an instant, he spun, the cane flicking up and across Dunn's face, lightly cutting his cheek. A small line of blood appeared. Dunn raised his hand and wiped it across the wound. He looked at the blood on his hand. He nodded as though the punishment was fair.

Delovich sniffed, cocked his head, and returned to his spot beside Blalock.

"I think I'm beginning to understand," Delovich said. "But in any case, Mr. Thigpen, my association with Josef Adolpho is of no concern to you."

Blalock wiped sweat from his forehead and dried his hand on his pant leg.

"You see," Delovich continued, "I've gotten word that you're off limits – no hit man's going to make you a mark, no matter what the price."

Dunn shot a glance at me.

Dunn knew why, but he wasn't going to say. *Yeah, see Mr, Delovich, it's like this – they're scared because not only does this guy refuse to die, he's not afraid of death. That's dangerous. Puts knives through his hand. Maybe he can't be killed!*

"No hit man?" I asked. "Are you sure? Because Norton tried."

"The word came out after that, I presume," Delovich told me. "And therefore I believe you must have connections in high places. A hit on you will result in retribution. Perfectly understandable. It's much the same in my own organization."

Norton must've gotten the word out about me, that I was bad for their business.

What do they have, a hit man hotline?

I wondered why Delovich was telling me all this. Because he didn't expect me to walk out alive?

No, he's too much the businessman.

I figured he must be playing nice because I might be someone he could make a deal with, perhaps expand his empire through my connections. "So, you're a big crime kingpin," I said, rocking my head side to side, mocking him, "and you can't even hire someone to kill me."

Blalock opened his mouth as though to volunteer, but he kept quiet.

"Not precisely correct," Delovich said. "I said that hit men won't come after you. I have other men perfectly willing to perform this function, if necessary."

Okay, so maybe he's not afraid of telling me these things because he knows he can have me killed.

Delovich scowled. "But I'm not some gutter criminal. I'm not a killer, Mr. Thigpen. My rules are simple. Don't talk, and play things straight with me. It's the only way to run a business."

"You're talking to me now," I pointed out.

"Yes, well, we'll get to that. One, you're obviously not who you claim to be. Blalock, isn't that correct?"

Blalock nodded.

Delovich's smile was almost warm. "Blalock believed you represented police authorities from Europe. Interpol, to be precise."

That's why he asked Ellie if she'd been to Europe.

"Of course," Delovich continued, "I knew that there was someone from Interpol in the area. It was an unofficial investigation—fact gathering. Turns out it was Sloan. And even though I wasn't the primary target of the investigation, I knew he was acting as a mole. I don't like moles. They're not playing it straight."

"And what happens if people don't play it straight?" I asked.

"In the case of a mole, the severest penalty. Why don't you ask Derek Sloan?"

"Sloan's dead," I pointed out. "And you're telling me that he was Interpol?"

That might explain why his murder hasn't been in the news ...

Delovich shrugged. "I'm not saying anything, except that the problem's solved. Sloan's dead. His house has burned to the ground." He stepped toward me, stopped in the middle of the room, and calmly planted his cane. "On the other hand, if someone were to, say, be skimming profits from me, I'd think Sloan's fate would be equally appropriate." He turned to Dunn. "We don't have any skimming here, do we?"

"No, sir, Mr. Delovich," Dunn said. "The numbers have been adding up, haven't they?"

"For the most part. Sloan was cashing more checks from you than I care for, but I'm sure it was legitimate business."

"It was!" Dunn said. "Sloan was bringing me a lot of insurance business. Car repairs. He needed a cut."

"I'm not buying this," I said. "You say you don't go around killing people who play by your rules, but you must have enemies—people not on your side, people who don't want to cooperate."

"One mustn't go around shooting up a town," Delovich said. "Very unprofitable. No, I find it's more efficient if I make a deal. Everybody wants to be part of the action, and there's nothing wrong with that. Greed gets in the way, I suppose, for a few people. But for most, a bribe or a cut is an effective persuasion tool. Of course, the threat of financial ruin works well, too."

"Why are you telling me these things?" I asked. I no longer cared about the mechanisms by which people made money. Not only was it no longer relevant to me, it seemed about as important as pondering the treachery of an ancestral ape, one that had perhaps touched Kubrick's monolith. "You don't know that I won't talk. It seems like after all you've told me, you'd want me dead."

"Oh, I don't think I've told you anything you don't already know," Delovich said. "In fact, I believe you know much more than you're letting on. That's what got Blalock all excited. Except Blalock doesn't understand things. He doesn't put them in perspective."

"I'm just an insurance fraud investigator."

"Then why would someone put a contract out on you?"

"Because I was investigating fraud at Josef's Repair Shop. You've got a stake in things there. Maybe you figured I'd go up the food chain until I started finding out things about you."

Delovich waved off the concern. "You're stretching your investigative abilities, I think. Anyway, there are many people on my payroll, people in high places. Investigations can get sidetracked, underfunded, and if need be, canceled. Besides, why risk a murder charge instead of fraud? It makes no sense, Mr. Thigpen, and so I believe you're not being totally honest with me. I've been very generous so far, but I'd appreciate some reciprocation."

"What do you want from me?" I asked.

"Tell me who you're working for."

"I'm an independent investigator. I was working on a case for Alliance Insurance when I got shot and Hal got killed."
I glanced at Blalock, but he appeared uninterested in the conversation.

"I see," Delovich said. "And did you go to the police and

report being shot?"

"No," I told him.

"And you uncovered fraud at the repair shop?"

"I did."

"Did you report it?"

"No. I didn't have a chance."

"And did you tell the authorities about Sloan's death?"

"No."

"Once I explained to Blalock your lack of reporting to authorities, he understood that you weren't a threat." Delovich turned to Blalock. "Correct?"

"Yeah, I get it now," Blalock said. "But I still think you should give me credit for protecting your interests."

Delovich sighed. "So much drive, so little horsepower." He pointed the cane at me. "He was trying to scare you and your wife off, and it wasn't necessary because you're not Interpol and you're not going to the authorities." He planted his cane again as though to drive the point home.

"So what if I haven't gone to the police? Maybe I will later."

"Well, you see, Mr. Thigpen, you say you're a simple fraud investigator, and yet you haven't gone to the authorities about getting shot, nor about the fraud you've uncovered, Nor about Hal, nor about anything, in fact. Maybe your investigative service is a front."

"For what?" I asked.

"For someone who is assessing the situation in Metro Detroit."

Assessing what situation?

The turf war?

Think, Jack – you got to be quick on this.

"I'm always assessing things," I said. "That's my nature."

"I can assure you that I have things under control."

"Control? I saw what happened at Josef's Repair Shop."

Delovich's grip tightened on his cane. "I admit there've been some difficulties. However, my original offer stands."

What offer?

Who the hell did Delovich think I was?

Someone who assesses ...

"I'm sure your offer is being considered," I said.

Delovich nodded almost imperceptibly.

Delovich thinks I'm someone special, someone he can deal with. Maybe I can end this power struggle. Maybe that'll take the threat away from Ellie (and Tom).

I decided to play along.

"You sound like a rational businessman," I said.

"That's precisely what I am," Delovich said. "A capitalist."

"You sound Russian."

"I became an American citizen over ten years ago. I admire America. It is filled with hard workers, and people work harder when they can get a piece of the action. It's not like that in Russia."

No, because in Russia, most of the money goes to the Mafiya. There's no spirit of enterprise, just an iron grip.

"Russia has a proud history but a questionable future," Delovich said. "America has many more opportunities."

"Especially for someone who can bend rules, break laws, cut off fingers, have people shot."

"I heard about Josef's fingers," Delovich said. His knuckles turned white as he gripped his cane even tighter. "He was being squeezed, but he wouldn't say by whom." He strode over to Dunn. "Are you being squeezed?"

"No, Mr. Delovich. You know I'd tell you the moment anyone tried moving in."

"But someone is trying to move in." He stared at me. "You know who. Look at his methods. He blows up repair shops, maims people. You want that kind of operation? Sloppy work, I tell you. The avtoritet can't want this."

Avtoritet? The way Delovich said the word made me think that whoever was assessing the situation (me, in Delovich's eyes) would report to this person, although I supposed the avtoritet could've been an organization.

I can have Tom look the word up.

"This guy trying to move in—he has different methods," I admitted.

Delovich shook his head. "He's getting panicky."

Okay, it's a "he".

"But," Delovich continued, "I admit that he's had some degree of success. So much so that I had to interrupt my schedule to come up here and take care of this personally. I'm getting real fucking annoyed about it, and I get ugly when I'm annoyed."

"If I knew anything," Dunn said, "I'd say so."

"Not if you were playing both sides," Delovich told him.

Dunn, whose face had regained much of its color, turned ghostly white again. "It's not me. I wouldn't do that."

"Because I've heard things," Delovich said. "Nasty little rumors about people playing both sides."

"I know better than to try that shit," Dunn said.

"My other problem is," Delovich said, "I don't know who's in charge of the other side."

The other side. Could that be who put the contract out on me? Maybe Delovich was telling the truth. Maybe he hadn't ordered the hit.

"You know anything about this matter?" Delovich asked me.

"A little," I admitted.

Delovich nodded smugly as though he'd been correct that I wasn't merely a fraud investigator.

"I heard there's a turf war," I said. "And the Mafiya's involved. That'd be you, right?"

Delovich laughed. "You're a humorous man, Mr. Thigpen. No, as an assessor—from Moscow?—you might favor the other side. Can you tell me when the judgment will be reached, the razborka?"

"That's a determination of who controls the area, right?"

"Ah, I apologize. I didn't want to threaten your cover by tricking you into revealing that you understand Russian."

"Apology accepted," I said.

"To be fair to you, then, I'll explain the situation. The Mafiya sends their own man, a point man, to gain control."

"And later someone assesses the situation to see who has control?" I asked.

"Precisely. This assessment goes to the avtoritet in Moscow. I simply want the avtoritet to understand that the Mafiya point man will never be successful. My organization is too tight."

"But as you yourself suggested," I said, "this Mafiya point man is having some success."

Delovich rapped the floor with his cane. "A few minor traitors have turned on me. He'll never succeed without control of the casino. That's what matters most. Now, can I have your assurance that the Mafiya will accurately evaluate their point man's efforts? The Mafiya might make more profits if they moved him in, but at what cost? They'd waste valuable resources that could be used elsewhere. If they accept my offer, they have less profits but with much less effort. Still, you have to understand—I'm a businessman, and they get nothing for free. If I send them a cut, they must help me expand. Chicago, perhaps."

"I need to talk to this point man," I said. "And I don't know who it is."

Delovich began rubbing the end of his cane. "You don't?"

"No. Maybe you and I should cooperate on finding out who it is."

"To what end?" Delovich asked.

"This point man—he set me up to have me killed. And so I'd like to offer my services to you; in return, I want to know who's moving in on your turf."

Delovich squinted at me. It was the first time his face showed his confusion.

He's thinking he was wrong. You're no assessor, Jack. He's onto you.

"Maybe you're the one being squeezed," Delovich said. "I'm not sure I trust you. What will you do with this knowledge?"

"I just want a crack at him."

"I'll take your offer under advisement," Delovich said thoughtfully. "Anything else?"

"No. This is personal."

"Ah! Of course it is."

Okay, Jack, you still got him on your side. He thinks maybe you're not the assessor, but he also believes you're not here to rat him out.

"He put out a contract on me," I said. "And my best friend got killed."

Delovich nodded. "And you're probably worried that he'll come after you again."

"Or go after anyone I know," I said, glaring at Blalock, remembering how he'd threatened Ellie.

"Yes, this Mafiya," Delovich said, "they're a band of thugs. They kidnap relatives, even children. No ethics. I'd watch your back if I were you, Mr. Thigpen."

So far, it's been two bullets in my front. It's not my back that I'm worried about.

"I'm not sure I'd place you especially high on the morality chart," I said.

"Bah!" Delovich said. "You heard about the school explosion in Russia last year? Dozens of children killed! That's what the Mafiya does, Mr. Thigpen. Cutthroats, that's what they are. They have no morals, no rules."

"I take it you know," I said, "that I'm playing straight with you. I just want to get the guy who put out the contract on me."

Delovich looked at Dunn. "What do you think?"

"I'd want Thigpen on my side," Dunn said.

"That's right," I said. "Mr. Dunn knows just how much pain I can withstand. Isn't that right?"

Dunn nodded.

"And that I'm not afraid of dying."

"No, not of that," Dunn agreed.

"And that my interest in finding the man who ordered me shot is for personal reasons that have little to do with Mr. Delovich's operations."

"I'm certain of it," Dunn said.

Delovich strode over to Dunn and clapped him on the back of his neck. "Dunn and I go way back. We have our little problems—" Delovich touched Dunn's cheek near the line of blood that was starting to congeal. "—but I place a lot of trust in him." He pushed Dunn's head down, kissed the top of it, and returned to Blalock's side.

Delovich nodded at me. "Give me your phone number. Mr. Thigpen. If I have any leads for you, I'll call. You understand, though, that I still believe you might be the one assessing this situation. I suggest you take my offer seriously, despite any predilection you might have for wanting the Mafiya point man to succeed."

I took the new cell phone out of my pocket and read the phone number to Delovich. He blinked once after I finished as though the eye movement helped him to commit the number to memory. "In return, you'll give me any information that you find."

"How'll I get in touch with you?" I asked. I wanted to spit at the thought of working with such scum, but I had no saliva. Still, the distaste in my mouth made me swallow.

"Call Mr. Dunn. He'll relay a message." Delovich turned to Dunn. "You'll relay it promptly. Understood?"

"Yes, sir, Mr. Delovich."

"Now," Delovich said, turning to me, "is there anything else?"

"Not that I can think of at the moment," I told him.

"Good. Now, if you'll excuse me, I have other appointments." Delovich turned to leave. Blalock reached for the door handle, but Delovich grabbed his arm. "Wait." He peered back at me. "You know, there could be another reason the contract on you was canceled."

"And what would that be?" I asked.

"Someone other than the hit man knew that the first attempt was botched."

Botched wasn't exactly the right word. But I suppose it hadn't gone as planned.

"Nobody other than Norton knew," I said, quickly adding, "and Dunn."

"Mr. Dunn isn't playing both sides," Delovich said. "You heard him yourself, yes? Besides, I've checked him out. And as for Norton, well, he has no business sense. Good hunter, though."

Yeah, I heard he's going to be focusing on car sales for the foreseeable future.

Dunn cleared his throat. "I thought Blalock knew, too."

"So what?" Blalock said. "That don't mean shit."

"Hold on a minute," I said. "Blalock, why were you threatening Ellie?"

"Like Mr. Delovich said, I thought you was investigating his organization."

"Why'd you ask her if she'd been to Europe?"

"The Mafiya's involved."

"They have spread across Europe," Delovich noted. "And so of course America's a logical progression."

Although I was looking at Delovich, I pointed at Blalock. "And that's what he meant by asking me to back off, that this was bigger than I thought?"

"I believe he was trying to protect my organization," Delovich said.

"Why's he working at Alliance Insurance?"

Delovich rolled his eyes. "I tried sending him someplace to work where I thought he wouldn't do much damage." He sighed, and his hand rubbed the top of his cane, which I now saw had been carved into the shape of a fist. "His parents died tragically, and their deaths meant an end to their business. I have a soft heart, so I took him into my organization."

"Yeah, but see, someone set me up," I said. "Ted Meade—he runs the fraud department at Alliance—sounded surprised when I called him back."

"Surprised you were alive?" Delovich asked.

"Maybe. I told him I wanted to follow Sloan into Detroit. He told me to wait, like he had to check with someone, then told me to go ahead. I figure maybe he called the guy who had the contract out on me. Maybe he even called Norton himself. You said yourself that you heard rumors about people playing both sides. Maybe Ted Meade's one of them."

"Perhaps," Delovich said. He turned to Blalock. "What do you think?"

"I don't know, Mr. Delovich."

"And another thing," I said, "you pointed out that I haven't gone to the authorities. You suggested I couldn't get anywhere near you with my investigation, but the police might get near if they were investigating a murder."

"Your friend's murder, Mr. Thigpen?" Delovich asked.

"I was the target. If I'd been killed, the police would find out I was murdered while investigating one of your operations. If nothing else, it'd be putting a squeeze on you, right?"

Delovich squinted. He tapped the cane several times as though starting a mental calculation. "Perhaps."

"They'd have subpoena power, the whole nine yards."

"But that would take time," Delovich said. "And from what I've seen, this entire squeeze is being accelerated. It's as though they can't wait beyond tomorrow. The pressure is, shall we say, threatening to crumble certain aspects of my business."

"Maybe the deadline's been moved up," I suggested.

"I know of no deadlines. However, once the squeezing became accelerated, I had to protect my assets, especially the new riverboat casino. I had the opening moved up."

"The casino's yours?"

"No, of course not."

"But you get a cut of the profits."

"Let's just say I have business relationships with the casino's management."

"How'd you get them to move it up?" I asked.

Delovich shrugged. "I make suggestions. People listen."

"Why would the casino matter so much?" I asked.

"Do you know what the annual profits of a casino this size are?" he asked.

"Not really. Millions, I imagine."

"Approaching a billion, Mr. Thigpen. Of course, I don't own the casino, but my interests are covered there. And control of this casino goes to whoever controls the Metro Detroit area."

"So maybe that's why the contract on me was called off—the casino opening was moved up."

"It all ties in to the casino," Delovich murmured. In a louder voice, he said, "Influence with the casino buys connections. Connections are of ultimate importance in the business world. Why do you think, for example, so many crime rings are run by families? Trust. Connections."

There were plenty of familiar crime families—Genovese, Gambino, Luchese, Bonanno. I remembered Tom's story about the Purple Gang and how they'd lost their grip on the city when a gang from out east moved in.

Delovich is afraid of losing his grip. If he loses the casino, the rest of his empire crumbles.

"Yes," Delovich said, nodding. "Controlling the casino will be like controlling the oil in a Middle Eastern nation. It fuels everything."

Especially corruption, I thought. A lot of money can be laundered in a place like a casino.

Delovich turned to Blalock. "You wouldn't know, would you, of anyone with an interest in having influence in the casino?"

"Nobody except you, Mr. Delovich."

"Because it occurs to me that even though you're family, you're fairly new in my organization."

"I know I've made a few mistakes."

"Maybe more than a few. I've come to think that perhaps you've made a few critical errors in judgment."

"What do you mean?" Blalock asked. "I haven't done much of anything, and you've nevah even given me credit for the things I do."

"I haven't given you much to do. But it occurs to me that you might have been in an excellent position to set up Mr. Thigpen. You, along with Ted Meade."

"Meade was losing too much money to fraud. He picked Thigpen's number out of the phone book."

"And if you were playing Thigpen to get murdered, to put the squeeze on me, I'd have to wonder if someone put you up to it or if you were just being inventive on your own."

Blalock began edging toward the door. "I don't like the way this is going. Everyone's talking crazy. I'll be in the cah."

Blalock turned and left hurriedly.

Delovich looked at me and smiled. "He's learning fast."

"You knew all along," I said, "that Blalock was playing both sides."

"One is never sure about these things. But I've always understood that Blalock is too ambitious for his own good. Also, he knew things I haven't told him."

"I don't think he'll be in the car," I said.

"No."

"Aren't you going to stop him?" I asked.

"No," Delovich said. "He's not very bright. He might lead me to the person I really want to speak to."

I nodded. "Me, too."

A visit to Alliance Insurance might be profitable, as well.

I wonder how surprised Ted Meade will be to see me. And just how well does he know Blalock?

CHAPTER TWENTY EIGHT

Of course, I trusted Delovich about as far as I could spit.

I glanced at Dunn. He was gently touching his face, probing for the wound, glancing at his finger to judge the amount of blood.

"What about him?" I asked Delovich, nodding at Dunn.

"What do you mean?" Delovich asked.

"Are you planning to cut him any more?"

"Of course not! I'm not an animal, Mr. Thigpen. I'm simply a stickler for discipline."

"Good," I said. "I don't think Mr. Dunn will cause any more problems for you. He's probably a decent guy. Probably has a family."

"Yes," Delovich said, "and I'm sure he'll explain the cut on his face in some innocuous fashion."

Dunn nodded. "It must've been some sharp object in the service department. Some tool wasn't properly stored."

I didn't want anyone killed (at least anyone that didn't deserve a good and thorough killing, such as the Mafiya's point man). I figured Dunn was going to be all right, as long as he didn't become a talker.

I brushed by Delovich. "I've got to go."

"I'm sure we'll be in touch soon," Delovich said.

"If we do," I said, pausing in the hall outside Dunn's office, "just don't call me a talker." The two thugs stared at me like they wanted to wrap their hands around my throat—although this might've been their normal antagonistic state.

"Not if it's just me that you talk to," Delovich said.

I turned and walked out of the dealership, onto the sales lot, where music played, flags flapped, and customers sought emotional satisfaction by way of spending money. My mouth felt filled with bile, the result of a distasteful upheaval, courtesy of my stomach as a reaction to working with Delovich (who no doubt believed that the crimes his cronies committed to be completely victimless).

I made it to Tom's truck without the hassle of a sales pitch and drove off the lot, toward Roseville.

Traffic slowed, then stopped. There was a traffic jam ahead, resulting from what looked like a fender bender. It occurred to me that it might be an insurance scam, but I didn't care. It was amazing how few things really mattered when everything was life or death.

Taking advantage of stalled traffic, I took out the cell phone and called Tom.

"Was Delovich the guy?" Tom asked immediately.

"No," I said, my voice sounding tired. I worried that my vocal cords were wearing out. "But you were right that this is a turf war. It's like a contest! Each one wants to be Mister Big. People are getting killed and mutilated all because some asshole wants the brass ring."

It occurred to me that Delovich probably didn't want me saying much about the situation to anyone.

"So, what's next?" Tom asked.

"I'm heading back to Alliance Insurance. There's someone I need to talk to."

"Tell me more about what happened at Dunn Ford," Tom said.

I considered telling him everything that had happened. But he'd already heard enough. He might decide to take it upon himself to try some stunt like he'd had at the Norton Chevrolet dealership. "I've said enough."

"I need to know what's going on," Tom said. "How can I help if I'm in the dark?"

In the dark. Is that what 'true death' is? Eternal darkness? Will I see the tunnel of light?

I had to keep going as though I would. I had to *believe.*

"Jack?"

"I don't have any light for you, Tom. Not now. I'm sorry."

"Hey—I didn't mean it like that."

"I know. Listen, I need you to look up a word on the Internet. I think it's Russian. Avtoritet."

"Say it again."

"Av-tor-it-et."

"Hold on. It'll just take a second. Got the website bookmarked."

I could hear his footsteps grow fainter.

It's not right to rely on him so much. I'm going to be dead. But Tom? He's got a long life ahead of him, and this nasty business might haunt him the rest of it.

The footsteps returned.

"Jack—yeah, it's Russian. Avtoritet—it means authority. Someone in charge of the new profit-oriented Mafiya."

"Kinda what I thought. A Godfather type. Only Russian."

"I don't like the sound of this."

"Listen, Tom, traffic's starting back up. Gotta go. Just make sure I call in an hour or two. Otherwise, ..."

"Yeah, yeah, I know."

I ended the call and accelerated along with the rest of the traffic, the car with the dented fender now off on the side of the road.

With traffic resuming its normal breakneck speed, I was able to reach Utica Road in ten minutes.

I'd only been to the Kalahan Building once in my life, and that was when I got my assignment from Ted Meade to conduct the surveillance of Josef's Repair Shop. Looking forward to seeing what Ted Meade had to say about the whole affair, I parked and walked toward the Kalahan entrance. I had an eerie sensation, a vision of going to a pearly gate that was dripping like a clock in one of Dali's paintings, and Ted Meade was there with a rubber stamp that revealed DAMNED in indelible ink when he thumped it onto my application for admission.

I opened the door, walked in, and got in the elevator. The music must've been on a short loop, because it was the same as when I'd left a few days ago. *The Girl From Ipanema.*

The receptionist, nearly choking on her gum as she tried to speak, jumped to her feet as I strode past her desk. "Sir, can I help you? Sir?"

I waved her off. "You look tired. Take a vacation. I hear the beaches in Brazil are good."

At least when I pass her, she sees me, unlike the poor sap in Ipanema.

"But—"

"Ted's expecting me. No need to get up—I know the way."

I went through the maze of cubicles to Ted's office.

The wrinkles in Ted Meade's face looked even more etched in stone than when I'd first met him. Was this an indication of a guilty conscious?

He looked up from his desk as I stood in the doorway. "Jack! Thank God you're alive. Did you get hurt? Come in, have a seat." He slipped a pad of paper into the top folder on one of the stacks.

I sat across from him and stared.

"You don't look good, Jack. Did the explosion at Josef's hit you?"

I said nothing.

"What's wrong?" Meade asked.

"It's just I didn't really expect to be here," I said. "I mean, considering what happened."

"Well, I'm glad you're all right."

I studied him. His surprise appeared to result from seeing me alive after the explosion, not from surviving a hit man. But I wasn't sure. "I knew you had problems with the insurance payouts, Meade, and the fake air bags were putting a crimp in your profits, but did you have to blow the place up?"

"Oh, c'mon Jack, you're joking, right?"

"Do I look like I'm joking?"

Meade leaned forward, hands on his desk. "To be honest, you look sick, Mr. Thigpen. Were you there when it happened? Maybe you got a bit of a concussion. Maybe you should see a doctor."

"I've just lost a bit of blood."

"Well, look, if this is about your fee, I think we can work something out. I mean, of course the down payment is yours to keep. We can prorate the rest on another assignment. Get your five days of work in."

"It's not the money," I said. "In fact, I won't be cashing the check."

"But you did a couple days of work, didn't you?" Meade asked.

"It's on the house—on one condition. You tell me the truth."

"The truth about what?"

Very slowly, I said, "I want you to tell me all about my assignment."

"Sure."

"And I want to know what happened on the day I called and asked you if I should follow Derek Sloan, to leave the repair shop that I was staking out."

"If you say so, Jack. No problem. Where do you want me to start?"

"Did you know who Derek Sloan was?"

"No. Not until I looked up the plate number you told me over the phone."

"How did you pick me for this assignment?"

"Your ad says you specialize in insurance fraud."

"And that's all? No one gave you my name?"

"No. What's this about, Jack?"

I shook my head. "Just answer the questions. That should be worth the money you'll save by not paying me. Now, why didn't you call after you heard about the explosion at Josef's?"

"I just figured you'd be in touch. I mean, maybe you were still following leads with Derek Sloan."

"No one's going to be following Sloan anymore."

Meade looked at me quizzically.

"Never mind. Turns out he wasn't exactly what he appeared to be. Seems like there's a lot of that going around."

It was Meade's turn to shake his head. "I'm not following."

"Were you going to report the dead body to the police?" I asked.

"What dead body? From the repair shop? By the time I heard about it, the police had been there for hours."

"Okay, never mind about that. I want you to tell me how much interest Blalock showed in my assignment."

"Blalock?"

"Yeah, the Boston Bruins fan."

"Hell, Jack, no interest that I know about. I mean, I suppose he probably heard about it when I was giving you the case. He was out in the hallway, wasn't he?"

"Yes, indeed he was."

"That's all I know. Honest. Anyway, Blalock—that son of a bitch—just turned in his resignation. No notice, no nothing. Poof, he's out of here."

"That seems odd," I said.

"Odd? Hell, it's not just odd, it's a downright pain in the ass to the HR Department. Me, too. As you can see, I have more than enough paperwork without worrying about closing out his employment here."

"When did he turn in his resignation?"

"Twenty minutes ago!"

So, Mr. Blalock's feeling the heat. Maybe he was the one who was going to call and report the dead body (my body!), the one that would lead the police to Josef Adolpho, then to Delovich. As it was, they couldn't tie Hal Booker to anything other than perhaps a street gang.

"Remember when I asked about following Sloan?" I asked.

"Yeah, sure."

"It seems to me you had to check with someone before giving me the go-ahead."

Meade frowned. "Come to think of it ..."

"Tell me."

"A friend of mine was interested in the repair shop. Said he had a business interest in it, and wanted to know everything—and I mean everything—involved with your investigation."

"What kind of business interest?" I asked.

Meade shrugged. "This guy owns a helluva lot of businesses. You know, one of those guys who's so rich, they light cigars with twenty-dollar bills. He's all right, though. Been friendly to me, that's for sure."

"How'd he get his money?" I asked.

"Oh, hell, I don't know. From his businesses, I suppose. There're a few who say he's a bit of a *Great Gatsby* character, someone with a lot of money and a bit of a mysterious past, but I think that's just jealousy talking."

"And you told him I was proposing to follow Sloan?"

"Yeah."

"What did he say?"

"He made me wait a few minutes. Hey—you're right; I remember getting the feeling that he was calling someone else to check on something."

Yeah, he was calling Archibald Norton to see what'd be best for the hit.

"What'd he say next?" I asked.

"He told me to go ahead and let you do it."

"I see. What's your friend's name?"

"Oh, you probably know him—"

Meade's head jerked up. I looked out the doorway and saw someone's back as he hurried down an aisle between cubicles. Meade jumped out of his chair. "Hold on a second, Mr. Thigpen. I got things to tell this Blalock."

Blalock again!

I stood and followed Meade out of the office. As I retraced my path through the cubicle maze toward the receptionist, the way I'd been set up to be killed began coming into focus.

Ted Meade was at best a dunderhead who apparently, while trying to wade his way through piles of paperwork of scams and fraud, had innocently hired me to investigate a certain repair shop. Then (lo and behold!), there just happens to be a rat on the payroll, a Bostonian by the name of Blalock, who's playing both sides of a turf war. Blalock tells the Mafiya point man that someone's investigating Josef's. Why tell him? Because it's part of the normal reporting scheme. Information is power in the underworld (and most other places, too). The point man, feeling pressured, knowing there's going to be a razborka judgment from some unknown assessor, figures he can pressure Delovich—the crime kingpin from Indianapolis, a Russian expatriate—by getting a police investigation started into the murder of a fraud investigator named Jack Thigpen. But something went wrong. I didn't die.

By the time I caught up to Meade, he was at the elevators. Blalock was standing inside, with Meade holding the door open. The doors tried to close, hit Meade's hand, and whooshed back fully open.

"I got a word or two to say before you leave," Meade said.

The girl from Ipanema goes ...

"Back off," Blalock said. "I'm in a hurry." He was holding a box the size of a lunchbox with a few items from his desk in it. His personal effects, I assumed. It didn't look like he had intended to stay long.

Whoosh.

"Back off? Now you listen here. I—"

Blalock leaned forward and thrust his palm against the center of Meade's chest, giving him an abrupt shove. Meade backpedaled.

The elevator doors closed, Blalock standing inside, giving Meade an odd look and the thumbs-up sign.

"Shit," Meade said, his face red (and expanding somewhat with anger, smoothing out a few of the wrinkles). He ran to the stairwell door, opened it, and rushed downstairs, his shoes slapping the steps as he descended.

I followed Meade down the stairs. Maybe it was because I was trying to hurry, but it felt like I was a clown on stilts taking a staircase challenge, immensely aware of the pull of gravity on my body.

Able to reach the bottom floor without tripping over my feet, the steps, or any subconscious obstacle, I walked as quickly as I could manage out of the building, into the parking lot. I felt weak but didn't know if it was from loss of blood or CJD.

Meade was standing beside Blalock, beside the same black BMW I'd seen near Bonnie's condo. Meade was talking in a loud, throaty voice. "I want to see what's in the box. You can't just walk out. Who the hell do you think you are?"

Blalock smiled. "What the fuck's the big deal? Go ahead. Look at the box. It's all my stuff."

Meade grabbed the box and poked around in it. From what I could see, there wasn't much in it. A couple of desktop picture frames, his Boston Bruins coffee mug, some index cards, a few pens.

Blalock took a cell phone out of his pocket and punched a speed-dial. By the time I got to Meade's side, Blalock was speaking into the phone. "Yeah, he's heah now." He nodded, listening. "No, can't wait. Got somethin' to do." He paused again, then into the phone said, "Look, I've got a sheethead giving me a bunch of crap. I've done everything I can. It's up to you now." Blalock ended the call.

"Hey, Meade," I said, "I need to hear the rest of your answer to my question."

"What question?" Meade asked sharply. Then, realizing it was me and not Blalock, he softened his tone. "Sorry, Jack. It's just that I went out of my way to welcome this guy, and this is the thanks I get."

"People sometimes need to leave suddenly" I told him. "Sometimes they have no choice."

Meade finished his inspection of the box and held it out to Blalock, who jerked it out of Meade's hand. "You know, Mr. Blalock, I'm going to have your computer station checked out. If you planted any virus or screwed it up in any way—"

"The computah's clean," Blalock said, opening the door to his BMW.

"You got anything ordered on a corporate account?" Meade asked.

"Nothing."

"Because disgruntled employees usually try to screw things up, one way or another."

"I'm not disgruntled," Blalock said, climbing into the driver's seat. "I'm just late." He closed the door, started the engine, and drove off.

"Asshole," Meade muttered.

"About that answer ...," I said.

"Huh? Oh yeah—you wanted to know who was interested in the fraud at Josef's. John LaPointe."

"LaPointe? The businessman from Grosse Pointe?" I remembered seeing him when I'd gone to say good-bye to Ellie at the Club. "You're sure?"

"Yeah. I figure he must be having some real bad problems at the repair shop. And you know, he's got a lot of contacts, so I figured I'd keep him happy on this one and maybe he'd bring some business my way."

"How'd he find out about the case?" I asked.

"Oh, he said he'd 'heard' about it, but he didn't go into details. I didn't really think about it. Why are you asking, Jack? What's this all about?"

"Nothing," I said, thinking, Blalock told him. "I, uh, I'm just wondering why it was that he wanted me to follow Sloan into Detroit."

Meade shrugged. "With someone like LaPointe, I don't ask a lot of questions. He even mentioned that he was interested in future business dealings with Alliance. What was I going to say?"

I remembered that when I'd seen him at the Club, Octavia had spoken to him. She'd pointed at me. LaPointe had nodded, one of those little movements of the elite to acknowledge someone's presence.

He hadn't seemed surprised to see me. Still, he'd realized that I had returned from following Sloan into Detroit—he'd known the hit had been botched.

CHAPTER TWENTY NINE

"Maybe people should question LaPointe more," I told Meade. "Maybe the answers would be surprising."

How does one go about accusing a respected businessman of being a point man for the Mafiya?

I remembered, though, what Meade had said. LaPointe was a modern-age Gatsby. If I remembered correctly, Gatsby was rich and respected, a smooth talker. In an effort to win his girlfriend's heart, he'd gone off to make his millions. And indeed he had. But the source of his money had been nebulous. Bootlegging had been a possibility, if I remembered correctly.

Just like the Purple Gang.

Except, maybe for LaPointe, it was Russian vodka.

Meade's face was returning to a normal color, his anger fading, his wrinkles deepening again. "So I can cancel that check, right?" he asked.

"Yeah. Cancel it. Cancel everything." I turned and returned to Tom's truck, wanting to learn more about LaPointe. How long had he been in the Detroit area? Had he ever visited Europe? What was his native language?

The best place to start, I figured, was the Club. Everyone there knew LaPointe, at least in passing, and the place usually operated as a rumor mill. Most of the rumors weren't completely accurate, but there was usually a grain of truth in them.

I pulled out of the parking lot and headed south toward Grosse Pointe.

In keeping up with my newfound tradition, I called my brother.

"Tom, I'm heading to the Grosse Pointe Athletic Club."

"Are you going to tell me what happened at Dunn Ford's

now?" he asked.

"No. It was a dead end, though."

"Very funny, Jack."

"Seriously, it didn't help me find the man who wanted me killed. I've got a new lead, though, and I'm chasing it down right now."

"That's why you're going to the Club?"

"Yeah."

"So it must be someone there."

"Stop helping, Tom. You're my backup, and I'll call if I need you, but I don't right now."

"Don't hesitate to call if you need backup, though, okay? Hey, there's more news about that explosion at the repair shop. Remember that they reported four survivors? They all went to the hospital. Three of them died this morning. The police say the deaths are 'suspicious.' The fourth person is missing."

"Sounds to me like maybe someone went in to finish the job."

"I've heard of turf wars, but these guys sound like they're going to tear down Detroit in the process."

"It'll be over soon," I said. "It's like a damn contest. There's a judge, and a winner might be declared when the new casino opens."

"Maybe you should wait until then to chase this guy down," Tom suggested. "Sounds like it'd be safer."

"I might not be around. I've got to take care of this now. Today."

"I know, Jack."

"I'll call."

"Okay."

I put the phone back in my pocket and accelerated.

Not much time left, Jack. You can feel it, can't you? Maybe it'll be just like going to sleep.

But I was afraid it wouldn't be. I was afraid I'd be horribly aware of the degenerative disease, which had already taken root, spreading its deadly tentacles into my brain, snaking its way across my central nervous system.

I passed a road sign that read NO OUTLET. Years earlier, it had read DEAD END, but people wanted the sign changed, uncomfortable with seeing the word DEAD every day.

When I got to the Club, I had a hard time finding a parking spot. There were people all over. Then I remembered. Tennis matches today. Had Octavia played yet? Was she on her way to the Nationals?

In a way, these questions were pointless. Tennis wasn't a matter of life and death, after all. Still, however her match turned out, I hoped Octavia had played well. I hoped she was happy. Maybe that's all I could hope for anyone.

I found a spot at the far end of the parking lot and began walking toward the Club entrance, taking the Louisville Slugger with me. Most of the people at the Club were used to seeing me carry around a tennis racket. I figured the change in sports gear wouldn't bring me undue attention.

Feeling suddenly weaker, walking became problematic. It felt like I was dragging both legs along, that I was a car battery giving its last ounce of juice in a final attempt to start an engine on a cold winter morning.

Rrrrr ... rrrrr ... click ... silence.

Gradually, I regained some measure of strength, though, perhaps simply by force of will. Before reaching the Club entrance, I spotted Octavia's opponent in the day's main match, Cheryl Baine. She was sitting in the front passenger seat of the family car, a dark gray Cadillac. Her father, Howard Baine, was in the driver's seat. Although unable to hear him, I could tell he was shouting at her. His right hand was pointing at her, angling up, then pointing at her again as though emphasizing certain words. His mouth moved in exaggerated motions. Cheryl cowered in her seat, leaning to her right, against the car door, getting as far away from him as she could.

I was only about ten feet away from the car when Cheryl turned to her father and shouted loud enough for me to hear, "Leave me alone!"

That's when he slapped her face.

I felt a burning sensation in my chest, an accelerated heart rate, my body priming itself for a confrontation. I stormed to the driver's side of the car and—changing aim at the last second, thinking if I went at the window beside Baine's head, some of the safety glass might spray inward and hit Cheryl—swung the bat at the back seat window. The window instantly broke into hundreds of glass bits that scattered across the back seat.

Cheryl screamed.

Baine looked back, his eyes so wide they seemed to wrap around the sides of his head.

I took off my sunglasses and pointed at him. "You ever touch her again, and I'll kill you, you son of a bitch!"

I put my sunglasses back on, stepped forward, and swung the bat down, on top of the hood, putting in a deep dent.

Baine wasn't about to stay and argue parenting rights or property damage. He started the car, slammed the engine into gear, and sped off. As the car drove toward the exit, Cheryl turned, briefly, with relieved eyes and a small but thankful smile.

I looked around. People had heard the commotion, but I was carrying a baseball bat and I suppose nobody felt compelled to come up and challenge me to explain what had happened.

I stood motionless, trying to decide whether or not I should proceed inside. I kicked a few bits of glass that had fallen outside the car.

Then I saw Octavia. She was near the entrance to the main tennis court, walking toward the Club, her racket hanging limply in her hand. She wore a matching lime-green outfit—headband, top, and skirt.

Maybe she wouldn't have seen me had I not just bashed in a car window, but more than a few people were staring at me, and this undoubtedly made Octavia look in my direction.

"Jack!" she shouted.

She ran toward me.

The way she had looked before she'd acknowledged me, I figured she must've lost the match. The fact that Baine had been chastising Cheryl was not necessarily an indication that his daughter had lost. He was always critical, overly so, and seemed to enjoy berating her.

She slowed when she was within a few feet of me. "Jack, what's wrong? You look so tired!"

"Too much baseball," I said, tilting the bat at her. "How was your match?"

"Oh, I won," she said, rolling her eyes. "But that's it. I'm done. No more tennis."

"What? You're going to Nationals!"

"I don't care. I have a situation. I'm going to quit tennis altogether."

A situation? "Tell me what's going on."

"I'd rather not talk about it."

I knew that she did want to talk, though. I looked at the Club. There could very well be a monster inside, one that appeared normal, even respectable.

What the hell's more important, Jack? Getting a monster off the streets or helping a little girl who'll probably keep playing tennis anyway?

"Look, Octavia, I don't want to diminish your situation, but don't you think you can work this one out on your own?"

"How? No one understands me, Jack. No one except you."

"What about your parents?"

Octavia glanced at the Club and glared. "They had another big fight last night. It got really loud this time. And it's all my fault."

"Are you afraid they'll get a divorce?"

"I wish they would. I'm the only reason they're staying together—to see me play tennis."

"Look, we need to talk, but not here. I, uh, think maybe I'll be in trouble if I stay much longer."

She looked at me, her mouth the perfect pout.

"I can help you, Octavia, but not for much longer. Time's running out for me."

The ensuing silence lengthened. An ability to stay silent for a long period of time wasn't one of Octavia's strengths.

"Tell ya what, there's a Slushy Freeze just around the corner from here," I said. "Meet you there in five minutes."

She nodded eagerly, although her eagerness failed to dampen the sad look in her eyes. "Okay, Jack. I've got to stop at my locker first and grab my bag."

She turned and walked away, swinging her racket as though clearing a path through Mogul hordes. Her braided hair swished behind her. Her pleated lime green skirt swayed gracefully, as though choreographed by her innate sense of rhythm.

And so, unable to pass through the gathering crowd and go inside to find out anything about LaPointe, I headed back toward where I'd parked. I was nearly the deadest walking man on the planet, and I was going off to help a young girl unequalled in her zest for life.

CHAPTER THIRTY

The Slushy Freeze had several tables out front, round plastic with three legs, and a dozen more in a patio area beside it. The parking lot was in back. There were tall oaks nearby, providing shade. It was a warm day, and there were only a few tables free. Most of the patrons were teenagers dressed in bathing suits.

I parked in back and called Tom.

"Hey, Jack, still at the Club?"

"I'm just around the corner, at the Slushy Freeze. Tom, I'd like you to come and meet someone."

"You found the guy who put out the contract on you? I'll take him out if you want."

"No, not him. Octavia Papadakis. You know, my young tennis friend? She thinks of me as her mentor, and I'm not going to be around much longer. I want her to have someone she can turn to if there's any trouble."

"What kind of trouble?" Tom asked.

"I've just seen some parental abuse, and I worry."

"Hey, if her folks are physically abusing the girl, we need to—"

"Not her parents, Tom. Another kid's. Octavia's parents are fine, as far as I know. I just ..., I'd just feel better knowing she had someone to turn to."

"Okay, Jack."

"How fast can you get here?"

"Twenty-five minutes if I'm lucky."

"Good. See you then."

I put the cell phone away, quickly gargled with mouthwash, and got out of the pickup. I spit out the mouthwash and walked toward the tables. Octavia was just leaving the order window. She carried her drink to one of the open tables on the side and sat down, placing a large handbag (the handle of her tennis racket rising diagonally from it) on the concrete beside her chair. She sipped the drink and scanned the road out front.

She turned, spotted me, and waved me over.

I sat opposite her.

"What's wrong with your arm, Jack? You're holding it funny."

"Maybe I don't want to talk about it. Maybe I was playing chicken with a bus and lost."

"Don't try to make me laugh. I'm not feeling good."

"Humor can help any situation."

"You're right, of course," Octavia said. She sighed. "You're always right. I'm the one who's wrong. My whole life is wrong."

"Octavia, a lot of kids blame themselves for their parents' problems. Don't fall into that trap."

"It's just gotten worse and worse lately. I can't stand it."

"Maybe they're just working through some issues. The fact that they're trying to stay together for you shows how much they care."

She harrumphed. "They're unhappy because of me. If I stop playing tennis, the problem's solved."

I shook my head. "The world doesn't work that way. They'll blame themselves, just like you're blaming yourself now. They'll think they ruined your tennis career."

"Maybe I don't want a tennis career."

"Look, Octavia, don't pull that on me. I know you, and I know you want to be a pro player someday. Remember how many times you asked me about the pro circuit?"

She nodded timidly and sipped her drink.

"I never even explained half of how exciting it is. The whole world's yours, and there's only yourself to stand in your way."

She looked at my right hand and grabbed it before I could jerk it away. "You've got a splinter, Jack. Let me get it out."

"Oh, could you?" I asked. Why she reacted to a splinter in one hand and not to the stitched gash in my other hand was curious. I held up my left hand, giving her a better view of the stitches. "I've been having hand problems lately."

"What'd you do?"

"Cut myself. Silly me."

She reached into her handbag, fished around in the contents (a handheld computer game, skin care products, headbands, tennis balls, and dozens of other odds and ends), and pulled out a pair of eyebrow tweezers. "Hold still," she said.

Leaning forward, I held my hand—palm up—on the table. The position was uncomfortable, almost painful, but it gave Octavia the best view to operate.

"How'd you get it?" Octavia asked, tweezers poised over my hand. "The splinter, I mean."

"I'm not sure. I had a little incident with a penknife and a desk yesterday. Maybe that's how."

"You have to pull these or they'll get infected."

"If you can ruin your future, I can certainly ruin mine."

"I'm not ruining my future. I'm stopping my parents from fighting."

"Look, Octavia, both of your parents are pushing you hard, right? They want you to be a pro."

"That's right."

"But it's your dream, too."

She shrugged.

"Then why don't you at least wait until after Nationals before making a decision. That way, maybe your parents won't feel so much pressure. Tournament pressure does strange things to people, even to non-players."

"I know. It's weird. Kathy's father had a nervous breakdown last year when she lost."

She flicked her wrist and pulled the splinter out. "Got it!"

I pulled my hand quickly back and rubbed it. "Thanks. You saved me from certain infection."

She dropped the tweezers in her handbag. "You're welcome."

"Octavia, you know Ellie and me are splitting up."

She nodded in the direction of the Club. "I heard."

"So I can speak from experience. Trust me, no one's happy going through a divorce. It's one of the most painful experiences there is."

"Well, I've been thinking about what you said. Maybe I'll wait until after Nationals. I mean, they did mention that their money problems would be a lot better by then."

"It's probably their money problems that's causing them to fight, not you."

She nodded slightly and sipped her drink. "Maybe. But what am I going to say to my parents? I don't want to pretend that I can't hear them arguing."

"Tell them the truth. Say you don't want them to stay together just for you."

"But—"

"And then stretch it out. Tell 'em that your tennis career will be hampered if they stay together and they're unhappy. I mean, really, if they were decent parents at all, they'd get a divorce!"

She smiled, then laughed. "Sometimes you crack me up, Jack."

"Then you'll play?"

She nodded.

"Good. Now, remember the other day when I saw you in the Club?"

"Yes. Is that when you and Ellie broke up?"

"More or less. Anyway, I saw you talking to John LaPointe. How well do you know him?"

"Oh, he's pretty nice. You know, he paid for the indoor tennis courts at the Club."

I nodded.

"I see him there sometimes. My folks and I went to his house last year. A whole lot of people did. He was christening a new speed boat. He had a big shindig."

"Where's he live?"

"On Lake Shore Drive. You know that big gated estate just north of here? The one with the big L on the front gate?"

"Yeah, and let me guess. It stands for LaPointe?"

"You got it."

"Has he ever done anything ... strange?"

She cocked her head for a moment. "Not that I can think of. What's this about, Jack?"

"Just curious. Now, remember how I said I might be going away? That it'll be hard to get in touch with me?"

"Uh huh."

"I'm going to introduce you to my brother. His name's Tom.

Tom Bass."

"If he's your brother, how come his last name's not Thigpen?" she asked suspiciously.

"His father, a Bass, left, and then his mother married a Thigpen—my father—and had me soon after."

She lightly smacked her forehead. "Duh! I should've known that."

"Tom's a good guy. If you ever have any trouble, give him a call, okay?"

"Yeah, okay, but when are you going to introduce me?"

"He should be here any minute now. Hold on." I took out my cell phone and tried calling him, but there was no answer.

"I'd better get back to the Club," Octavia said. "Everyone's going to start worrying soon."

Although wanting to introduce her to Tom, I knew she was right. "Okay."

She stood and picked up her bag.

"Remember—Tom Bass. Thomas B-A-S-S. His number's in the book."

She put the bag down, took out a notepad and pen, and wrote the name. "Thanks, Jack." She put the pen and notepad back into the handbag and picked it up. "And hey, you should put a Band-Aid on that splinter. You should cover up those stitches, too."

"All I've got is duct tape," I said.

"Maybe that'll work. I heard it can hold just about anything together."

I looked at the road, hoping to see my Explorer with Tom inside. No luck.

"Bye, Jack. Thanks."

"Good luck in the Nationals."

She nodded and bounced away at her usual jog, heading toward the sidewalk.

I took out my cell phone and entered Tom's number again, imagining the next self-help title on a bookstore shelf: *Duct Tape For The Soul.*

CHAPTER THIRTY ONE

Tom didn't pick up the call.

There was a clock in the Slushy Freeze, and I waited five minutes before hitting the redial button. Still no answer. I hit redial twice more after waiting five minutes before each.

After I waited another minute, a motorcycle pulled in, a Triumph with a red gas tank on which *Tom Terrific* was written.

Tom turned off the engine and hung his helmet on the backrest. He hurried over to my table and flopped down in a chair. He looked harried, his eyes red, his rattail even more disheveled than the last time I'd seen him. His bandana was crooked. "Got here as soon as I could."

"What happened?" I asked.

"I started out in your Explorer. It died—I mean, the engine quit."

I suppose I must've looked stricken with fear, because Tom reached over and put a hand on my arm. "Jack, I know it seems bad. It's going to work out for the best, though."

I shrugged.

"Where's Octavia?"

"She had to get back to the Club. I told her to call you if she ever needs help. That's mostly all she needs, someone to talk to."

"I can handle that."

"Yeah, I know—you're a good listener. One other thing, though, she says her parents are arguing. She blames herself, ... and her tennis playing. If she calls, tell her that she should tell her parents to get some counseling—family counseling, something like that."

"Okay, Jack."

"And if she sounds like she's in trouble, maybe you should be ready to call the police or social services."

"Right." Tom glanced at colorful posters on the side of the Slushy Freeze windows. "Hey, mind if I get a Slushy?"

"Go ahead. I'm trying to figure out what to do next."

He stood, straightened his bandana, and walked toward the order window.

What … to … do … next …

By the time Tom returned with a red Slushy, I still had no answers. He sat and sipped the drink through a straw.

"I just don't care about this turf war," I said.

"But you need to find out who put out the contract on you, right?" Tom asked. "That's who's responsible for Hal getting murdered."

"If I take him out, he'll just be replaced by someone else. It's a violent world, and there's not a damn thing I can do about it."

"But there is something you can do," Tom argued. "You've got a say in this turf war. I'm not sure how, but it seems like you might be able to dictate who wins."

"Why would I want to do that?" I asked.

"I'm not sure. Is there one side that's 'better' than the other?"

"I suppose Delovich doesn't use murder and mayhem quite so much as ... the Mafiya." I'd almost said LaPointe. But I still didn't quite believe that such a rich, prominent businessman who lived in Grosse Pointe (as opposed to owning a trucking company in Indianapolis) could be a point man for the Mafiya, a crime king wannabe.

"Well, there you go," Tom said. "If you tilt the balance in favor of Delovich, there's no telling how many lives you'll save."

I believed Tom might be right. "Okay. We'll see. Have you been watching the news?"

"Some. Still no news about Sloan. And there're no updates on the repair shop story. They've sent the bodies of the three that died at the hospital off for autopsies. The hospital's complaining that they're getting blamed for something that the police should've handled better."

"Someone's tying up loose ends."

"There were a few reports on the upsurge in violence today – arsons, assaults, murders. The cops are scratching their heads. One called it a statistical anomaly."

A turf war, by any other name.

"Oh, and the strike's over," Tom said.

"When did that happen?" I asked.

"The union still has to vote on it, but you know how that goes—mostly it's the higher-ups that decide what is and isn't a good deal. Of course, both sides are claiming victory."

"Just wait a while before you think about buying a car."

"Yeah, I know all about those cars made during strikes," Tom said. "What should I do about the Explorer?"

"It's going to be yours soon, so whatever you think is best."

"Jack—"

I waved him off. "It's all right. By the way, make sure you tell Uncle Bob—the Colonel—thanks."

"I will, Jack."

"And buy a cell phone. You gotta join the modern world."

"Okay."

Tom finished his drink. He stood and took it to a waste receptacle, where he was distracted by a young woman wearing a one-piece bathing suit.

If only I had enough life left in me to be so distracted.

When he got back, he said, "There's at least one good thing about your stay. You'll be able to see Lynne the Pin. She's on a flight."

"Didn't I say not to tell her?"

"I didn't tell her anything about you. She called. I knew she was crying, even though she was trying to hide it. I think she caught that asshole Craig screwing around again."

I shook my head. It felt heavier.

"She confronted him and he threatened her," Tom added.

"What?"

"Yeah, threatened her. I got worried. I mean, you and I both know that she grew up with two big brothers, and I don't think she'll back down from a fight. If it came to blows, she'd lose, so I insisted she leave."

"Don't let her go to my place for a while," I said. "Not until all this blows over."

"Okay."

My cell phone vibrated. I frowned, figuring it was Octavia. Maybe she'd tried to call Tom but nobody answered. I took the phone from my pocket and answered, "Hello?"

"Mr. Thigpen?"

"Yeah. What do you want, Delovich?"

"I'm relaying a message to you. I'm sure you're aware that our previous agreement about helping each other still holds?"

He was trying to sound level headed, impassionate, but I could hear the tension in his words. "Yeah, yeah, what's the message?"

"Someone wants to speak to you. It's the man who is, shall we say, trying to horn in on my business."

The Mafiya point man.

"Why doesn't he give me a call?" I asked.

"Oh, he didn't speak to me directly. His associates have been creating havoc all over the city, squeezing." I heard a rap over the phone and realized Delovich was striking something (or someone) with his cane.

"Yeah, all this squeezing is on the news," I said.

"My people are starting to question my ability to protect them."

Rap.

"That's a shame," I said. I could sense that Delovich felt he had to do something. If there was an assessment going on, a razborka, his inaction would be seen as weakness. Instead, Delovich would want to project strength.

"They've left word that unless this man speaks to you today, my people will suffer the consequences." Rap, rap. "His associates pulled this stunt on our mutual friend—Bob Dunn. Mr. Dunn called me immediately."

Sure he did. Dunn knew Delovich was watching closely. (Did he still have all his fingers? Was that the standard penalty for staying with Delovich and not switching allegiance?)

"So the Mafiya point man wants to talk to me?"

"That's correct."

"What's his name?" I asked.

"No name was given," Delovich said.

Rap.

I knew Delovich was trying to stay calm, but he was struggling. I could envision his cane lashing out, hitting something, anything, in an effort to vent his frustration.

"Why does he want to talk to me?" I asked. It probably

wasn't to kill me—if the contract was canceled. Except, maybe he'd changed his mind.

Was it LaPointe?

"I suspect he wishes to lay out his side of things," Delovich said.

"So I can assess the situation from his viewpoint for the razborka?"

"Correct. If you give him the nod, the Mafiya *will* bring in more men, more resources, and he'll be running the entire show soon. I'd like to hear your assurance that you're still cooperative with me and will remain so. You still see things my way."

He was asking me if I'd side with him over the Mafiya. "Yeah, sign me up. These other guys are thugs. No business sense."

"Very well, then. He suggested you go directly to the Kalahan Building. Stand outside, near the front door. I'll relay a message back through Mr. Dunn that you'll be there."

"Why the Kalahan Building?"

"I'm assuming that he wants you to feel safer by meeting at a public building."

"Otherwise I might not go."

"Correct. And Mr. Thigpen, you will call Mr. Dunn after your meeting. Understood?"

I ended the call. Tom was looking at me, his eyebrows knotted. "Who was that?" he asked.

"Delovich." I stood. "Time to go."

"I take it you don't want me to come with you?"

"You take it right."

"I figured as much." He stood and headed toward his motorcycle. "I suppose I'd better head back home and wait for your call."

"Yeah."

As I walked toward the pickup, I wondered what I might put on my gravestone, if I were to be buried instead of cremated.

A pithy remembrance? Perhaps a few words of wisdom?

One thing I didn't want—*Jack Thigpen, dead guy.*

CHAPTER THIRTY TWO

I parked at Roseville's Kalahan Building again, the second time in a day, and thought about going inside and having another word with Ted Meade, and maybe the receptionist, too—not that I had anything in particular to say to either of them. In a way, I just wanted to reminisce. They were two of the people I'd last spoken with before hearing about my impending death. Maybe I'd ask what they would remember me by, what sort of man did I come across as. What did they think I should have etched in my gravestone?

Instead, I climbed out and walked around the parking lot. There was no sign of a Mafiya point man anywhere.

After I waited ten minutes, standing on the sidewalk between the parking lot and the building, a line of five black Land Rovers pulled into the lot. They drove toward me and stopped beside the sidewalk, the third vehicle nearest to me.

I backed away onto the building's grass skirt as stony-faced men, ten in all, climbed out of all but the middle vehicle. They surrounded me, but not in an attack; they appeared more like a casual ring of goons getting ready to do the hokey pokey (not threatening, but not wanting to let me escape, either). They wore loose fitting clothes—open collar shirts (some white, some gray) and elastic band khaki pants (a few pulled up on them as though they were used to wearing belts; a couple of others pulled down as though un-sticking them from their asses). I stopped, folded my arms, and waited.

The back door of the third Land Rover opened and John LaPointe, wearing the standard Wall Street three-piece blue pinstripe suit, stepped out. He adjusted his tie and said, "Good afternoon, Mr. Thigpen. You're an extremely hard man to catch up with."

"Fuck you," I told him.

The entourage of goons (at least they weren't wearing sunglasses) shifted uneasily on their feet. A couple of them tilted their heads to the side as though to undo kinks.

"All you had to do was call," I added.

"I've been calling all morning," LaPointe said.

"Oh, right. I had to change phones. My old one went for a swim."

"I don't have much time," LaPointe said, "so let me tell you straight up. We can play this easy or difficult."

His black hair was thicker than I remembered, and I hadn't noticed before how grainy and pockmarked his face appeared. He'd probably pass for handsome except for the close-up photos.

"What's the difficult way?" I asked.

"People you know will die."

"Why not just kill me? You tried once already."

The left side of LaPointe's upper lip lifted up briefly as though pulled by a marionette's string (or a line attached to a fishhook). Although his expression appeared measured, the twitch suggested he was feeling pressure. A deadline loomed. The razborka. Maybe he was about to buckle from the strain. (Or, maybe the movement of his lip was simply a tic.)

"Have you ever seen someone die slowly, Mr. Thigpen, the kind of death that torture brings about?"

No, but I shall be my own witness soon.

"It can be gruesome—especially if it's someone you know personally. Are you squeamish at all? Is this something you would enjoy watching?"

Not backing down, I waved my hand (the unstitched one) back toward the building. "Anyone can be watching us right now, out any one of those windows. You can't do anything here."

"What would they see? That you were being threatened? Maybe so, but it might also appear that I was coming to your assistance, negotiating perhaps. That would be my story and all of my men would back it up."

His upper lip did the fishhook grab again.

"I don't believe you're Mafiya." I said. "You don't sound

Russian. You have no accent."

"Many people have voice training. They can change their speech patterns in an instant. You'd be surprised."

"Why'd you put out the contract on me?"

LaPointe took a quick step toward me, his hands tightening into fists, his black eyes flaring. He looked like he wanted to snap my neck. He stopped just beyond the perimeter of his cronies. "I don't have time for this. You're going to call your pal Delovich and tell him to send word down through his organization that I give the orders now."

"Why do you think he'd listen to me?" I asked.

"Don't fuck with me, Thigpen. I heard what Blalock said. I heard what Dunn said. You admitted you're his right-hand man at Josef's Repair shop. You've got Delovich's ear. You're like his *consigliore*, except he's even a bit afraid of you."

I looked at the faces of LaPointe's entourage. None of them looked me in the eye. They appeared nervous, but not because they were involved with crime—they were afraid of me. Still, perhaps they figured that the numbers were in their favor. A hit man might not take me on, but ten of the Mafiya's finest might think I could be taken down.

Except they looked like they didn't want to go down that path at all. Maybe the word from Norton (and Dunn) had gotten out to them—*here's a guy who just keeps bleeding; he doesn't die; he's a goddam Energizer bunny that keeps going, and going, and going ...*

"I don't have Delovich's number," I said. *Go ahead, Jack. Let them meet. Maybe they'll kill each other.* "But I know how to get in touch with him."

LaPointe smiled briefly, a sort of Robert Redford kind of smile, self confident and fully aware. "Do it now."

"What's the rush?" I asked.

This time, LaPointe didn't smile. "You know damn well what the rush is. That asshole moved up the opening of the casino. Why he moved up the date is beyond me. I had everything—" He stopped and shook his head. "Never mind that. Just call. Now."

I took out the cell phone and looked calmly at LaPointe. "*Suka*," I said, sneering.

LaPointe exhaled sharply.

"Filthy *swinya*."

His hands clenched. Then he drew in a deep breath and adjusted his tie again (even though it had been perfectly aligned). "I haven't the time, Thigpen; either make the call or don't. Your choice. I'll tell you this once—you don't want to fuck with me. I guarantee you don't."

I tilted my head side to side mockingly. But I punched in Dunn's number on the cell phone.

"Bill Dunn here."

"Dunn, it's me. Jack Thigpen. How's your day been going? It's got to be better than mine."

"Thigpen!" LaPointe shouted. "Get on with it."

I held my hand out toward him, palm down, and waved it down in short patting motions. *Quiet down, you friggin' moron.*

"Whatcha want, Thigpen?" Dunn asked. "Get to the point."

I knew Dunn was under orders to listen for a call from me. Delovich would be upset if Dunn hung up. So I said, "Hold on a sec."

I looked toward LaPointe, holding the phone behind my back. "Just tell me one thing, and I'll do as you ask."

"Make it quick," LaPointe said.

"Why'd you put a hit on me?"

"To take Delovich down with a murder investigation. Now talk to Dunn. I'm losing my patience."

I wished I had the Louisville Slugger with me. Even if the hokey-pokey guys tried to stop me, I figured I might be able to fling it at LaPointe and perhaps get lucky, sweet spot to temple, and knock this guy's lights out—permanently.

I took the phone out from behind my back. "Dunn?"

"Yeah. C'mon, Thigpen, tell me what you want."

"Get in touch with Delovich. Tell him I have vital information concerning his competition. I'll meet him at your place in about thirty minutes."

"Here?" Dunn asked. "Why here?"

"Because I like cars, dammit. Just shut up and relay the message. Christ!" I turned the phone off and put it in my pocket.

LaPointe's lip did the jerk again. "You didn't do like I asked."

"One—I don't take orders from the likes of you. Two—Delovich won't do as I say unless I tell him face to face."

He eyed me suspiciously. "You're up to something."

"Me? Why would I be up to something? All you ever did to me was try to have me killed!"

"A misunderstanding," LaPointe said. "I apologize. I had no idea who you were. Now, step into my Rover and we'll drive to Dunn's."

"I don't think so," I said.

"I insist."

"Look, I'm not trying to bail out on you. I don't want to miss this. I'll meet you there." I wasn't afraid of LaPointe; it's just that I found him too repulsive to tolerate in close proximity.

"Not good enough," LaPointe said. He glanced at his (shiny) gold Rolex. "I'll give you ten seconds to start walking to the Land Rover. If you fail to do that, my men will throw you in."

His men shifted uneasily.

"When's my time start?" I asked.

There was a tug on LaPointe's lip.

"Five seconds," he said.

"Is that five seconds until my time starts or five seconds left?" I asked.

LaPointe looked up from his watch. "Put him in my Rover."

The men scratched their heads. A couple of them took a tentative step toward me.

"What the fuck's wrong with you?" LaPointe asked, eyes bulging. He pointed at the man nearest him. "I said put him in!"

The sound of a motorcycle engine roared to life, becoming deafening as the bike rounded the corner of the Kalahan Building, accelerating on the grass skirt, kicking up of a stretch of sod.

Tom Terrific.

LaPointe's men were frozen by the sight, as though they'd never seen a motorcycle action rescue before. Even LaPointe looked befuddled, confusion settling his mouth's tic, disbelief calming the bulge in his eyes.

Tom aimed the bike between two of the thugs. He was already braking as he passed between them. Once past them, he turned sharply on the handlebar, kicking the rear wheel around. The bike came to a complete stop, pointing at the same gap in the perimeter through which he'd entered the circle.

I grabbed his waist and pulled myself behind him onto the seat and wrapped my arms around his waist. I pulled my feet up as best I could.

Tom opened the throttle, popping a wheelie, the front tire passing through the gap between goons as though it were a battering ram.

I wanted to wave back at LaPointe, to rub it in, but I was too afraid of falling off.

Tom pulled out onto the main road, accelerated to the next traffic light, and turned right. He sped to the second traffic light and turned right again. Halfway down the block, he turned left into a McDonald's parking lot and parked behind it, near the drive-through speaker.

He turned the engine off, swung the kickstand down, and hopped off. "You okay?" he asked, pulling off his helmet.

"What the hell are you doing?" I asked. "You said you were going back to your house."

"Well, yeah, I was. Just taking the scenic route."

"One that happened to come by the Kalahan Building?"

"Bingo."

"You knew where I was going because you overheard me during the call at the Slushy Freeze."

"It's not like you were whispering."

I shook my head. "Tom, how many times do I have to ask you not to get involved?"

"But that's bullshit, Jack!"

"I won't have you risking your life."

"But you were in trouble, right? You were outnumbered."

"I was handling the situation just fine."

"Didn't look like it to me."

"You were watching the whole time?"

"Yeah. I stopped down the block and walked it up to the

Kalahan Building real quiet-like. I parked on the side of the building and then watched you from around the corner. Are you telling me that those guys weren't threatening you?"

"Of course they were threatening me. But like I said, I was handling it."

Tom took a deep breath and looked at his feet.

I didn't have any taste in my mouth, and I didn't have any intuitive feeling that it'd be my last meeting with my brother. On the other hand, I wasn't going to last forever. The end was coming sooner rather than later.

"You're right—I guess I wasn't handling it all that well," I said. "Hey, we make a great team, don't we?"

Tom nodded.

"A new-age dynamic duo. The Dead Guy and Tom Terrific."

Tom chuckled. "I never thought about it like that."

"You know, we just escaped from the Mafiya's finest. Vastly outnumbered, we pulled it off."

"Yeah. That was cool."

"We're better than Batman and Robin, the Lone Ranger and Tonto, ..."

"Moose and Squirrel."

It took me a moment to remember the cartoon characters—Rocky and Bullwinkle (and their appropriately Russian nemesis, Boris Badenov). I laughed. "Yeah, even Moose and Squirrel."

I got off the bike and hugged him. "Thanks, Tom. Thanks for everything."

He held me tightly. "I'd do anything for you, Jack."

We embraced a few more seconds before I broke away. "I need to get going. Those guys'll be gone by now. Take me back to the pickup."

He frowned. "You sure?"

"They're going to be in a rush to go somewhere. They've got an appointment."

"Where'll you be going?"

"Same place."

"Care to tell me where?"

"Can't do it. And you've got to promise me that you're not going to follow."

"But—"

"Promise me, Tom."

"Okay, Jack, I won't follow. I promise."

"And if I don't see Lynne, tell her she's the best sister in the world. Tell her I missed her. Tell her we'll just have to wait to meet in the afterlife. But it'll be great. She'll see."

"Geez, Jack, it sounds like—" He paused, then continued, "Okay, Jack, I'll tell her."

"And no matter what happens, keep your head up. Keep looking ahead. Live a full life. Keep the faith."

"Semper Fi."

"Absolutely."

I climbed onto the back seat. "Let's ride."

CHAPTER THIRTY THREE

Tom dropped me off at the Kalahan Building and gave a short wave as he roared off on his Tom Terrific Triumph. We didn't say anything, as though we'd already expressed everything we wanted to. There was no sense in dragging things out.

I drove well over the speed limit to Dunn's Ford. I had a sense that my soul was unraveling (much like Tom's rattail), and that little wisps of me were slipping away in the wind of time.

I wanted the uncertainty to end, although I feared that when the end finally did come, my soul would be dispersed into a great void, and I would no longer be aware.

I knew I had to try to end the turf war. As bad as Delovich was, LaPointe was worse. He had no regard for human life. Yes, he wanted power and money, as did Delovich, but while Delovich negotiated, LaPointe coerced by torturing, maiming, and killing those who didn't play his way.

After pulling into the parking lot, I realized there was nobody in sight. No sales staff. No customers. No black Land Rovers, no limousines. It looked like a ghost lot.

Streamers hung limply between lampposts. A large banner taped across the front door of the showroom announced the reason for the lack of activity.

> CLOSED TODAY IN PREPARATION FOR OUR
> ALL DAY MARATHON SALES EVENT TOMORROW.
> HUGE SAVINGS ON ALL CARS.

Why the hell call it an event? They were just selling cars. They made it sound like some kind of new holiday, another glorification of the consumer.

The emptiness of the place chilled me.

It's that unknown factor again, Jack. You don't know where Delovich and LaPointe are, just like you don't know what's going to happen to you ...

"Yeah," I muttered, "but there's not a damn thing I can do about it."

I parked near the door to the parts department. I approached the door, bat in hand, and hesitated as I reached for the handle.

Just what are you prepared to do, Jack, to stop LaPointe? Kill him? Would that be murder?

I could call it retroactive self-defense. LaPointe had aimed a weapon (a hit man who went by the name of Norton) at me and pulled the trigger.

I had no answers. I didn't know how far I would go, how far I could go. I wanted to kill him, as it was the only way I'd know he'd be stopped. But the act would seem so ... cold-blooded.

I opened the door and walked inside, holding the bat up. The service counter was directly ahead. No one there. I walked down the hallway to my right, past Bill Dunn's empty office (noticing the knife marks on his desk), into the showroom. No one there, either. There was no music, only the soft hum of the air conditioning. The cars were shiny, polished, but like whores visiting a church attended by the truly devoted, finding no one interested in their wares.

I noticed security cameras in the upper corners of the room.

They're probably watching me right now.

I walked back down the hallway, continuing past the parts department, into the repair bays.

There was a center aisle with five repair bays on each side, their roll-up doors closed. Halfway down the aisle were the first people I'd seen since entering the dealership.

As the door closed behind me, I glanced back and saw someone crouched near the parts counter.

Ahead, LaPointe, Dunn, and three of LaPointe's henchmen were standing near a vertical support beam. I walked toward them, past tool carts and pneumatic controls for the repair bay lifts. Hoods were open on the cars in for service. There were tool carts with open drawers, as though the mechanics had left suddenly. (The sales event must've been hastily concocted.) There were hoses dangling from the ceiling in several of the bays—air hoses for pneumatic tools and lubricants for oil changes. The atmosphere was thick, eerily somber, like at an open casket funeral.

Two of the repair bays had no cars in them. I noticed that four of the vehicles in occupied bays were black Land Rovers. The fact that there weren't five Land Rovers made me uneasy. I wasn't sure why, because with only four, it seemed to me that the numbers would be more in my favor, one against six or seven instead of one against ten (eleven, counting LaPointe).

I stopped when I was still twenty feet from the group. They were all watching me, waiting. The henchmen (two white shirts, one gray) looked fidgety. Gray Shirt edged farther away from me as though afraid of my toxic reach. LaPointe was peering at me, his mouth set with grim determination (perhaps to defend against the tic). One of the White Shirts had a handgun held against Dunn's side, just above the third rib from the bottom. The underarms of Dunn's shirt were stained with sweat.

"Come here, Thigpen," LaPointe said. "At least you're a man of your word."

"I'll stay right here, thank you."

"Where's Delovich?"

"How the hell should I know? Have Dunn call him and ask."

"I think not. Even if he didn't directly warn Delovich, he might have a code word. He might reveal a clue about what's happening here."

"I guess you're screwed then," I told him.

LaPointe shook his head. "I'm just getting warmed up." His cell phone had begun beeping when he'd said *getting*. He took the phone from his pocket and answered.

I looked at Dunn. "You all right?"

He nodded, blinking, sweat rolling down into his eyes (although I had to admit his square jaw still looked firmly set). "They ain't gonna turn me. I'm loyal to Mr. Delovich. Loyal to the end. You tell him that if I don't see him."

LaPointe laughed, lowering the cell phone. "Mr. Dunn, I'm going to show Thigpen how effective my persuasion techniques can be. Thigpen, you're going to convince Delovich to side with me. If I can turn Dunn, I can turn anyone."

"Except Delovich," I said.

Ignoring me, LaPointe again spoke into the cell phone.

"You've got to stop him, Thigpen," Dunn said.

"Why?" I asked. "So your organization can have the profits instead of his?"

"No. You don't understand. You don't know what the Mafiya's all about. You don't know their methods."

Yeah, that's what Delovich was saying.

I agreed—LaPointe needed to be stopped, but what could I do?

Kill him.

I tapped the bat against my palm, wondering if his men were too fearful to tear me apart with their bullets.

"Stop him, Thigpen," Dunn urged. "I know you can do it."

LaPointe ended his call. He nodded at one of the gray-shirted thugs and pointed at the nearest empty bay, "Open the door."

The gray-shirted thug went to the wall and pushed a button. The door rolled up, and a black Land Rover—the fifth—pulled into the bay, its roof just clearing the rising door.

The Rover stopped. The door was lowered. Once the bottom edge clanked against the concrete door, the Land Rover doors flew open. There was a flurry of motion. Three of LaPointe's goons came out of the Rover—and one other man. He looked familiar, a tall redheaded man. Then I remembered. He'd been at Josef's Repair Shop. And he'd been the tow truck driver for the scam in Detroit I'd watched just before Hal got shot.

The redheaded man had a glazed look and his legs appeared weak and wobbly, with two of the goons holding him up, gripping his arms. The third stood in front, looking at LaPointe.

The door behind me opened. I turned and watched Blalock entering the service area. Wearing his standard Boston Bruins hockey jersey, mostly black with gold trim and the B logo in the middle, he brushed past me (apparently believing I wasn't toxic) and looked directly at my sunglasses. I couldn't read his expression. It seemed like he was trying to read me, penetrate the dark lenses and get a sense of the man behind them. He continued past me and stood beside LaPointe.

"What took you so long?" LaPointe asked.

"This Detroit traffic is bad. Too many big cahs."

LaPointe rolled his eyes. He walked over to Dunn, stared at him, inches away from his face, then took a few steps toward me. "See the redheaded fool over there? We found him outside the hospital. He must've gotten out while my men were taking care of the others. His name's Federov. Came from Russia only last year."

"He doesn't work for Delovich," I said. "He's just a scam artist."

"He's in Delovich's organization. And since Josef Adolpho wouldn't turn, Mr. Federov will now have to pay for that mistake."

LaPointe returned to face Dunn. "Your fate will be similar. I suggest you reconsider."

Dunn blinked and licked his lips as though trying to wet them in order to say something, but he remained silent. Maybe he was considering the offer.

LaPointe turned toward the goon (white-shirted) in front of Federov. "Strap him to the lift."

Although Federov had a glazed, drugged look to him, he vigorously shook his head. "No. Don't."

"That's not necessary," I said.

LaPointe smiled, his lip not showing any sign of a tic. "I won't harm you, and Delovich is protected, but nobody said anything about his men. Fair game, as far as I know."

"Hey!" Federov shouted. "Somebody help! Stop! Goddammit, get your fuckin' hands off me!"

"Quiet!" LaPointe shouted.

Held down on the floor by LaPointe's thugs, Federov spat at him, the saliva traveling not much farther than his lips. "You son of a bitch, you motherfuckin' piece of shit."

"Convince him to be quiet," LaPointe told his men.

One of them threw a fist across Federov's chin. His eyes rolled. Blood trailed from the corner of his mouth. His head began rolling side to side as though he were struggling to stay conscious, as though his life depended on it (perhaps it did).

One of the men opened the back of the Land Rover and took out a handful of long cable ties. Another man opened the door, and the third backed the Rover halfway outside the bay. The first and second men dragged Federov to the lift, which conveniently had four extensions, one for each limb, and strapped him to it. He looked like someone nailed down in preparation for crucifixion.

"Bring the Rover in and close the door."

While his thugs complied, I took a couple of steps toward LaPointe and asked, "How many people are you going to kill, LaPointe?"

"As many as necessary."

As the Rover stopped over Federov, LaPointe said, "He's lucky there's so much clearance."

"And when's it going to stop?" I asked.

"I don't believe it ever will," LaPointe said. He smiled cruelly at me. "But perhaps it won't be so bad if you can convince Dunn and Delovich to cooperate. How badly do you want to help?"

"I'm not sure Delovich will listen to me."

"Tsk tsk. Then things will get messy."

LaPointe turned to his three men, who were now standing in front of the Land Rover. Below it, an occasional moan escaped. The door behind me opened and someone shouted, "It's Delovich."

LaPointe turned, visibly pleased. "Show him in. Tell him I'm willing to negotiate."

I couldn't believe that Delovich would walk into what appeared to be a trap, but he strode into the bay area, rapping his cane every other step. He strode past me, barely giving me a glance, and nearing Dunn he stopped, planting his cane firmly on the floor. His face reddened as he looked at the gun pressed against Dunn's side.

"What do you think you're doing here, LaPointe? What the fuck's this all about?" He was squinting, as though trying to contain his anger.

"What I am doing, Delovich, is preparing to convince you to call your entire organization and tell them you've struck a deal with me, and that I'm running the show now. John LaPointe."

"You? You're working for the Mafiya?"

"Let's just say I'm laying the foundation for their operations. Now, are you prepared to start making your calls?"

"That's not going to happen," Delovich said.

LaPointe turned to me. "Mr. Delovich doesn't want to cooperate."

"Did you think he would?" I asked. "Why don't you just shoot him?"

Delovich glared briefly at me.

LaPointe shook his head. "Word has come from Moscow, from the avtoritet. Both Mr. Delovich and I are to refrain from killing one another, at least until the razborka is complete."

"Sounds fair to me," I said. Of course, they didn't have to obey the avtoritet, but I imagined there'd be consequences to such insubordination, unpleasant ones. No, whoever won this war apparently needed to be in the Mafiya's good graces.

"Hey, Thigpen," Dunn said, nodding at the guy holding a gun on him. "Help me out here, okay?"

"I can't believe this," I said. "It's like people interviewing for a CEO's job."

Delovich rapped his cane on the concrete floor. "Thigpen, you said you wanted to talk. You didn't say you were bringing the point man here."

I shrugged. "You said you wanted to know who he was. Well, I found out. Anyway, I figured you'd want to meet up with him."

"Shut up," LaPointe said. "Thigpen, I think you can now see that neither Dunn nor Delovich is responding to my demand."

"I'll never cooperate with you, LaPointe," Delovich said. "And neither will Mr. Dunn."

"According to the casino's management," LaPointe said, "Mr. Dunn has direct connections with casino operations. He intends to launder Delovich's money through the casino. So, Thigpen, you must pressure Dunn into switching allegiance."

I pointed the Louisville Slugger at LaPointe. "You know, I can apply a little pressure, too."

"I want to be perfectly clear," LaPointe continued. "Either Dunn or Delovich will begin seeing things my way. Your choice, for starters. Understand?"

Sure, even if I convinced only Dunn (and not Delovich), LaPointe might gain control of the casino. After that, all of the other dominos would fall. It'd be a wrap. Turf war over. Oh, there might be a few skirmishes remaining here and there, but once the razborka was made and LaPointe was given control of the area, Delovich was toast.

Still, I knew Delovich could flick his cane and seriously wound the man with the gun trained on Bill Dunn, which might provide enough of a distraction that I could take a swing with my bat.

"I don't think he'll listen to me," I said. Delovich had thought I was the assessor. Surely by now he knew he'd been mistaken. Still, I was the only one in the room (other than Dunn) who might take his side.

"I believe he will," LaPointe said. "You will try."

LaPointe had threatened everyone I knew. He'd said they'd all die if I didn't cooperate. But still I kept quiet, hoping LaPointe would make a mistake.

Federov moaned beneath the Land Rover.

"What's that?" Delovich asked.

"They strapped a man named Federov to the lift," I said. "He's from Josef's. They intend to kill him."

Delovich's hands tightened on the cane. He stooped and glanced under the Land Rover.

"Dunn is next," LaPointe said.

"You're sloppy," Delovich said. "You think the Mafiya will let you run things?"

"I've been with them a long time. I *am* the Mafiya."

Delovich snorted. "Then why did the avtoritet signal me that he was considering my offer?"

"Because up till now I've been too slow, too careful. I admit your organization is more loyal than I believed possible. I should've applied more pressure long ago." LaPointe pointed at one of the three henchmen near the Rover. "Get ready to raise the lift." The thug stepped over to the hydraulic control.

"Wait," I said. "Tell you what, LaPointe—I asked you a question at the Kalahan Building. You answered the question, and I did as you asked. I'm willing to do the same here, but this time I'd like you to answer more than one question."

"How many?" LaPointe asked impatiently. "I don't have all day."

"I didn't count them, for Christ's sake. Do I look like a mathematician? Give me five minutes of answers."

"I'll give you two," LaPointe said. He held out his palm to the man at the hydraulic lift control—*not yet.*

"When's my time start?" I asked.

"One minute, fifty seconds," LaPointe answered.

Oh hell, Jack, don't go through this again.

"All right, tell me what happened at Josef's."

"My guys fucked up. They were pressuring Adolpho, but they weren't supposed to blow the place up until later, as a last resort. We asked a survivor at the hospital, and he said the suitcase latch malfunctioned. An explosive device fell out and detonated."

"What happened to the men at the hospital?" I asked.

"They failed me. Nobody fails me twice. I run a tight ship, Thigpen. Very tight. The razborka will be in my favor." He flipped his hand toward Delovich. "Delovich is a buffoon, nothing more than a wimpy businessman."

"Don't eat into my time," I said.

"At least I can add," Delovich said. "And I could always count on your mother to suck my cock."

"Shut up, Delovich," I said.

Delovich opened his mouth to say something but stopped.

"See," LaPointe said. "He listens to you."

"Next question," I said. "Why? You live in a mansion, so I assume you have money. Why risk it?"

"The estate doesn't belong to me. The Mafiya purchased it. I'm here acting on their behalf."

"Then why would the Mafiya consider working with Delovich?"

LaPointe's lip was tugged upward by the tic. "How the fuck should I know?"

"They like to cover all bases, that's why," Delovich said. "Not only is my offer generous, they get to avoid the trouble and publicity this asshole's creating."

"Quiet," I said. "Now, LaPointe, tell me how this works in precise terms. Someone will call you with the results from the person assessing the situation?"

"In a word, yes. A call from the Mafiya boss. The avtoritet."

"Did Blalock always work for you?"

"He played both sides. He believes himself to be more important than he really is, but now I trust him more than these idiots who're afraid of you." He glared briefly at his men.

"Okay, but—"

"Time's up. Now convince Delovich."

I turned to Delovich and said, "I suggest you turn your organization over to LaPointe. At least the casino. You'll probably save Federov's life."

"I turn nothing over," Delovich said. "You know as well as I that he'll kill Federov anyway. He just admitted to killing three of his loyal—if somewhat incompetent—men. If he runs things, many, many more people will die."

"There's no chance I can convince you?"

"No."

I turned to LaPointe and shrugged. "I tried."

"You're not saying the right things. Is there a code word you use? Blalock said Delovich would listen to you."

"I don't get it," Blalock said. "Maybe ya oughta see if he can convince Dunn."

I held out my hand and turned to Dunn. "How about it? You gonna listen to me?"

Dunn shook his hand. "You know I'd like to, Thigpen," he said. He glanced at Delovich and added, "But it just wouldn't be wise."

LaPointe's breathing grew more rapid. He pointed at Delovich. "You are going to lose your business." Then he pointed at Dunn. "You are going to lose everything." Finally, he pointed at me. "You are going to lose someone very dear to you."

What? What's he mean?

"Now, we start," LaPointe said. He glared at Dunn. "You'll follow Federov on the ride up." LaPointe nodded sharply to the man at the lift control. He pushed a lever up.

The lift started to rise.

Federov's weak voice drifted out from under the Land Rover—"No! Stop!"

I jogged toward the man at the controls, raising my bat, but one of the thugs caught me, held me tight, pinning my arms behind my back.

"Please!" Federov cried from under the vehicle.

The Land Rover nudged upward.

Federov screamed.

I snapped my head backward, striking the nose of the guy holding me. He released me. His handgun clattered to the floor. I grabbed it and turned, knowing I couldn't win a shoot-out while so outnumbered.

Federov's scream intensified into a blood-chortling cry.

I pointed the handgun at myself, at where Norton had shot me, and fired.

There was a squishing sound from under the Land Rover, then the horrible crunch of breaking bones. The Land Rover came off the floor. Blood spilled across the concrete in a spreading pool.

I screamed, running ahead a few steps. "You fuckin' idiots. You're messing with the wrong guy. You messing with a guy who's already dead."

The man at the controls lowered the lever, not taking his eyes from the front of my sweatshirt, blood seeping across it.

The silence lengthened.

Most of the henchmen had jaws reaching down toward their knees. Then they all began jabbering in Russian. Another group burst through the door from the parts department, men who must've been on look-out duty in other parts of the dealership. The thug who'd fired the gun pointed a shaking finger at me and shouted, "Upir."

From their terrified expressions—and the way they pronounced the word—I had the impression they'd identified me as a vampire or some equivalent creature. And what they were seeing confirmed what they'd heard about me, someone who can't be killed.

Men ran from all directions around the bays to the Land Rovers, slapping buttons on their way to roll up the doors. They scrambled over each other, into the vehicles, backing out as soon as the vehicles gained clearance under the rising doors.

Even LaPointe was backing away.

One of his men, climbing into the last Rover (with faithful ol' Blalock already behind the wheel), said, "Sorry, Mr. LaPointe, but we cannot deal with this—we can't fight a devil."

LaPointe, evidently realizing he was losing support fast, climbed in before the Rover began reversing out of the bay. He rolled down the window and shook his cell phone at me. "You'll be getting a call, Thigpen. This isn't over yet. Remember—you're the one who's being difficult. This'll be on your hands."

Someone very dear. Oh no—Ellie!

But she was safely out of town, wasn't she?

Only Delovich and Dunn remained.

"I'll be a son of a bitch," Delovich said. "How'd you know that would work?"

"I didn't. All I know is that people keep shooting me and I don't die." Of course, if the aim was slightly better, Norton could have killed me twice over.

Delovich cocked his head as though trying to understand. He turned to Dunn and pointed at Federov's crushed body—a bloody pulp, some of which was falling into the service pit below the lift. "You'll have to call someone to clean up this mess."

Dunn was wiping sweat from his brow. He appeared unable to stop the flow. "Y-Y-Yeah."

My cell phone vibrated.

Not now, Tom!

"Does this mean you win?" I asked Delovich.

"I'm not sure, but it certainly tilts the situation in my favor." He paused, rubbing the top of his cane. "He's grown careless. It's almost over for him."

"It seems like he'd rather die than lose this razborka."

"I complained to the avtoritet. I said that I feared LaPointe would not accept the razborka if it were in my favor. I was assured that if it was necessary, LaPointe would be removed."

"Does LaPointe know that?"

Delovich shrugged. "It would explain his behavior."

My cell phone beeped.

It had to be Tom, I thought. He was the only one beside Delovich with the new cell phone number. I took the phone from my pocket. "Tom?" But as soon as I said my brother's name, I realized—my hand clenching the phone—that there was one other person who had the number.

The voice sounded Russian. "Thigpen, we got someone here. We'll kill her unless control of the casino is in LaPointe's hands."

"What? Wait—"

Oh God, no. Don't let it be true.

Another voice spoke over the phone, a young girl's voice, the words coming out between sobs. "Jack? Is that you?"

"Octavia?"

"I'm scared, Jack."

Think fast, Jack.

"Where are you?"

"I'm blindfolded."

"Do you hear any cars?"

"No."

"Hear any boats?"

"Yes—"

The Russian voice returned. "Have Delovich contact the casino and give the word that Mr. LaPointe's in charge. Delovich will direct the casino management to contact Mr. LaPointe and confirm the change. I suggest you hurry. The girl might die of fright before we get a chance to do anything to her. Understand? By the end of the day. Mr. LaPointe will be waiting."

The call ended.

I turned to Delovich. "They kidnapped a little girl. A kid!"

Delovich shrugged. "That's the way of the Mafiya. They believe abductions of children are often more effective for coercion. They have so much life left. Adults—not so much."

I grabbed his lapels. "Turn it over," I yelled at him. "Turn it all over to him."

Delovich knocked me away. "Who'd be next, Thigpen? You think LaPointe will stop with your little girl? Whose daughter will die next because he's running the show?"

"I can't let her die." I imagined that because Octavia knew LaPointe, he'd been able to lure her away. He'd talked to her, asking her about the tournament or something else that was relevant, and his thugs had come up from behind, grabbed her, suppressed her screams.

"LaPointe won't let her go anyway," Delovich said. "She knows too much."

The truth of his statement terrified me.

"I have to save her. She's got to be at LaPointe's estate. She said she heard boats."

"You'll need backup," Delovich said.

I looked at him, wondering if I could trust him, afraid that Octavia would be harmed in crossfire if the turf war was brought to LaPointe's doorstep.

And remember, Jack, you were acting weird when you were last with her at the Club, where everyone could see. And you'd just smashed Baine's car window. If she turns up dead somewhere, you'll probably be suspect number one.

"Okay," I said. "Do you know where LaPointe's estate is?"

"I believe so."

"I'll meet you at the gate. Bring some of your men."

"What's your plan?"

I hope to have one by the time I get there.

Instead of letting Delovich know I was playing this by ear, I said, "He's bound to have security measures, cameras, defenses. A direct approach is best."

"We can't go in shooting up the place."

"I don't think we'll have to." I turned toward the parts department door. "Hurry."

CHAPTER THIRTY FOUR

Although I wanted to leave immediately, I figured I'd need to keep myself together enough in case I had to carry Octavia out of danger. I crawled into the truck, took off my sweatshirt, and tossed it onto the passenger seat. I rummaged through the duffel bag and took out a bandage and the roll of duct tape. I unrolled a one-foot length, bit into the edge of the tape, and ripped the piece free. I looked at my chest.

There was a piece of rib showing, splintered yellowish-white curved bone. The flesh hadn't been puckered much, perhaps because of the scar tissue that had developed since Norton had shot me. It looked like the hole in a coffee can punched with a screwdriver. I wrapped the bandage around my midsection, then placed the tape diagonally over the wound. I tore off three more pieces of tape, crisscrossed them across the wound, then wrapped a length of tape around my entire midsection.

As I ripped the next piece of tape from the roll, a curious tickling sensation affected my eyes. I wiped a finger across my cheek and looked at it.

Nothing.

No tears.

Octavia. I'd get her out of LaPointe's reach no matter what, no matter how many times I was shot. The duct tape wrapped around my torso would keep me together.

My cell phone vibrated again. I took it out. There was a text message. I quickly retrieved it.

CHECK UNDER SEAT. FORGOT TO TELL YOU. LEFT GIFT. -TOM

I peered under the passenger seat, found a shirt-size box, and pulled it out. Tom had left me a Kevlar vest.

"Timing's a bit off, Tom," I whispered.

But maybe the timing was perfect. The goons had seen a bullet penetrate my body. They didn't think I was wearing one. If they saw me take some bullets, it would feed their image of me—a Upir.

I put on the Kevlar vest, tightened the straps, then slipped on my sweatshirt.

Please, no head shots, for Octavia's sake ...

I started the pickup and drove off the lot.

My hands clenched the steering wheel all the way to I-94. I got on the highway and headed toward Detroit.

Doubt nagged at me.

Why would LaPointe risk holding a hostage at his estate? Isn't that foolish?

But maybe more of his men were abandoning him. After all, LaPointe was going up against a devil, a upir.

A devil ...

I didn't care what I was, what manner of being. All I wanted was to save Octavia's life.

I turned off I-94 in Harper Woods and took Vernier to Lake Shore Drive, where I turned south. Lake St. Clair was on my left.

I passed the sign that indicated I was entering Grosse Pointe Farms and slowed to the posted limit.

LaPointe's estate was just ahead.

A direct approach is best, Jack. Your advantage is their fear of you. They believe they can't kill you.

I figured there'd be a security guard at the gate. I tried picturing the gate, which I'd driven by probably a thousand times. Most likely, there was some kind of structure just beyond the gate, a small building, perhaps a booth to protect the guard from the elements. There wasn't one visible from the road (from what I could remember), but the estate was lined with trees and shrubs. There was a hedge outside the fence, which was tall—over fifteen feet—and constructed with black wrought-iron. I figured there had to be motion sensors near the fence, because it could be climbed, although perhaps not so easily by me.

"I'm going to have to trust myself," I said, needing to hear my voice. My thoughts were getting too jumbled. And I wasn't sure—but there seemed to be a tingling sensation in my nerves.

"I can do this."

Was Octavia still alive?

"He needs Octavia alive for leverage. It's all he has left."

True, but he's unpredictable. Anything can happen.

"Just get inside the house. Find Octavia. Tell 'em that bullets can't stop you. Play up the upir angle. Scare 'em off. Untie Octavia—she's gonna be tied up—or maybe cut the ropes. Carry her outside, protect her from gunfire with your body."

It was a plan, but I didn't like it. How would I find Octavia? It was a huge house—a mansion. Dozens of rooms. Maybe hidden passageways, too, since the Mafiya owned it.

"What about Delovich and his men?"

I don't know.

I turned left at LaPointe's driveway and parked on it near the road. Other than those driving along Lake Shore behind me, there were no cars in sight. The tall gate was at least twenty yards ahead, set well off the road, shrouded in shadows from the groves of trees on the estate. On each side, stone pillars and walls extended for ten feet, where they again met with wrought iron. Fifteen feet high, the gate's hinges were set into these stone structures. The gate opened at the middle. There was a guard booth just inside, on the left side of the driveway.

I opened the pickup's door, stepped outside, and grabbed the baseball bat. I hesitated, then threw the car keys under the front seat.

I didn't think I'd be needing them anymore.

Hearing a loud car behind me, I slammed the door shut and turned.

The car drove past on Lake Shore.

C'mon, Delovich, where the hell are you?

I waited another minute, which wasn't a long time, but I was anxious to enter the estate. Just when I was ready to head in, Delovich's limousine slid in beside me.

Delovich hurried out and strode toward me, not even bothering to strike his cane onto the driveway as he walked.

There were two others with him. They wore blue jeans and T-shirts. Both chewed gum and wore sunglasses. They looked about expectantly.

The driver turned the vehicle around and left.

"This is all the help you could bring?" I asked.

"It was short notice," Delovich told me. "And, uh, the word's gotten out, evidently, about you. I swear I said nothing. Me? Personally, I don't care what you are. This is business."

"Where's the car going?"

"To a marina north of here. I'll have a boat waiting offshore. They'll have binoculars trained on the estate's waterfront. At my signal, they'll come and pick us up. I figure if things fall apart, the police might arrive on the scene."

I nodded. "Yeah, that's good thinking."

"I've done this kind of thing before."

I glanced at the pickup. "Have the pickup moved if I don't make it out. Take it to the Kalahan Building and leave the keys under the front seat. That's where they are now." *Tom'll look for you, Jack, at all the places you've been and he'll find the truck there.*

Delovich nodded. "I'll make a call."

I turned and studied the two henchmen, who looked too young and too much like they needed baths.

"They any good?"

"They're good," Delovich said. "But not the best."

"Long distance aim?"

Delovich looked at the two men. One of them said, "With rifles, yeah, but not with handguns. Can't guarantee a hit on any shot over fifty yards, and that'd have to be a stationary target."

"That's not good enough," I said, thinking to suggest they try to get a shot at LaPointe from outside, perhaps from up in a tree. *Delovich doesn't want to kill LaPointe, though, Jack. You gotta remember that.*

"What's your plan?" Delovich asked.

"What if we called the police?"

"I think they'd want to know who you are before checking out the home of John LaPointe. Are you prepared to be scrutinized?"

"We don't have time," I said. "Here's the deal. These guys are afraid of me, but they might shoot anyway. I've got a Kevlar vest on now. That'll support their upir beliefs if I get hit but don't go down. I want you to wait twenty minutes, then follow me."

"You want us to come in with guns blazing?"

"This isn't a movie," I said. "Octavia might get hit."

"What if we hear shots before the twenty minutes are up?"

"Wait twenty minutes. Period. Got it?"

Delovich nodded.

I walked toward the gate and turned my head back. "The twenty minutes will start once I'm on the other side of the gate."

"Got it," Delovich said, taking out his cell phone. "Good luck."

The wrought-iron bars loomed in front of me as I entered the shadows. The foliage absorbed the sounds of the traffic behind me, and it seemed for a moment like I was at the gate of a primeval forest. A couple of blue jays squawked as I reached the gate, staring at the L, half of which was on the left gate, half on the right.

There, to my left, was the guard's booth, perhaps four feet by five. On one of its windows was a small air conditioning unit. The man inside didn't wear a uniform. It was apparently one of LaPointe's thugs (this one wearing a white shirt). I didn't recognize him, though, as someone who'd been at the Dunn Ford dealership.

The guard was staring at me. He opened the door and stood on the mansion side of the booth. He looked ready to make a run for it.

"Are you going to let me in?" I asked.

"I ain't supposed to let no one in," he said.

"But I'm not *no one*. I'm someone. And if you don't open this fuckin' gate, I'm going to chase you down and eat your soul for dinner."

The man started shaking. He stepped slowly back to the door, reached inside, and pushed a button.

"That's all I do for you," he said, taking off at a fast run toward the mansion.

I stepped through the gate, which was opening via electric motors from within the stone pillars.

Twenty minutes, Jack. Not much time.

I walked to my left, into the wooded part of the lawn, then

worked my way toward the mansion, ducking behind trees, spurting ahead when there was no cover (*dammit, the legs feel tight*).

There could be a marksman anywhere ahead, hiding. If I wasn't careful, a quick burst from an automatic weapon could slice through my legs.

I glanced back at the gate. Delovich and his two men were at the guard booth. Delovich pushed a button. Motors whirred as the gates began to close.

"Good idea, Delovich," I muttered.

There was a fair distance between each of the tree trunks (too far for comfort, too distant to fully conceal an approach), but it was even worse farther to my left, where there was an open lawn, the grass full, lush, manicured like a expensive golf course.

I advanced, feeling like I was in a war movie, maneuvering toward an enemy machine gun nest.

The mansion was another hundred yards ahead, at the end of the slightly curving driveway. Garden beds lined the asphalt, although the flowers were pitiful, as though the gardener had mistakenly planted flowers requiring direct sunlight.

The ground was clear of obstacles, though, weed-free grass, and at the base of each tree there was a circle of cedar chips. There were a few patches of shrubs, and I tried angling toward them to help conceal my approach.

Time was short, but the closer I got to the mansion before being spotted, the better my chances of everyone seeing a bullet hit me and my not going down.

The mansion didn't look haunted—but it did look bleak, especially when clouds cast it in shadow. It rose up before me as I approached, a three-story brick structure, and I realized that it was built at the top of a slight slope. Trees off to my right continued past the house, where the land sloped down again.

When I got to the tree nearest the mansion's front door, about twenty yards ahead, I paused and looked back. I shook my head, dumbfounded. Delovich was peering at me from beside the next tree.

"I told you twenty minutes!" I said.

His two henchmen behind him, Delovich glanced at his

watch. "It's been twenty-four."

Dammit, Jack, you're losing your sense of time. It's all slipping away ...

"Wait there."

I turned and studied the mansion. There was a large balcony on the third floor. A large colonnaded portico spread out before me at the front door. Stucco white, it reminded me of the White House.

In a wide carport to the right of the mansion, there were four black Land Rovers.

Maybe only one Rover's worth of men had given up on LaPointe. Just one. Maybe he'd steeled the rest into fighting against the upir, the devil man.

The front door opened. Lapointe's voice called out, "I know you're there, Thigpen. Come closer so we can have a talk."

I hesitated then stepped away from the tree and marched toward the portico. When I reached the driveway, I stopped.

"Give me Octavia," I said. "She's got nothing to do with this."

"I'm waiting for a confirmation call from the casino," LaPointe said. "You and the girl are lucky that the razborka isn't finished yet. Have you made Delovich cooperate yet?"

"I told you all along he wouldn't listen to me."

"Find a way—be creative—or the girl dies."

I glanced back. Delovich was staring at me. His two men were peering at the house. I slightly shook my head, hoping they'd understand that I wanted to handle this by myself.

"You've gone too far, LaPointe," I said. "Everyone's going to know you killed Octavia."

"In my opinion, no."

"Let me see her. How do I know she's still alive?"

"Come inside. See for yourself."

"No—bring her out."

There was a few seconds of silence, and then a sharp command—"Go out and convince him to come inside."

LaPointe's thugs began filing out the front door, handguns trained on me. They aligned themselves in a semicircle, on the outskirts of the portico.

I counted nine (ten, including LaPointe).

Not great odds, Jack, not great at all.

One of them fired his handgun into the air. "You come inside now," he said.

"Don't worry, Thigpen," LaPointe called out. "I'm not going to kill you; but if you don't convince Delovich, I am going to test your threshold of pain."

I took a step ahead and began thumping the end of the baseball bat down onto the asphalt. "What have we here? Dinner? I've been so fuckin' hungry for so many centuries. Don't look so scared, gentlemen. It won't hurt. But upirs gotta feed every now and then, and I haven't tasted good Russian blood in centuries. *Da?* What's the matter?"

"Stay back," one of them said.

"Go get him!" LaPointe ordered.

"Who'll be first?" I asked, taking off my sunglasses. I shoved them in my pants pocket and tucked my lower lip behind my upper teeth. I made a sucking sound. "A feast—I can't wait! You've all heard of the upir, yes, but I'm a super badass upir cause I'll take any cross you show me and shove it up your ass!"

"That's all bullshit!" LaPointe cried. "Don't listen."

I held the bat between my knees and rubbed my hands together. "Vintage Russian blood. This is going to be good!"

The thugs looked more than nervous; they looked terrified—knees quivering, eyes squeezing shut, hands trembling, saying quick prayers in urgent hushed voices—all except one, that is. Even so, as he walked toward me, his steps were tentative. "You are bluffing," he said, taking one last step so that he was only three feet in front of me, aiming the handgun at my heart.

He paused, his smile not very big, as though he'd thought the shot at Dunn Ford's might have missed, and at this range he wouldn't make that mistake.

He pulled the trigger.

The impact knocked me back a couple of steps, and for a few moments, I couldn't breathe. The pain was incredible, like someone had swung a sledgehammer against my chest. I tried keeping my face as calm as possible.

The bat had fallen on the ground. I bent forward, picked it

up with my left hand, and probed the bullet hole with my right hand's index finger.

I sneered at the man who'd just shot me. "You can't kill me, you son of a bitch. Now get the fuck out of my way or I'm going to have you for lunch."

He blinked twice, his entire body trembling. He took one step back, staring at my sweatshirt, then turned and ran toward the carport, his comrades racing him there.

"Stop!" LaPointe screamed. "It's a trick!"

They didn't bother to respond.

I looked back at Delovich and signaled him over toward the carport. *Keep them there, out of trouble. Anyway, Delovich, if you win this contest, they'll be your thugs.*

Maybe.

I looked at the front door.

I started walking. Leaning forward, I was able to propel myself a bit faster, not at a jog, but I knew every second counted.

The moment I passed through the arched doorway, shots began firing from somewhere ahead, and the bullets began hitting me. The shots sounded loud, unnatural, with an ethereal chugging quality—*chug, chug, chug ...*

They might've knocked me back if I hadn't been leaning forward. The bullets straightened me up a bit, but I continued pressing ahead down the main hallway, an oak staircase to my right, the silhouetted figure of LaPointe in a room at the far end. One bullet hit my leg, just above the knee (missing the bone). Blood began seeping down my sweatpants leg.

I don't know how many shots were fired, or how long it took me to travel the length of the hallway (during which I could hear LaPointe's anger-filled voice—"Why ... won't ... you ... fuckin' ... die!), but as I neared the end, LaPointe ran.

I heard footsteps receding to the right, and when I rounded the corner, there was an open door ahead of me with steps leading down.

I hurried down the staircase.

At the bottom of the steps, I paused and listened.

Nothing. No noise. Only empty silence.

There. A noise. A whimper?

I followed the sound down the hallway ahead and slowed as I neared an open door on my left. Cautiously I looked inside.

It was a billiards room, cavernous, and on its gleaming polished floor there was a Ping Pong table, pool table, and a dozen arcade video games. At the far end were scattered sofas and chairs and a flat panel TV screen. Just beyond the arcade games was a curved bar, its wood highly polished, with padded bar stools neatly lined up in front. There were several dartboards on the wood paneling to my right.

Edging into the room, I was able to see more of the room to the left. Near the Ping Pong table was a game table and in a chair at the table, Octavia sat. She was blindfolded with blue strips of cloth. Her hands were tied behind her back, and her feet were bound together.

She heard the shots, Jack. She thinks someone's coming to kill her. She's listening ...

Her handbag was beside the chair, on the tiled floor, her tennis racket still in it.

He must've gotten her not long after I saw her at the Slushy Freeze.

She whimpered again.

She doesn't know you're here, Jack. Don't call out to her. She'll give you away. LaPointe's got to be in here somewhere.

Where?

Behind an arcade game? Behind the bar?

The card table was more than ten feet from any place that LaPointe could be hiding; I decided that I might be able to free her quickly enough so that LaPointe couldn't jump me. Then, if LaPointe did appear, I could shield her from any more shots and get her out.

I took a step to my right, then began edging along the arcade games, peering over to look in back of each as I passed.

When I was parallel to Octavia, I stop and whispered, "Octavia, it's me—Jack."

She immediately straightened her back. Her head turned alertly as she tried to pinpoint my position. "Where are you?"

"Shhh. I'm going to get you out of here, but we'll have to be quick."

"Oh, Jack, hurry and get me out of here. I'm scared. They hit me. They said they'd kill me."

"Don't be scared. You got to do some thinking. I'm not thinking so well now. I'm trying. Really. But, I-I-I'm just not feeling right anymore."

"I heard gunshots. Tell me what to do, Jack."

She was restrained with tie-wraps. I thought my penknife could cut the plastic. Holding the bat in my left hand, I reached with my right and took out the penknife. I unfolded the blade. "I'm going to cross the room and cut your bindings. I'm going to use a sawing motion. Hold your hands and legs steady, but apply pressure to the blade. Don't fight it. Okay?"

"Okay, Jack." She sniffed.

"That's my girl. We'll be out of here lickety split."

She nodded.

"Know who kidnapped you?"

"No. I was talking to Mr. LaPointe and—"

"It was LaPointe."

"But—"

"So when I take off your blindfold, you watch for him, okay?"

"But someone grabbed me from behind. Mr. LaPointe was telling them to leave me alone and trying to pull me away!"

"He was just covering himself in case anyone was watching. You're in his basement."

She sniffed again.

"Octavia, I need you to understand what happened."

She nodded hesitantly. "Okay."

"So stay away from LaPointe."

"Yes, Jack."

I took one more long look around the room, trying to find an odd shadow, a shoe sticking out from beyond some corner, but the room still looked empty except for Octavia and me.

"Ready?" I asked.

"Yes, Jack."

I put the knife down a moment, reached into my pocket, took out my sunglasses, and put them back on.

"On three," I said, picking up the knife. "One ..., two ..., three—"

I stumbled over the tiled floor to her side, dropped the bat, and tore off her blindfold. Scanning the room, I shimmied around behind her, then lowered my gaze and began sawing at the tie-wrap that strapped her wrists together.

"How are we getting out of here, Jack?" Octavia asked.

"Shhh."

The knife finally snapped through the last of the plastic, and Octavia's hands were free.

I looked up. Still no one in sight. I moved around to the front of Octavia's chair.

"Jack—you're all shot up!"

"Quiet."

I started cutting the tie-wrap binding her ankles together.

"Jack!"

I heard Octavia's warning at the same time as I heard shoes slapping the linoleum.

Reaching for the bat, I started to rise, turning, glimpsing a two by four, and that's when a blow to my back made me fall on my stomach. It didn't hurt, but neither could I resist the force.

I could hear my bat rolling away.

I tried pushing myself up to my feet.

LaPointe hit me again, squarely in the back. I was forced down again, *whoosh.* Again and again, faster and faster, LaPointe struck my back, whacking away like a crazed lumberjack, shouting, "Motherfucker, you goddam motherfucker!"

I began to fade.

Time?

What was time?

What was life?

An illusion.

Jack ...

Jack ...

"Jack!"

Octavia's voice. She was screaming as LaPointe continued battering my back. I turned my head and looked at her. Her eyes widened with fear (perhaps because I looked like I couldn't get up) and then her expression hardened and she reached into her handbag, pulled out her tennis racket and swung.

Whack.

The pounding on my back stopped.

"You little shit!" LaPointe said.

I swung my arm, rolled myself over, found the bat, and swung. LaPointe was swinging his piece of lumber at me again (a two by four), but my Louisville Slugger slammed into the side of his ankle first.

The two by four hit the floor directly beside my head.

LaPointe cried out in pain.

His breaths came rapidly, and as I sat up, I could see the pain in his face. He was standing mostly on one leg, with little pressure on the other.

His head jerked around as though he was looking for something to kill me with, something that might work.

But maybe now he suspected that nothing would. He limped to his left, grabbed the edge of the Ping Pong table, and flipped it over. The table crashed down on me.

As I struggled to get the table off, Octavia screamed. "Jack—he's got me!"

I pushed my head to my right so that I could see out from under the edge of the table.

LaPointe was moving a little faster, limping toward the door. He held Octavia over his shoulder. She pounded her fists on his back. "Jack—help!"

"I'm coming," I said, the weakness of my voice disheartening, sounding more like a death knell.

"I'm coming."

CHAPTER THIRTY FIVE

Somehow I was able to crawl out from under the Ping Pong table and regain my feet.

I hurriedly closed the penknife, shoved it in my pocket, grabbed the bat, and rushed out the door and up the steps as best I could.

I heard another scream and followed it, crossing the hallway and entering a large drawing room. To my left, I saw a grand piano, with open patio doors beyond. I ran hobbled through the room, past bookshelves and the piano, and went through the patio doors. To my right, Delovich was rounding the side of the mansion, from the carport side.

He approached me, tapping his cane, scanning left and right. One of his men trailed closely behind, still chewing his gum like a cow with its cud. He was wiping his hands on his jeans as though he hated dealing with this situation and was trying to cleanse himself.

I pointed down the hill, where LaPointe—still carrying a flailing Octavia—was racing with an uneven gait toward a boathouse a hundred yards below. It was built on pilings and jutted fifty feet out into the lake. A pier ran alongside to the boathouse door. The boathouse had windows, and I could see a boat sitting in the water within.

On the pier, Blalock stood with arms folded across his chest.

"LaPointe's got Octavia," I yelled at Delovich. It looked like about a forty-yard shot. "Have your man shoot him."

"Can't guarantee I wouldn't hit the girl," the gum-chewer shouted back.

"Do it as the boat leaves the dock," I said. "You'll have a clean shot."

Delovich stepped next to me on the porch, his cane rapping on the slate surface. He glanced at my bullet-riddled sweatshirt, hesitated, then peered down the hill at LaPointe and seemed to consider the odds of a successful shot.

"We're not here to kill LaPointe," Delovich said.

"Then what are you here for?" I demanded.

"To stop him, not to kill him. I suggest we head for the lake." He looked out to the lake and waved with his cane.

His boat. Maybe we've got a chance ...

I took off down the hill.

LaPointe was almost to the dock.

"Blalock!" I shouted. "Don't help him—you picked the wrong side!"

"Mr. LaPointe is quite resourceful," Blalock called smugly, 'resourceful' sounding like resawsful. "I haven't given up on 'im yet."

I looked over my shoulder. Delovich and his man were coming, but at a slow pace.

"Hurry up!" I shouted.

Delovich shrugged as though he wouldn't risk falling in order to save Octavia's life.

LaPointe ran down the pier and went inside the boathouse. Blalock followed close behind. I could now hear the boat's idling engine. It sounded powerful—an impatient chugging.

Approaching land quickly, Delovich's boat looked like a fast one, long and sleek, a cabin cruiser constructed for speed.

LaPointe's boat began surging out of the dock, then it accelerated even more, its bow lifting up. A racing boat, white, cigar shaped, designed to slice through the water. It didn't appear to even have a cabin. I imagined it would make an excellent boat for running drugs.

LaPointe's boat continued accelerating until it looked almost to be flying across the lake.

I waved at Delovich's boat—*hurry!*

Delovich and his man reached my side. We stepped onto the dock, hurried to the end, and waited for his boat.

"Where's LaPointe going?" I asked.

"I don't know," Delovich said. "Maybe Canada."

"If he goes to Canada, isn't this razborka decided?"

"I would think so, but it's not up to me."

"Why take Octavia? I don't understand!"

"Whatever his intentions, he's certainly afraid of you." He peered at me, his eyes lingering on the numerous bullet holes in my sweatsuit and the blood trailing down my leg. "I believe I would be, too. Whatever his intention, he still wants insurance. Leverage."

Finally Delovich's boat reached the pier. The gum chewer pushed at the boat, stopping its forward momentum and holding it steady. Delovich and I climbed aboard. The captain had a tan, rawhide face that looked perpetually grim and flat, as though he'd spent his life on a fast boat and the wind had flattened his features. He shifted the engines into REVERSE. The gum chewer pushed, getting the boat away from the pier, then hopped aboard.

"Catch the boat that just left," Delovich told the captain.

I flopped onto a white-cushioned port-side seat.

There were two seats up front, behind a low-angle windshield and a dashboard with rows of round gauges. Between the seats there was a control panel with four levers topped with red balls. The pilot grimly pushed two of the levers forward, putting the engines into FORWARD. He gradually worked the two other levers forward—dual engines, port and starboard, each lever controlling one—and the boat surged ahead.

The boat plowed over waves and slapped down on the water, jarring me.

I clutched the edge of my seat as the boat was pushed faster and faster, striking the water—*wham, wham, wham*—the captain gritting his teeth and staring ahead.

I was the only one present willing to kill LaPointe in order to save Octavia, but I was the one in most danger of getting tossed overboard. My grasp was weakening.

Delovich opened the top of a storage bin, and threw me a life preserver.

Yeah, big misnomer there—

I snapped it on. "Got any binoculars?" I asked.

The driver reached under the dashboard and handed them back without turning his taut face.

Delovich took the binoculars. One hand holding the top of his seat, he peered ahead. "Difficult to get a good look. I can see him, but they're pretty far ahead."

"Are we gaining?"

"Don't know yet. We don't appear to be falling behind, at least not much."

"Can you see Octavia?"

"No."

The boat hit a large wave—*wham*.

"Patience, Mr. Thigpen," Delovich suggested.

"I'm out of patience," I said.

He nodded as though commiserating.

"It appears that he's following the shoreline," Delovich said. "Perhaps he's not going to Canada."

"Blalock said he's resourceful. What could he do, backed against the wall, to get this razborka resolved in his favor?"

Delovich glanced at his cane, which he had tucked below the passenger seat in front, as though wanting to tap it, needing to tap it in order to think. "To me, the game's over. However, I suppose if he could get the support of the casino owners now, even at this late stage, ... well, it's his only chance."

"It's a riverboat casino," I pointed out. "If he heads down the Detroit River, he can board it."

Delovich's face scrunched up as though he was trying to calculate an impossibly complex equation. "What are you saying—he's going to demand they pledge allegiance to him?"

"The grand opening's tomorrow. The owners might be there."

"Yes, but why would they agree to such a demand?"

"Because he'll murder a little girl if they don't. Bad publicity! Do these owners have the phone number of the avtoritet?"

"Perhaps."

"Then it's his only hope. You said he's likely to get killed if he doesn't win this turf war."

"Which is why, if I were him, I would head for Canada," Delovich said. "If he lies low, he might live a long and healthy life."

"You look like you don't think LaPointe will do that, though."

"No, I'm afraid not. See, I didn't know who the Mafiya man was. When I found out it was LaPointe— "

"Wait," I interrupted. "Take another look."

Delovich raised the binoculars and aimed them ahead. He looked for a few seconds and lowered them. "I'm afraid we're falling farther behind."

"What if we called the police? Maybe they could catch him."

"I won't be calling the police," Delovich said. "And I won't allow you to do that, either."

I didn't think the police would do any good. I imagined at the first sign of the police, Octavia would be weighed down with something and thrown over the side of LaPointe's boat. A feeling of nausea welled up inside me—grief, a physical manifestation of the utter horror I felt when I thought about Octavia—and it pummeled my senses—*wham wham wham*—as the cabin cruiser plowed through waves. "We've got to keep going," I said.

"We will, Mr. Thigpen. We will."

"What were you going to say about LaPointe?"

"Only that I've heard a lot about him—not in a criminal sense, of course. I mean, he's been coming into a lot of money lately, and I heard he's very aggressive when it comes to gaining power—political power. Lots of deals under the table."

"That's not necessarily criminal. Look at Washington."

"Correct—politicians are susceptible to bribes and intimidation and blackmail. None of them wants a scandal, and those are the tactics of the Mafiya. LaPointe is using them in a dangerous way."

"All of this stuff you've heard about LaPointe makes sense now, right?" I asked.

Delovich nodded. "But I don't think you quite understand. If LaPointe were to gain control of my organization and the Mafiya supports him, his ambition might very well take him beyond profits."

The way he said profits made me think he was saying the

name of a god he worshipped.

"I thought that's all you guys gave a shit about," I said.

"Please, Mr. Thigpen. You don't see me running around threatening an innocent girl."

"Maybe I don't know you all that well."

"Then let me tell you something. All I want is a profitable organization, one in which there's no unnecessary violence and everyone wins. My game is victimless crimes."

Yeah, tell that to Melissa.

"What's LaPointe's game?"

"Ask yourself what would make someone like him risk all that he owned."

"I thought the Mafiya owned that estate, not LaPointe."

"Even so, LaPointe's filthy rich, and he certainly has hidden money stashed away somewhere. He could live a luxurious life. But he isn't just interested in money. He wants more, and it includes intimidation and power—perhaps even global power. He will enable the Mafiya to fly under the political radar and then grasp control. First Metro Detroit, then Michigan, then maybe even the country."

Under the radar, like Alliance Insurance. Sneaking up on the Big Boys.

"Sounds like you guys believe in some whacked-out code, a criminal Darwinism," I said.

Delovich shrugged. "Once they gain power, anyone who opposes them dies. Survival of the compliant. But that's not it precisely." He sighed.

"Why didn't you just shoot him?" I asked.

"Because I'm not stupid. I value my life. I play the cards I'm dealt. Besides, I intend this razborka to be in my favor."

At the cost of a little girl.

"You know, I think you're a real son of a bitch. You talk a good game, but you're willing to watch LaPointe kill her. You're about as close to evil as you can be."

"Not as close as LaPointe. Now look here, Thigpen, I'm taking quite a few risks by siding with you. I'm an excellent judge of character, but even I make mistakes."

"Fuck off."

"Tell me, Thigpen, who precisely are you?"

"I am what I am. Nothing more."

"Of course, I know now you're not sent from Russia. You're not involved with the razborka; still, you avoid the police."

"I had my reasons," I said, "but now I don't care." I looked ahead, carefully standing for a second before sitting back down. "Check the binoculars again."

Delovich nodded. "Quite a ways behind—somewhere close to a half-mile. We'll be entering the Detroit River soon."

"How long to the Ambassador Bridge?" I asked, remembering that the riverboat casino was near the bridge.

"Perhaps twenty minutes," Delovich said. He turned to me. "So, care to clarify your position on who you are? Because if it's a new drug, I'd like to negotiate a deal with you."

"Drug?"

"I've seen people high on PCP take bullets and keep on going like they've been bitten by mosquitoes. But nothing like what you've taken. Nothing that allows someone to ignore so much pain. Is it an experimental military drug?"

"It's not a drug," I told Delovich. "It's a disease."

Delovich sighed. "Too bad."

I began seeing the Canadian shoreline on the other side of Lake St. Clair, which was narrowing, funneling into the Detroit River. We were following the shoreline of Michigan, which actually curved west here, at the bottom of Michigan's thumb. Here, Canada was actually south of us.

Ahead was an island—Belle Isle—in the middle of the river, with the RenCen's black towers rising in the distance. I was fairly sure that the river's main channel was on the Canadian side of Belle Isle, but LaPointe was continuing along the Michigan shore.

Delovich's cell phone chimed.

He answered it and spoke for less than a minute before tucking it back inside his suit.

"Well, well," he said, "it appears that Mr. LaPointe is about to lose."

"What do you mean?" I asked.

"I just had a message relayed from Moscow, from the

avtoritet. He's been in touch with the assessor. The assessor told him that the razborka will be completed by tonight."

"Hey!" the pilot shouted above the roar of the engines. "He's slowing down."

I tried standing but fell. "Shit," I said, grabbing the storage bin. I steadied myself, pulled myself up, and peered ahead. LaPointe's boat was still too far ahead for me to see with any detail.

Delovich lowered the binoculars. "He's heading directly for Belle Isle, but he seems to be stopping offshore. It is time for the end game, I believe."

"Belle Isle? What the hell's there?"

"I don't know. Maybe someone's meeting him there."

I squinted, everything looking hazy, fuzzy—*like I was dying*.

I hoped my blood supply held out.

CHAPTER THIRTY SIX

Delovich turned to his gum-chewing henchman. "Get your gun out."

The man reached under his shirt and pulled it out from a shoulder holster.

"When was the razborka supposed to be completed?" I asked, worried that if it was completed before we rescued Octavia, we'd be too late. As long as it wasn't decided, LaPointe needed her for leverage.

"A month from now," Delovich said. "At least that's what I'd been led to believe."

"Why's it been moved up?"

"I don't know. Maybe the assessor has heard how careless LaPointe's become."

The cabin cruiser quickly caught up to LaPointe's boat. The captain throttled down, and we slowed until we were within a few yards of LaPointe's speedboat. Just beyond, slightly to the left, the tree-lined shore of Belle Isle was only a hundred yards away.

I could see LaPointe, Blalock, and Octavia in the speedboat's cockpit now. Octavia's ankles were still bound with the tie-wrap. LaPointe had found another blindfold, a thick strip of white cloth. Her arms were tied behind her with yellow rope. Near the side of the cockpit closest to us, LaPointe picked her up, still favoring one foot, and slung her over his shoulder. That's when I saw the yellow rope was tied to something else. An anchor.

There was about a four-foot stretch of rope from Octavia's hands to the end of the anchor, which looked gray and had three triangular spikes that were folded up. LaPointe was holding it in his hand, swinging it slowly, over the edge of the boat and back.

LaPointe sneered at me. "Now you can watch her drown." His voice jerked me away from staring at Octavia.

That's when I noticed Blalock had a gun drawn. He held it at his side, allowing the threat to speak for itself.

"Tell your man to throw his gun in the water," LaPointe demanded.

Delovich turned and said, "Put it back in your holster."

After he complied, Delovich turned back to LaPointe. "That'll have to do. I'm not going to kill you, LaPointe. And unlike you, I'm a man of my word."

For a moment, LaPointe gritted his teeth in a way that made Delovich's pilot look relaxed in comparison. Then he smiled and seemed to enjoy himself for a few moments.

He's thinking. He doesn't have a plan. He's making this up as he goes.

Our boats drifted downstream slowly. I could hear boat sounds, the clangs of a bell somewhere on the island.

"What about Blalock?" I whispered. "You can kill him, can't you?"

Delovich's eyes scanned the bullet holes in my sweatshirt. "True enough, but from what I can see, Blalock is just standing there. LaPointe's our problem, not Blalock. He's powerless without LaPointe."

LaPoint called out: "I'm guessing you heard, Delovich."

"About the razborka?"

"You know that's what I mean. Don't play stupid."

"I'm just trying to be clear, to use precise language. You, on the other hand, seem to crave sloppiness."

"It's not over yet," LaPointe said. "But I see you think it is. It's not—I have the rest of the day."

"I wouldn't presume it's over yet. But the odds do seem in my favor. What is it exactly you're trying to accomplish with this stunt?"

I climbed forward, out of the cockpit and slid along the narrow deck between the cabin and the small aluminum railing that was only a few inches above the deck.

LaPointe nodded at me. "What do you think you're doing?"

I didn't respond.

"Stop there," LaPointe said, "or the anchor goes overboard. The girl follows."

Delovich's boat began drifting farther away from LaPointe, closer to the swifter current in the middle of the channel. I stared back at the pilot. "Keep us close!"

He engaged the engine and turned the steering wheel. The boat turned, angling slightly upstream, until we barely bumped the speedboat. "Watch it!" I shouted.

"I almost slipped there," LaPointe said. He grinned. "I think I'd like to see the reaction on your face, Thigpen, when she makes her big splash."

I heard Delovich say to his henchman, "If LaPointe tries to leave, put some bullets in his hull. Try to hit the engine."

"It's over, LaPointe," I said. "Give it up."

"You don't look so good, Thigpen," he said.

I shook my head. "I don't matter. Octavia does. If you leave her with us and make a run to Canada, you just might escape with your life. The Mafiya might not want to spend a lot of time and resources to chase you down. You'd be quitting at the right time."

"Will you cry?" LaPointe asked. "I mean, later when they dredge her up and you hold her lifeless body in your arms, will it affect you?"

Octavia squirmed briefly. She looked like she wanted to resist more, but she was too exhausted. I didn't doubt that she'd fought LaPointe and her bindings the entire trip in the boat.

Ignoring LaPointe's taunting, I said, "But if you persist in this, the Mafiya will hunt you down."

"That's right," Delovich added. "They'll see it as an effort to ruin their dealings with me. They'll hunt you down. You can't go against the Mafiya's ruling—the razborka."

"Bullshit," LaPointe said, growing more animated. His foot slipped, but he caught his balance. His face was growing taut and red. "I'm their best man. And I'm going to win this."

"You have an ugliness about you," I said. "See how it's coming out now? If you don't care about human life, your soul turns black and ugly."

LaPointe looked at me as though I were insane. Then he shook his head. "I'm no different from Delovich in that respect."

"Not true," Delovich said. "I don't go around killing people, unless perhaps they turn on me. But not innocents, and especially not innocent little girls."

"Oh, I'm going to enjoy so much watching her go down. And after that, Delovich, after Thigpen here takes a dive and tries to save her, I'm going to have Blalock shoot you." He grinned as though he'd just thought of the plan and was saying it out loud so that he could listen and see if it sounded like it made sense. Evidently, to LaPointe, it did.

Blalock raised his handgun to his shoulder but didn't point it at anyone yet.

Delovich shook his head. "I'm under Mafiya protection."

"I don't give a fuck." He put a foot on the edge of the boat, steadying himself, compensating for an unsteady (swelling) ankle. He began swaying, swinging the anchor back and forth in wider arcs.

Gotta time it right. Throw the bat. Hit him when the anchor's over the boat.

"I'll say it was accidental," LaPointe said, nodding in agreement with himself. "I was trying to stop Thigpen from killing her."

He's going to do it!

Breathing faster, panting, he looked over his shoulder at the Detroit skyline. "You're mine, goddammit! Mine!"

I tried to think of a way to stop his insanity, to stop LaPointe cold, but despite the urgency with which I wanted to save Octavia, I felt like an empty shell casing, spent, discarded, powerless.

"Ready, Thigpen? You're pretty good at not dying, but I don't think the girl is."

"Don't do it," I said.

"Such a sweet little girl."

"I'm begging you."

"That's good, Thigpen. Keep trying."

"Please don't kill her."

He shook his head.

"Please."

LaPointe stared at me. "Go to hell." He swung the anchor far behind him in final preparation to fling it away from the boat.

I leaned forward, dropping the bat, clutching the aluminum rail, hoping to use it to help propel me down more quickly into the water.

Blalock suddenly raised his arm, put the barrel of his handgun against LaPointe's neck—right along the spine—and pulled the trigger.

The explosion was violent. Blood and tissue shot out, spraying the white hull.

Octavia screamed as she dropped safely onto the deck, thudding an instant after the anchor's metallic *clank*. LaPointe collapsed onto the side of the boat, draping over it, his hands trailing listlessly in the water. Blood streamed down the side of the hull.

"Well I'll be a son of a bitch," Delovich said.

Slowly I leaned back, staring at Blalock, who looked repulsed as he stared at LaPointe.

He glanced up at me and said, his voice losing all of its Boston accent (and gaining a slight Russian one), "Consider the razborka complete."

CHAPTER THIRTY SEVEN

I clambered the rest of the way to the front of the cabin cruiser, reached my right foot over to the speedboat, and jumped into its cockpit. Blood was spattered everywhere. Octavia was covered with it.

She was whimpering, trembling, shaking, and for a moment I thought she might be in shock. My hands were trembling, too, as I began untying her gag.

"Nice shot," Delovich called. "What name, precisely, do you really go by?"

"Call me Blalock. It's as good as any."

"You're the assessor," Delovich said, looking stunned for the first time. He shook his head in disbelief.

Blalock shrugged and looked down at LaPointe. "Now I give up on him." He stepped forward, put his shoe on LaPointe's rear end, and kicked the body overboard. "So this is what you Americans say is sleeping with fishes, yes?"

"Sometimes it is quite literal," Delovich said.

I finally got Octavia's gag off. She gulped in air. I pulled off her blindfold. Her eyes were so puffy that I wondered if she could see. She started crying again, her chest heaving as though she couldn't get enough oxygen to cry and shiver at the same time.

"Easy, Octavia," I whispered. I reached into my pocket and grabbed my penknife. "Deep breaths."

She nodded, although she was shaking so violently that it was difficult to tell.

I cut the rope quickly, removing the threat of the anchor, then finished cutting the tie-wrap around her ankles. She hugged me tightly, and for a moment I forgot that I had a fatal disease.

She's so warm, so full of life …

I gently nudged her away. "You're safe now," I said.

She nodded and began gingerly rubbing her ankles. "I wwwas s-s-so scared."

"It's over now," I told her. "LaPointe's dead."

She blinked rapidly and said, "He was g-g-going to k-kill me."

"He can't hurt you now." I stood, my feet wide apart, knees bent, to steady myself against the rocking motion of the waves. "We're going over to the other boat now."

"Okay, Jack."

Blalock had found a bucket and was throwing water onto the deck and the side of the boat to wash away the blood. He glanced downstream every few moments, and I could see LaPointe's body bobbing, drifting out toward the middle of the channel, gaining speed.

I held Octavia's arm, led her to the side of the cockpit, and helped her climb across to the cabin cruiser. She grabbed the aluminum railing and effortlessly clambered past the cabin to the seats.

About to follow her, I paused and asked Blalock, "So, ... Delovich wins?"

"Yes. It is my judgment that the Mafiya will be better off with Delovich running things here."

"How much of your existence is a ruse?" I asked.

"Everything. But that's not so very different from many other people, *da*?"

I nodded.

True enough.

"But," Blalock said, "I despised that accent." He looked downstream at LaPointe's body again and shouted, "*Suka*!"

"I know what that means," I said.

Blalock smiled briefly. "It is so nice to speak a little of the mother tongue again."

"Why'd you shoot him?" I asked.

"He was out of control. With him, there was too much chaos, too much disorder. It was all bespredel."

I nodded. Bespredel. I didn't need to know Russian to translate—*all fucked up.*

I climbed over to the cabin cruiser. Delovich was trying to give me his cool business look, but his eyes were gleaming victoriously.

"What was his plan?" Delovich asked Blalock. "Why'd he take Octavia?"

Blalock spat into the river. "He was planning to go to the casino and force the owners to call the avtoritet and tell him that LaPointe had won their allegiance. Slim chance, but I called Moscow and told them I'd decide by the end of the day. I was therefore obliged to wait until nighttime to make my judgment."

"You didn't wait," I pointed out.

He glared at LaPointe's body. "My disgust level reached the breaking point. The avtoritet called him, before he called Delovich, and LaPointe knew he had no time left. He decided to make a stand."

"But he never had a chance, did he?" I asked.

"He did. He had more armtwisters coming next week. Delovich moved the opening of the casino up, upsetting LaPointe's plans."

"You look like you want to add something else," I noted.

Blalock shrugged. "I admit that Mr. Delovich's organization is tighter than I anticipated."

"Even for someone who's supposed to make a razborka?" I asked.

"Indeed so," he said.

He shot LaPointe because of bespredel, but he did it also—I believed—because he wanted to save Octavia's life.

He's good at playing roles, but he can't hide the truth in his eyes.

Blalock leaned forward and reached across the side of his boat. Delovich stepped over to the side of the cabin cruiser, reached across, and shook Blalock's hand. "So, am I to understand that we're in business?"

"I can't guarantee anything. But the avtoritet has always followed my judgment, my razborka."

"Don't look so disappointed," Delovich said. "Think of it as a natural outcome of globalization."

"Perhaps it is," Blalock said. "We had wanted LaPointe to gain control. He was a true Russian. That's why I helped him as much as I could while maintaining my neutrality of decision making."

"Delovich moved here from Russia," I said. "The fact that he's now an American shouldn't be held against him."

Blalock smiled mirthlessly. Without responding, he turned and walked to the steering wheel. He turned a key and the engine started. He moved the levers forward and the boat surged downriver, running over LaPointe's bobbing body.

I wasn't sure, but it looked like I saw a brief spray of blood in the wake.

CHAPTER THIRTY EIGHT

"Take us to the yacht club over there," I said, pointing.

"Do what he wants," Delovich told the pilot.

He engaged the engine and we cruised ahead through the choppy waves.

"What's next, Jack?" Octavia asked.

"I'm going to drop you off at that pier. You're going to go into that boat store. See it? Good. You're going to go in and tell them what happened. LaPointe kidnapped you. You don't know why. Your bag is still at his house. That'll be proof."

"What about you?" She looked at Delovich, then the gum-chewing henchman. "And everyone else?"

"You don't know these people. Tell the police to ask me. I'm the one who saved you, after all." I looked at Delovich a moment, then whispered to Octavia, "Hold on a second."

I walked over to Delovich and quietly said, "I'm going to clear the way for you. You'll have nothing to worry about."

"On what condition?" Delovich asked.

"That you institute a new rule in your organization."

"I enjoy having few rules," he said as though that was about all his people could comprehend.

"Well, you're going to have to add one," I told him. "If anyone hurts—or kills—an innocent during their scams, their extortions, their thefts, then that person's out of the organization and is blacklisted."

It was the first time I'd seen Delovich frown. "I don't know, Mr. Thigpen. Accidents happen."

"You know what I'm capable of. You know I've got certain talents, and I'm sure you're going to see the fairness of my offer. Am I right?"

He nervously tapped his cane against the hull. "But—"

"I'm insisting," I said.

I knew they were criminals, that I'd never convince them to obey laws, but with this new rule, someone like Melissa Jamison might not get paralyzed one dark and rainy night in the future.

"Very well, Mr. Thigpen. You have my word."

I returned to Octavia, reaching her just as the side of the cabin cruiser nudged the bumpers on the side of the pier, which was slightly above deck level.

Hurry—

I reached for Octavia's hand and helped her step onto the wooden planks. There were dozens of people visible in the marina. Some were sporting fishing poles farther down the pier. A couple of families had picnic spreads on the grass. Hikers walked along the road. Bicyclers sped along a bike path. There was a bustle of activity, and I knew she'd be safe here.

"Jack—"

I shook my head and held my finger to my mouth. "Shhh. I know. Don't worry."

"Where's your bat, Jack?"

That's when I knew she'd be more than just okay. She was already returning to her usual spunky self.

"Good-bye, Octavia. I'll always remember you." I turned and pointed downriver. "Take me that way."

"Jack!"

I couldn't turn to face her.

"Good-bye, Jack! Thanks for saving my life! You'll always be my hero!"

I nodded, hoping she would see me and know that I'd heard and that I appreciated the sentiment.

At my direction, Delovich had the driver steer the boat to the other end of Belle Isle, the river opening up before us, curving against the seawall and the RenCen towers. We backed into the Loop Canal. It was too shallow for the boat to proceed up the canal much farther than its outlet, but I could disembark here without risk of getting swept downriver.

I glanced at the skyline, the Ambassador Bridge spanning the river in the distance.

Not far from where this all started ...

After I reminded Delovich of his promise, I climbed out of the back of the boat, making my way carefully down the ladder, and waded ashore.

The cabin cruiser nudged out of the canal, then turned and sped upriver.

At this end of the island, there weren't nearly as many trees. There was a park, its centerpiece—Scott Fountain. I remained near the riverbank, keeping away from the walking paths, afraid someone might notice my condition and call for help. As I approached the end of the island farthest downriver, I paused and stared at the fountain, *water* shooting skyward out the top, and streaming out from numerous figures that were fashioned into the masonry—lions on pedestals and fish that circled the fountain's main column.

Water ...

I continued toward the end the island. The park was beautifully manicured, like a lush green oasis of land surrounded by the river.

The sun was out, and for a moment it warmed me.

I reached the end of the island and looked out at the river, considering continuing my trek, walking downriver, all the way out the St. Lawrence Seaway to the ocean, like a salmon after being spawned.

I reached into my pocket and took out the pebble.

Hello, Mr. Kubrik. Thanks for the ride. You helped me. I don't know how, but you did.

I reached back and tossed the pebble. It didn't travel far before plunking into the water.

Good-bye.

I was tired, so tired, but it didn't seem so bad, really, and I thought it would be so nice just to lie down.

And so that's what I did, stretching out on the grass, basking in the sunlight.

The world felt fuzzy and warm and nice, and I was so glad to be here, to be semi-alive and at the very least to enjoy this moment.

River water flowed past cheerily, the waves rhythmic, the pattern incredibly complex and wondrous. Whorls of clouds adorned a deep blue sky that cradled the earth. The grass was plush. It prodded me as though I could feel it growing.

It occurred to me that death wasn't sailing a ship by oneself, a lonely nighttime excursion—it was a moment of *becoming*, a release from the incomprehensible puzzle of life.

My vision began fading.

I could feel the underlying ripples of Nature, from which life bubbled forth into this world. The grass, the sky, the river—*they danced, they danced.*

Cascading streams of light washed over me, filling me, lifting me.

Wonderment ...

My eyes felt moist.

How could that be?

I reached up and felt my cheeks.

I was crying.

Why? Because I knew that I was going to live. The sirens from an ambulance were approaching, stopping nearby, and I was feeling stronger.

All in the same instant, I saw images of Hal and Melissa Jamison and Tom and Octavia and Lynne the Pin and Archie Norton and Cheryl Baine and I felt reverberations from them spreading all across the universe, reverberations from what I had done in the world, how I had changed it, how my *actions* and *interactions* had changed things, and that everything was interconnected, like notes in a symphony, except that it wasn't really a symphony—it was a mysterious interplay, the progression of something big, a design of music in which the final note hadn't yet been decided, and the world was sometimes discordant, and the final note was in danger at times of souring, that everyone had to try to harmonize that final note, or else it would be distorted by evil and a black noise that was screeching out on the periphery; but I knew that I'd done my part, that I had helped, and that I had more to do before I met death.

"C'mon, buddy, we'll fix you up," the paramedic said.

I nodded. "Good. I'm not a dead guy. Not yet."

Acknowledgements

The publication of The Dead Guy brings the grateful and loving acknowledgment of my wife, Robin, who guided me through four complete revisions, not to mention countless edits.

In fact, my entire family was supportive, and I would like to acknowledge my daughter Amy and my sons Andy and David. Other family members include Harve and Jane Hewitt, June (Mom) Adcock, Sara Paduchowski, Mike Robbel, Lynne (the Pin) Turner, Tom and Chuck Hewitt, and the Murkot crew.

Many friends offered ongoing support throughout the creative process, including Bob (the computer guy) Sykes, Linda (Ski) Zurawski, Vicky and Jerry at the Mayodan Post Office, Charlotte and the crew at the Mayodan library, and Julie Campbell and the Rockingham County Writers Group.

Acknowledgements also go out to the wonderful faculty at the University of North Carolina at Greensboro. They helped shape my literary outlook, especially Fred Chappell, Keith Cushman, Mark Smith-Soto, Bob Gingher, Charlie Headington, and Ben Ramsey.

I'm also grateful for the Writers Group of the Triad, especially members of the Novel Group, including Lynn Chandler-Willis, Julie Anne Parks, R.C. Smith, Charles Roberts, Julie Stanley, Paula Jordan, and newcomers Cindy Bullard and Demetria Gray.

My thanks would not be complete without Andy Zhang and Joan Roberts at Aberdeen Bay for their wonderful work in seeing the promise of The Dead Guy and getting it into print.

Doug Hewitt, October 2008

Doug Hewitt

Born and raised in Mt. Clemens, Michigan and the son of a Ford Motor retiree, Doug Hewitt often relies on the Detroit area for his fiction settings. With over 100 short stories published in the realm of speculative fiction, his work has appeared in anthologies such as 100 Wicked Little Witch Stories, Maelstrom, and The Dead Inn. Doug's first novel, SPEAR, was published in 2002 by Sands Publishing and received critical acclaim from Midwest Book Review. His publication credits have expanded into the chapbook realm, including the thriller Slipstream, which is available at Fictionwise.com along with several of his most popular short stories. Doug is currently working on the next Jack Thigpen novel.

The father of three, stepfather of two, and grandfather of five, Doug is also the author of the parenting book The Practical Guide to Weekend Parenting, released in 2005. He has continued his non-fiction work by co-authoring (with his wife, Robin) The Joyous Gift of Grandparenting in 2008, as well as Free Money for College: Finding and Winning Scholarships and Grants, which is due for release by Prufrock Press in July 2009. When he's not writing, Doug stays busy giving seminars for his business Teach, Learn, Connect, which is designed to help high school students find funding and success in college. Please visit Doug on the web at www.HewittsBooks.com or www.TeachLearnConnect.com.

If you have enjoyed reading this book, Aberdeen Bay also recommends--

Uncle Si's Secret

Author: M. M. Gornell
ISBN-13: 978-0-9814725-5-3
ISBN-10: 0-9814725-5-9

Belinda "Bella" Jones and her brother Bernard, owners of the Cedar Valley Residence, have put their hearts, souls, and a ton of cash into this dream endeavor. Now, after five years of hard work, their charming home is almost full of a lovable cast of residents and there's just one more building addition they want to do.

But then Lana Norris, a beautiful area resident is brutally murdered on Cedar Valley Trail just a few feet from their property line, and their world turns upside down. Things like this don't happen in Cedar Valley, and their residents are shocked—and afraid. Overnight their happy place has turned into a jumbled, unfamiliar world. Indeed, residents are checking out, belongings are mysteriously disappearing, the county government is on their back about raspberries of all things, and it seems that nothing will be right again until this homicidal maniac is captured.

Quickly, and to everyone's relief, the police arrest and charge Kirby Norris, Lana's husband. He has an alibi, but all the physical evidence points his way; and for motive, there's a million dollar life insurance policy. It's enough for the DA to indict, arraign, and bring to trial.

But Kirby swears he's innocent, and so does his mother, the eerily persistent Olive Norris. She engages a slick defense lawyer, but she also calls in Belinda, a past part-time investigator to find the real killer.

Belinda has had several modest successes in the crime arena, and her possibly psychic chef-brother thinks Kirby is innocent, and worse yet, the real killer is still loose and she should take the job. But once Belinda begins, she enters a turning labyrinth that not even she could foresee. Suddenly there's another gruesome murder, and some sudden surprises, and Belinda knows that she must solve this one fast—before she, or someone dear to her, becomes the next victim.

Printed in the United States
130778LV00002B/1-48/P

9 780981 472577